TIES
OF
FROST

SELINA R. GONZALEZ

TIES
OF
FROST

TETHERED HEARTS

GLOSSARY & PRONUNCIATION GUIDE

Find a glossary of terms and pronunciation guide at
https://SelinaRGonzalez.com/ties-of-frost-glossary

Or scan the QR code below

Laedreshian Empire

Wyveri Islands

Ithemorca Mountains

Glacori

Aizurgon Sea

Gamnica

Bryluthia

Avorn Mountains

Ravensburgh

Laedresh

Verdanya

N

Panth
Tri

Gryphoni Clan

Wolvus Kingdom

Neaston

Rupich

Nyksia

Shuallang

...thera ...ribe

Tullong

ONE

ZIDRA

My tankard was empty, which meant my cover for lingering alone in the crowded tavern was gone, and I was out of time. My informant hadn't shown, and if I didn't leave now, I'd be late. I'd have to be missing limbs and bleeding out in a ditch to be late.

Resigned, I stood and pulled my hood over my curly brown hair. I wove between jostling bodies, careful not to hit anyone with my sword's scabbard. At least I could finally get out of this void hole—no disrespect to the owners of the Lazy Mule. Wyveri preferred open skies and quiet. Even in my di'ora—my true, human-like form—I had un-usually keen shifter senses. I hated the smoky air that carried the scent of ale, savory food, and humans, elves, and shifters. Clattering dishes, conversations, laughter, and the squeak of chairs pushed on my ears. The people of the

Laedreshian Empire were certainly enjoying their holiday.

An elf with white hair and a sunburned nose turned and bumped into me, barely saving the three mugs he carried from spilling.

"Sorry, miss," he mumbled and scurried off.

At the door, I cast one last glance over the raucous crowd. An elf tossed her head, and her strawberry-blonde hair swung with the motion. A human with black skin used his watermage power to channel his ale into his mouth in a failed attempt to impress a girl with sleek dark hair framing her pale face. She rolled her eyes, and her pupils flashed, reflecting the candlelight with a yellow-green glow—probably a wolf shifter.

So many people, but not one wore a two-tone cloak.

Stifling a sigh, I stepped outside. Immediately, tension eased from my shoulders. Late afternoon sun shone through wisps of clouds, warming the late spring air with the promise of summer. Traffic along the wide dirt thoroughfare had thinned. Laedresh was always crowded, especially during holidays, and no holiday drew as many people to the capital as the three-day-long Dawning Festival. But this close to the Ceremony, many people were already at the imperial palace.

Where I was supposed to be.

I eyed the location of the sun and muttered a curse. The event was being held in my honor—well, not *my* honor specifically, although I did have hopes about that, but in honor of all rengiri.

The urge to shift into my di'yar rippled through me, but

too many people and merchant carts crowded the street to accommodate a fifteen-foot-tall wyvern. Even if I didn't cause injury or property damage, people would either panic or realize my identity. If I'd wanted to be recognized, my insignia of the Order of the Rengir—old Elvish for *sacred sword*—wouldn't have been stowed in the bag strapped to my thigh.

I joined the river of people moving toward the palace and tried not to visibly brood. People tended to become uncomfortable when a muscular woman in leather armor with a sword at her hip looked angry.

Still, keeping my frustration off my face was proving difficult. Over an hour wasted in that stinking tavern for nothing.

There could be many reasons my informant hadn't shown. He—or she—could have gotten lost in the sprawling streets. If this mysterious person did have information on Magistrate Nevros's death in the human kingdom of Neaston, he had to be a visitor to Laedresh. Yet the dark suspicion lingered that he'd been prevented from coming. Anyone who stopped someone from meeting a rengir had to be either insane or in a position of power.

My attention caught on a few men huddled together in the shadows between two buildings, glancing furtively at passersby. All of them wore swords and daggers. I subtly changed my course toward the possible troublemakers but then noticed the crossed spears embroidered in blue thread on their sleeves. Just city guards exchanging information.

I continued on my way, but my mouth tugged down

into a scowl. The city guard and criminal inspector in the city of Rupich had ruled that Magistrate Nevros's death was strange, but not murder. Lord Malvoy, the new magistrate, claimed his predecessor's death was tragic but not suspicious.

Rengiri weren't investigators by trade. We aided investigations and hunted down criminals when asked, but our primary occupation was monster hunters. So it didn't matter that Nevros falling on a forgotten pair of pruning shears neither made sense nor explained the bruises on his arms and his cracked knuckles. The inspector and Magistrate Malvoy were within their rights to dismiss my help, which they had.

But something—whether intuition or a prompting from Iskyr—told me Nevros's death was murder. Possibly assassination. Nevros had been a faithful patron of the Order of the Rengir and, from the one time I'd met him, a kind and unusually humble man who wasn't bothered that I was wyveri, unlike some people. He deserved to be honored in death, and that meant catching his killer. Not to mention catching a murderer would prove my worth. So, to Magistrate Malvoy's obvious displeasure, I'd kept investigating, although I'd tried to be subtle about it. I'd left Rupich only to attend the Dawning Festival in Laedresh.

Then yesterday, a note had been delivered to West Quarter Haven, the rengir common house where I was staying.

To Zidra Eilmaris.
The Lazy Mule. Two bells past noon. I know who killed Nevros.
I'll be wearing a cloak that is half blue, half red.

Yet the note-sender hadn't been there.

I kicked a pebble, drawing a judgmental look from an elderly light elf.

Dwelling on my frustration wouldn't provide answers, so I turned my attention to the sellers lining the streets. Where there were crowds, there was money to be made. Merchants called out their wares: food, drinks, toys, hand-painted fans, earthen dishware, embroidered tunics, and more.

Ahead, the flow of the crowd ebbed around a knot of revelers. Families with young children pressed close together around a small stage.

A woman with curly red hair and copious freckles sat on a stool. Behind her, a gigantic white sheet covered in colorful ink drawings stretched between two wood and plaster buildings. Her voice rose and fell as she moved her hands. Images of monsters and warriors peeled off the fabric and filled out, becoming three dimensional and moving under the sway of her magic. I smiled and hurried on. As much as I loved watching human inkmage storytellers, I had somewhere important to be.

"You're setting yourself up for disappointment," I muttered to myself.

But I couldn't help the longing twisting in my chest. I was a member of the Order of the Rengir and today was the Dawning Ceremony.

Only the most skilled and intelligent applicants could pass the rigorous tests to be admitted into Harcos Academy, the empire's oldest and foremost military college. After four years of study, only the best of Harcos's graduates were allowed to enter the two-year-long Rengir Course. Only those who passed the rigorous martial, magical, ethical, and religious tests were accepted into the Order.

Then the rengiri spent the rest of our lives, until we died or surrendered our insignia, serving our god Iskyr and the people of the empire. We didn't work for a salary. We owned nothing but what we could carry, and we asked for nothing but what those we served could spare. The peoples of the empire aided us because we protected them and kept watch for the return of Ascadrion the Earth-Shaker, the ancient dragon that had been driven to the void-between-worlds by the first emperor and his warriors nearly sixteen hundred years ago.

Every ten years, the Dawning Festival commemorated Emperor Syrzin's defeat of Ascadrion and the birth of the empire. While the Festival was celebrated across the continent, over half of the roughly three hundred rengiri came to Laedresh. For today, the final day, one rengir would be awarded the Emperor's Merit.

The Merit had been my dream since I was accepted into Harcos Academy seventeen years ago. Maybe if the medallion hung from my neck, I would finally feel like I had proven myself and redeemed my people. My mother would see that being a rengir wasn't a waste of my power, but the best use of it, and she would finally concede that my being a rengir honored my people. I'd be seen as equal to my younger sister. Or at least equal to my much older brother, who bred and trained hyzli, the gangly, wolf-hunting sighthounds coveted across the empire.

When I held the Merit in my hands, no one would question my motives as a wyveri. My family's praise would no longer be thinly disguised condemnation, full of hints that I could do better.

I tried to rein in my daydreams. I was probably too young, anyway. The youngest rengir to ever earn the Merit had been a human at age thirty-seven. Due to shifters' longer lifespans and slower maturation, my own seventy years was younger still, around thirty human years. I still had well over a century of service ahead of me—

"Touched by Zidra herself!"

My name jerked me out of my reverie. A seller beckoned passersby closer to a cart bedecked in colorful ribbons.

"Relics from great rengiri, sure to bring the blessings of Iskyr upon you!" The man—likely a half-human forest elf based on his coppery skin, vibrant green eyes, and shorter, more subtly pointed ears—held up a bowl. "This washbasin was used by the magnificent duo Kyrmaris after they killed the Serpent of Tullong. The blessed blood of holy warriors was cleansed in this bowl!"

Dragon fire stirred in my veins. It wasn't unusual for charlatans to make money selling rengir relics—body parts of long-dead heroes of the Order, as well as clothing worn or items used by rengiri living and deceased. While some relics held divine blessings, those were carefully guarded in sanctuaries. Street peddlers' relics were of questionable provenance and power, and I could hardly believe this seller was so crass as to sell possibly fake relics during the Festival.

That, however, was not what angered me. Even fake relics could comfort those who purchased them, and the practice wasn't illegal unless it could be proved the seller was lying—which was difficult. I didn't recognize the bowl, but washbasins weren't memorable.

No, what made my fangs grow was that awful name: Kyrmaris. A combination of Zidra Eilmaris and Kyrundar Ilifir—the name of my archrival. No, my nemesis. He had an irritating habit of getting himself involved in my missions. Storytellers and bards referring to us as a unit with a single, shared moniker, as if we *intended* to work together so often, was the sour milk in the bitter tea of our unfortunate continued acquaintance.

I forced my feet onward. I shouldn't care. A rengir wasn't supposed to crave glory.

But how was I supposed to earn the Emperor's Merit when that ice elf kept taking partial credit for my successes? We'd trained together at Harcos Academy, and he'd been annoying then, but he was worse now. Women constantly flirted with him, and he leveraged my reputation to bolster his own. We didn't even work together as often as the stories of "Kyrmaris" made it sound. Did we? Surely not.

Why was it part of his first name and part of my last name, anyway? Illogical, and it grated on me that his name came first. No one else cared. The accursed team name had stuck.

If I could get through the Ceremony without seeing Kyrundar, I'd be thrilled. *Wait—the Ceremony!*

I broke into a jog and soon reached the towering walls surrounding the city-within-a-city that was the imperial palace. I fished an oval pin the length of my forefinger from my thigh bag and pinned it on my shoulder. The pin featured an inlay of reddish sequoia wood. Set into the wood was a gold sword surrounded by flames of silver—the symbol of the Order.

I joined a short line of other rengiri at a side entrance. At least I wasn't late. Inside, the rengiri gathered in a marble plaza. Hundreds of wide steps rose from the plaza to the sprawling palace with its gleaming limestone columns and red-tiled roofs.

Rengiri trickled in, some from the crowds packed into the lawns that ran half a league to the main gate. Citizens fawned over them, flirtatious men and women pouting as the objects of their affections extricated themselves and passed the imperial guards to stand in the plaza. I spotted several I knew and had done missions with.

A willowy forest elf woman with light-bronze skin and silky dark hair caught my eye and smiled. I smiled back at Archon Aekyrdra, the leader of the Order. Her smile seemed encouraging, but even she didn't know who the emperor had chosen.

On a spacious landing halfway up the stairs, a podium stood between two ten-foot-tall crimson banners featuring the Order insignia in gold and silver thread. Trumpeters waited on the far edges of the landing.

Movement at the top of the staircase drew my attention. A tall light elf man with sparkling gold earrings emerged from the colonnade carrying a wide, shallow box. The trumpeters bugled. An expectant hush fell over the rengiri and the throng of citizens.

Vivid blue robes swirled around the ankles of the Grand Marshal of Imperial Events as he descended the long flight of stairs to the landing. The box he held was larger than made sense. Had the emperor changed the shape of the medallion? Tossing aside over one thousand years of tradition wasn't very elven.

The light elf emperors had kept the Laedreshian Empire intact in part because elves, who lived the longest of the three races, had a healthy respect for convention and stability. Then again, Valesiart was a mere eighty-five years old, barely an adult. An elf that young might be tempted to break a minor tradition.

The Grand Marshal set the box on the podium and picked up a bronze bullhorn. He spoke into the narrow mouthpiece, and his voice, magnified by the magic poured into the bullhorn by a metalmage, roared over the palace lawns.

"Today we gather to recognize the virtue and feats of our noble rengiri!"

The crowds roared their approval. My heart swelled. Our vows said we weren't to be *arrogant*. Pride in one's work and life wasn't arrogance.

"While we honor all rengiri," the Marshal continued, "the Emperor's Merit allows us to recognize the most active, fearsome, and noble member of our great protectors. For the last decade, imperial scribes have watched and listened. The rulers of the human kingdoms, elven kingdoms, and shifter nations have passed on their recommendations."

The wyveri queen would have asked the clan matriarchs for their input. Had my mother suggested me? Had she declined to answer? I wiped my clammy hands on my trousers.

"Noble patrons have given their opinions on which warriors are the most selfless, powerful, wise, and victorious. For the last several months, scribes have traveled the empire, collecting tales from bards and testimonies from cities and villages."

Internally, I scoffed. Bards were notorious for embellishing their tales. The more dramatic the story, the better they were paid. Nobles who opened their homes to rengiri paid lip service to honoring Iskyr and to the values of humble service and selfless giving, but many craved the acclaim and power that came with having rengiri as friends. While rengiri were to serve all people without favoritism, there was an implicit understanding that rengiri would give their hosts' lands extra protection.

It was why I refused to stay in anyone's home. I'd sleep outside if a Haven wasn't available.

To an extent, the Emperor's Merit was a popularity contest that honored the heroes who had the best public image. Even knowing that, I longed to receive the award.

"The reports have been considered by the emperor's trusted advisers," the Grand Marshal continued. "Our esteemed emperor has reviewed their findings and decided who among our honored rengiri has the greatest merit."

I kept my expression blank. Best not look too eager, as I likely wouldn't be chosen. Yet my racing pulse wasn't listening.

A flash of silver in my peripheral vision drew my attention from the Grand Marshal, who was reciting the rengir oaths. A tall elf with white hair hanging loose past his shoulders looked around. Sunlight glinted on the silver earrings and pale-blue gemstones adorning his ears from lobe to long point. Three rengiri stood between us, but still, his gaze caught mine. A smirk curved his mouth. He sent an exaggerated wink my way, a bit of magic making his blue eyes glow.

It had been too much to hope I could make it through the entire Dawning Festival without seeing Kyrundar.

My rival probably hoped *he* would receive the medallion. When we attended Harcos Academy together, we'd been something of friends—friends who constantly tried to one-up each other. One night we'd gotten personal in a game of truth or challenge, and we'd both admitted our desire to be the best rengir in the empire, perhaps in history. To Kyrundar's credit, he'd also appeared serious when he said his ultimate goal was serving those who could not protect themselves. But my mother had shown me that pleasant words could conceal selfish designs. Besides, that late-night admission had happened nearly fifteen years ago.

People changed.

That young elf with soft smiles and noble aspirations had become a rengir with flirtatious grins and an obsession with applause who constantly showed up where he was not wanted and got in my way.

Heat rose in my chest, and my fangs grew as scales appeared on my skin. I steadied myself, and my appearance returned to that of a human. Well, a human with small fangs.

The Grand Marshal read a declaration from Emperor Valesiart about the importance of recognizing the rengiri's efforts, then declared, "It is now time to announce the recipient of the Emperor's Merit!"

Cheers echoed like thunder.

I felt hot and cold all over. Did I look flushed? I felt flushed.

"Or shall I say…" The Grand Marshal paused, and everyone held their breath. Even me.

"The *recipients* of the Emperor's Merit."

I blinked, stunned. Whispers swirled around me. Never before had there been more than one recipient. Our young emperor was feeling a little rebellious.

"That is correct." By the sly tone of the Marshal's voice, he was enjoying himself. "His Exulted Royal Highness, Emperor Valesiart, has decreed that there are *two* rengiri who stand out above the rest, whose deeds and renown are so equal—and so frequently tied together—that to recognize one and not the other would be an affront to Iskyr."

A horrified intuition spread through me. My head turned of its own accord, instinct sending my gaze searching for a head of white hair.

He was looking for me, too.

Our eyes locked. The same question shone in his expression, but he looked curious, anticipatory—eager, in fact.

I turned back to the Grand Marshal so fast my neck popped. It couldn't be. It was someone else. *Anyone* else. Even if that meant I had to wait for the Merit.

"Today"—the Marshal's voice boomed over the palace—"in recognition of their bravery, comradery, selflessness, impressive feats, unwavering dedication to their calling, and the lives they have saved, Emperor Valesiart bestows the Emperor's Merit upon…"

Banners snapped in the breeze. The creak of armor sounded as rengiri fidgeted. My heart beat against my chest like it was trying to escape.

"Kyrmaris!"

The blood in my veins turned to sand. The Grand Marshal didn't even have the decency to refer to us by our own names? In the most important moment of my life?

A deafening cacophony of cheers, applause, and whistles filled the air. I braced myself, refusing to show how the sound pounded my senses. I made my way forward, past rengiri who clapped me on the back or gave me friendly punches on my pauldrons. Head held high, I focused on breathing slow and steady and smiling so they wouldn't realize how much I wanted to flee the overwhelming press of bodies.

A shadow fell over me, and I glanced up. Kyrundar flew over the heads of the other rengiri on a disk of ice that left a glittering trail of falling snow.

Show-off.

If I wanted to flaunt my power, I could, and honestly, I would win that contest. I could knock him out of the sky with a beat of my wings if I fancied doing so.

Which I did fairly often.

Fancied knocking him out of the sky, that is. I'd never actually done it.

I was a respectable rengir. I wasn't that petty.

Finally, I broke free of the suffocating crowd of rengiri and started up the steps—on foot. Like a normal person who understands how stairs work.

Kyrundar landed on the Grand Marshal's right with a flourish of icy swirls and a roguish grin, drawing applause. The way he posed and winked for the crowd, it was as if he had forgotten his name meant *beloved of god* and decided it meant *god's gift to all people*. I eyed the hundreds of steps between me and the podium and sighed. It would be more awkward if I made everyone wait for me to walk.

Comforting dragon fire raced through me as I shifted. My fingers grew and spread as my arms and hands transformed into leathery wings. My entire body swelled, and gray scales overtook my skin while two curving horns replaced my hair and a powerful tail sprouted. In di'yar, wyveri were the largest of all the shifters, and I towered over the other rengiri. My senses sharpened, making the cheers and exclamations of awe deafening.

I flew to the platform in a couple beats of my wings and landed where I wouldn't crush the Grand Marshal or my rival. For a moment I envisioned "accidentally" blocking Kyrundar with a massive wing.

Fine. Maybe I was a little petty.

He always got under my scales.

Instead, I shifted back to my di'ora and marched over. I bowed to the Marshal and ignored Kyrundar.

I barely heard the Marshal's congratulations as he shook our hands. He hung a gold medallion on a thick ribbon around Kyrundar's neck, because of course the pretty and charming elf was recognized first. Even at the moment of my greatest achievement, I still wasn't good enough.

The Grand Marshal stepped in front of me. Unlike Kyrundar, I didn't have to duck down as he easily reached over my head. The medallion thunked against my leather breastplate. Its weight pulled the ribbon down, crushing my curls. I managed to smile, desperately trying to feel proud.

The Marshal stepped into the gap between me and Kyrundar, grabbed one of each of our hands, and lifted them above our heads. "I present to you this Dawning Festival's recipients of the Emperor's Merit: Kyrmaris!"

My teeth hurt from clenching them behind my smile.

TWO

KYRUNDAR

lves lived the longest of all three races, often around seven hundred years, and we possessed the most powerful magic, so we were all staid, refined, and controlled. Always perfect examples of tradition, gentility, and respectability.

Ludicrous stereotype.

Back at the Riverfront Haven, a rengir common house in a wealthy district of Laedresh and one of my favorite Havens, I celebrated with enthusiasm. Rengiri didn't charge for our services, but we were allowed to accept gifts and donations. As I'd recently rescued a wealthy merchant's caravan, I had a little money to fund the revelry. I bought a whole hog, three baskets of fresh fruit, and several kegs of pear cider, my alcoholic beverage of choice.

All right, fine; sometimes I was a bit of an elven stereotype.

Even my earrings were a light elf tradition, so I looked like a typical elf in Bryluthia—aside from my ice elf white hair, blue eyes, and magic. Since elf magic was passed from father to son and mother to daughter, earrings were how I embraced my light elf mother's side of the family.

While I hadn't inherited my mother's magic, I had been blessed with her vocal talent, which I put to use leading the celebrating rengiri in songs about ancient battles. Sloshing more cider than I drank, I danced atop a table with three other warriors. Music and merriment echoed against the stone walls. I sang a rousing ballad and ignored the hollow feeling beneath the Emperor's Merit medallion tapping against my sternum.

Zidra hadn't so much as smiled at me. She'd shifted and flown out of the palace without a word. While I hoped she was partying in another Haven, I had a terrible feeling she wasn't. I wanted her to celebrate accomplishing a dream we'd both held since we attended the Academy to-gether. A dream we'd helped each other achieve.

More than anything, what I really wanted was for Zidra to be here, celebrating with me.

I sang louder, going a little off-key, to drown out my own thoughts. More rengiri arrived, bringing food, drinks, and musical instruments. Someone brought a small rubbery ball and started a game, hitting the ball with a wood paddle and bouncing it off the wall. I drifted between conversations until the music turned to romance and my appetite for food and company shriveled.

Rengiri filled every room and hall and even the gardens and courtyard of Riverfront Haven, spilling into the street. Zidra wasn't among them. I didn't realize I was looking for her until I reached the front gate a second time.

What was going on with her? She should have been glowing with pride, but she'd been the least animated I'd ever seen her during the Ceremony. She had to have known I would invite her to celebrate, but she hadn't given me the chance. Either something terrible was distracting her, or she was angry with me for reasons I couldn't imagine.

I wandered down the street. Revelers spilled out of taverns and homes, swayed arm in arm down the cobblestone roads, or talked in circles of golden light beneath street lanterns. People called congratulations as they recognized me, and a few men ran over to shake my hand.

"Congratulations, Rengir Ilifir! Is Rengir Eilmaris nearby?" A broad-shouldered shifter—I wasn't sure what kind, but the fangs gave him away—craned his neck to look around. His eager expression annoyed me. "Surely Kyrmaris is celebrating together? I hoped to meet her."

"Oh, we're...honoring different Havens with our presence," I said with a stiff grin. Not intentionally on my part, but he didn't need to know that.

"Ah, right." His shoulders sloped downward, and his feet dragged as he left.

"Surely Kyrmaris is celebrating together?"

The question rattled in my mind.

Sure, we were something of rivals, I supposed. We had

19

been ever since we had tied for first place in our Harcos entrance tests. Our eyes had locked, and there had been this spark in her eyes. At that moment, we'd had an unspoken agreement to push each other to be better. Every term, one of us was at the top of the class. We'd race to see the board where test results were posted. If I scored higher, she'd go a little bit wyvern—her fangs elongating or some scales poking through. Sometimes she'd snort a bit of smoke at me. If she scored higher, I'd flick snowflakes into her hair.

There's no top rank for being sworn into the Order of the Rengir. Either you're deemed worthy and take the oaths, or you're not. We were admitted at the same time, so in that, we were on equal footing, but we kept striving to be the best—and helping each other get there.

Nearly two months prior, I'd helped Zidra exterminate a nest of erphine. Nasty, aggressive, and carnivorous rodents that looked like a ferret but three times larger and gifted with saberteeth and a horrifying swarm attack. Tracking them all down was half the battle.

Zidra had blustered that she didn't need my help, but she had thanked me in the end. We always made a good team, after all. Zee was a bit proud, but I liked that about her.

"Rengir Ilifir!" A petite young woman with dark hair and pale skin bounced as she waved a silk kerchief. The group of young humans with her surged toward me.

I smiled and nodded, intending to continue on my way, but suddenly three women blocked my path, their congratulations and words of admiration spilling over each other.

"Oh, I wish I had ink and a quill to get your signature!" The young woman who had first caught my attention snagged my sleeve. "Rengir Ilifir, you're the best rengir alive!"

"The best ever!" effused another girl.

"Oh, I'm humbled you think so." I chuckled. "But Zidra is at least my equal—"

"And you're the handsomest," insisted the third young woman.

That I struggled to refute, and my lopsided smile and blush probably looked ridiculous.

"Can you do some ice magic?" one of the boys asked, leaning forward.

I almost said no, but arguing would delay me more than acquiescing. I formed three ice roses and gave them to the girls. With a little help from a suddenly icy road, I slipped past them.

I'd meant what I said, even if the humans hadn't been listening. Zidra was confident, hardworking, determined, and devout. If she got defensive at times about accepting help, I couldn't blame her. Her parents' disapproval and the prejudice some Laedreshians still held against wyveri made her feel like she had to prove herself, and prove herself she had. She deserved the Emperor's Merit more than I did.

Maybe not *all* the times I'd aided Zidra had been entirely selfless. We made a good team, yes. I loved fighting with her, yes. And as the only wyveri in the Order, she drew attention wherever she went. Attaching myself to her helped me stand out in a sea of elvish rengiri. I wasn't just riding on her cloak, though—besides being her equal in a fight, I made sure the bards and storytellers knew all about her bravery and skill and lauded her appropriately.

I needed to know why Zidra wasn't happy to have achieved her greatest ambition. I couldn't enjoy my accomplishment if she wasn't celebrating.

The West Quarter Haven was nearly a half hour's walk away. Zidra was staying there—that was the first thing I'd ascertained when I arrived in Laedresh before the Festival. I just hadn't thought of a good reason to visit her yet. Zidra would look at me like I'd lost my mind if I said I simply wanted to spend time with her. She liked everything to have a practical purpose, and I'd yet to convince her "friendship" counted as practical.

While *Is something wrong, or are you angry with me?* wasn't the reason I'd been looking for, at least it gave me a good excuse to see her.

The problem was, when I arrived at West Quarter Haven, it was oddly subdued. There were a dozen or so people, most of them other rengiri, lounging about the large common room. Someone was playing a lute. Once again, Zidra wasn't among them.

"Kyr!" A bellowing baritone carried over the noise. A small mountain of a man made his way toward me. His golden-brown skin wrinkled around his eyes, and a few threads of gray wove through his dark hair.

I grinned. "Sajen!"

"Congratulations!" Sajen pulled me into a crushing embrace, unbothered by the twin swords strapped to my back. Back when he'd spent a year teaching at Harcos, I'd once joked he should have been a bear shifter, not a gryphon shifter. Sajen had pretended to be concerned that I believed there was such a thing as bear shifters.

"Thank you," I gasped.

He released me and thumped my shoulder so hard I swayed to the side.

"Iskyr be praised; you deserve this honor. You and Zidra both." His wide smile cut deep lines into his cheeks. "I can't even be jealous that you earned an honor in eleven years that I haven't yet in forty-six. You were the two finest students I had the pleasure of teaching in the three rotations I served at Harcos, even if your rivalry gave me a couple of these gray hairs." He threw his head back and guffawed.

I joined in, his mirth infectious. "Say, speaking of Zee—I thought she was staying here, but I don't see her?"

"Oh, she is." Sajen's merriment fell away, and a furrow dug into his brow. "She joined us for the feasting, but..." He glanced around, then leaned in closer. "She was less celebratory than I'd expected. Like she had something on her mind. Then a message runner arrived with a letter, and she left."

Tension built behind my forehead. "As in, retired to the sleeping quarters?"

"No, she left the Haven."

So Zidra's odd demeanor really wasn't about me. An

uneasy feeling crept in. "Did she say where she was going?"

Sajen shook his head, his expression apologetic.

"No, but I know." A young man I didn't recognize, a forest elf by his dark hair and brilliantly green eyes, pushed off a pile of cushions. "I sneaked a glance at the letter over her shoulder. Rather odd. Just an apology for missing her earlier and a request to meet at Castle Grivolen as soon as possible. The sender didn't even sign their name."

Iskyr, is she in danger? Should I go after her?

The feeling of unease spread, along with a strong conviction I needed to be at Castle Grivolen. Cold swirled around my fingers. I blurted a thank-you and rushed back out into the night.

Castle Grivolen, or what was left of it, lay west of the city. Once the king of the wyveri's stronghold, the castle had been destroyed after the wyveri king and his army of supporters from across the continent had summoned and attempted to form an unholy alliance with Ascadrion the Earth-Shaker. After Ascadrion was cast into the void, Emperor Syrzin banished the wyveri to the islands. He built a new castle and founded Laedresh, which eventually became the imperial palace and the capital. Grivolen's ruins were left as a reminder not to repeat the mistakes of the past. No one with good intentions wanted to meet there at night, and certainly no respectable person asked a wyvern shifter to meet in that cursed place.

Whatever Zidra had gotten herself into, I wasn't about to let her face it alone.

THREE

ZIDRA

Something smelled wrong.

I lingered near an arch, the looming curve of mossy stone all that remained of the southern wall of Castle Grivolen. Jagged half-collapsed parapets, walls, and towers formed black silhouettes against the starry sky. It looked as dark and eerie as its cursed history. Meeting at the former seat of the Wyveri Kingdom would not have been my first choice, and the site reeked of illicit activities.

After circling the ruins as a wyvern and not seeing anyone, I'd landed. Even from the air, the smell had been offensive, and I'd shifted back to my di'ora in part to lessen my sense of smell. Traces of pipe smoke, strong drink, incense, mind-altering flowers and mushrooms, refuse, blood, and other pungent odors stung my nostrils. Humans, elves, and shifters had all been here within the last several days, as had fire-foxes and other animals.

With all those scents, it was impossible to determine if anyone was in the ruins. My hearing gave no clues, either. My mysterious contact could be inside alone, have failed to show up again, or be hiding in the shelter of a tree with a small contingent of attackers.

I hated going into a situation unprepared.

That had to be the cause of the tightness in my stomach. Right? Sure, something seemed off with the informant not appearing at the tavern and then asking to meet tonight of all nights at Grivolen of all places. But I couldn't leave.

With Magistrate Malvoy's lack of cooperation, this informant might be my last chance to find the truth. For all I knew, Malvoy himself was the murderer. Nevros deserved justice, and allowing a killer to roam free violated my vows to protect the empire. Worse, if I fled like a coward, I wouldn't deserve the medallion stuffed in my pack back at the Haven.

The thought of the Merit and the humiliation of earning it only because Kyrundar had tangled our fortunes strengthened my resolve. I would prove I was worthy of the Merit and that I didn't need anyone's patronizing aid to be an esteemed rengir.

I shifted my eyes to their wyvern form. The darkness lightened, tinged with red. Rocks, shrubs, and discarded wineskins and pottery shards littered the grounds. A frown pulled at my mouth. The ruins had been left as a warning but had become a harbor for new wickedness and carelessness. This wouldn't do. *I'll speak to the governor about this tomorrow.*

For now, I had an informant to find.

I drew my sword, reassured by its heft in my grip. As a rengir, I was bound by my oath to never harm innocents, never attack first without reasonable cause, and never kill except in self-defense or when absolutely necessary, but that didn't mean I shouldn't be prepared. A few seconds wasted drawing a weapon could be the difference between life and death.

Grass rustled beneath my boots as I stepped through the archway. Every step slow and purposeful, I stalked through the skeletal ruins.

A scent tickled my nose, stronger now. A person—I didn't know how to describe the subtle differences between a person and an animal, but I could tell. The scent was definitely a person. The source was too weak and my sense of smell too overwhelmed for me to pick out human, elf, or shifter, but someone was getting closer. The problem was, the scent was coming from outside the ruins.

Perhaps I'd beaten my informant here.

I backtracked to the arch and stood in the shadows.

The swishing scrape of ice accompanied the clear, clean scent of snow magic. An ice elf? My informant couldn't be Kyrundar. That wouldn't make any sense. Nor would Kyrundar be visiting Castle Grivolen alone when he could be reveling with a horde of adoring rengiri. Right?

Just outside the ruins, the ice elf skated to a stop in a swirl of tiny ice crystals, and my suspicions were realized.

Locking a growl behind my teeth, I stepped past the arch. "Ilifir. What under Iskyr's great sky are you doing here?"

"Good to see you, too," he mumbled. "I was worried about you. You're all right?"

"Of course I am! How did you find me, anyway?" He opened his mouth to answer, but I waved away his response. "Actually, it doesn't matter. You need to go before—"

"Who are you meeting?"

"Someone who claims to have information on a murder." Internally, I cringed. Why had I told him that much? I wanted to do this alone. "I was just going to look for them, and I won't have you scaring them away. Shoo."

"Why would they want to meet here? Now? Zee, I feel strongly unsettled in my spirit about this."

That gave me pause. While I wouldn't rank Kyrundar as the most pious person I knew, he was still devout, and everyone knew that when a member of a holy order felt a strong leading or premonition about something, you listened. Iskyr could guide and warn all people, but especially those who had dedicated their lives to his service. Between Kyrundar's unease and my own, perhaps I should abandon this meeting.

Kyrundar stepped forward. Weak moonlight glinted on the hilts of the two swords strapped to his back and glittered on the aquamarines dangling from his ears. "Let me come with you."

I huffed a dry laugh. "Oh, I see. You haven't had a premonition. You just want to steal my victory again."

He frowned. "I don't steal your victories. I've never once claimed sole credit for anything we did together, and

I've certainly never taken credit for anything you did on your own."

"No, you just insist on attaching your name to mine every chance you get." I bit back my theory that he was responsible for that awful Kyrmaris moniker. "I don't have time for this. My informant has already missed one meeting."

"And missing a meeting then calling another *here* isn't suspicious?"

I hesitated, unwilling to confess I shared his misgivings. "Someone with political power might be behind the murder I'm investigating. Whoever this witness is, he or she is afraid of being seen. They're skittish, and—"

"Then I'm definitely coming with you. I can help." Kyrundar walked past me into the ruins, sending tendrils of ice ahead of him along the ground. The magic's faint pale-blue glow illuminated his path.

Help, right. That's what my mother had claimed every time she'd tried to force me into her perception of wyveri greatness or criticized my choices. *I'm helping you. It's for your own good.*

A growl rumbled in my chest as my dragon fire stirred. I shoved it down and strode after him. "How, exactly?"

"I'm a more reassuring presence and better with people than you are." He flashed a winsome smile as if he hadn't just insulted me.

He was right, but that didn't mean I wasn't offended.

"Fine, but only because I'm done wasting time. Be quiet and stay out of my way for once."

"Oh please. When have I ever gotten in your way?"

No occasions jumped to mind, but I refused to admit that. "We don't have time to make a list."

Kyrundar chuckled. "You can't think of any instances because we're a great team."

"Oh, hush." I tromped past him, then realized I was making too much noise and softened my steps.

We slunk through the looming ruins, nothing but the occasional bird cry and the whisper of vegetation in the wind disrupting the silence.

My skin prickled, and I hated that I wasn't sure if it was because of the irritating man at my side, the eeriness of Grivolen, or a premonition.

A new smell snagged my attention, and I held out my hand to halt the ice elf. A person...or people? The scent was weak amid the general stench. The whiff of elf might just be Kyrundar. I closed my eyes and took a deeper breath through my nose. Definitely at least one human, somewhere ahead of us. I concentrated on my hearing.

"Someone is ahead," I murmured, my eyes still closed. "Possibly multiple people. Sounds of breathing are muffled, like they're behind something." If I shifted, I might be able to get a better reading, but the remaining walls were a little close for my di'yar. Besides, my sense of smell would improve with terrible consequences. I'd be trying to get the reek of this place out of my nose for days.

The soft rasp of steel against leather indicated Kyrundar drawing his swords.

I opened my eyes. "They might not be hostile."

He lifted an eyebrow. "Is that why you have your sword out?"

I didn't dignify that with a response. "Just—"

"Stay out of your way?"

If I detected a little hurt in his tone, I ignored it. Following the scents and sounds, I padded around a mostly intact wall and proceeded toward a low, square barrier. At one point, it must have been a smaller outbuilding. The scents became stronger, and I definitely heard at least three breathing patterns, but I still couldn't see anyone. That was impossible—

Something moved ahead, and I swung my sword up into guard. A figure emerged from the ground. The human woman wrung her hands and took a step closer.

"Zidra Eilmaris? Is that you? Who is with you?"

"I'm Zidra. Kyrundar Ilifir is with me."

The woman stiffened and eased back a step. "We know we can trust you, but can we trust him?"

I could practically feel Kyrundar bristling like a porcupine at my side. "We're Kyrmaris," he protested. "Co-recipients of the Emperor's Merit! If you trust her, you can trust me."

There were so many aggravating things about that pronouncement, but I stifled my reaction and focused on the woman. "You're not alone, either. Who is with you?"

"Other witnesses. We're terrified for our lives." She pointed behind her and down. "They're in the old root cellar."

Underground. The thick dirt explained why I struggled

31

to smell or hear them. I resisted the urge to fidget. I couldn't shift in a root cellar if this turned into a fight.

I turned to Kyrundar. "Keep watch up here. Don't interrupt unless I call for you, all right?"

His expression soured, but he nodded.

"What's your name?" I asked as I approached the woman.

"Jida. Are you going to sheathe your sword?"

My steps faltered. Sheathe my weapon and lose precious seconds if this was a trap? Or leave it out and risk panicking skittish informants into running, or worse, attacking?

"Right. Sorry. Rengir habit." I slid the blade into the sheath with a twinge of regret and followed the woman through a black hole into the ground.

FOUR

KYRUNDAR

Rengiri didn't panic. Before we took our vows, we spent years training and honing our reflexes. We studied tactics, tested our abilities in a variety of simulated and real challenges, and learned to read situations, people, and animals. Even after we left Harcos, we practiced in order to keep our skills sharp. When we weren't training, fighting, or serving, we spent time praying and reading holy texts. Rengiri had every reason to be confident and relaxed.

None of that changed the fact that my heart pounded and a cold sweat slicked my skin when Zidra's head of brown curls disappeared into the ground.

Whatever information she was looking for, if she didn't get it because I barged in, she would never forgive me. Assuming she would ever forgive me for whatever she was already angry with me about. But I'd agreed to keep watch.

Even if the urge to throw myself into the cellar in a cyclone of ice was growing, I would wait until she called for help.

That didn't mean I couldn't get a *little* closer, though. And call up just enough of my magic that it wouldn't be very noticeable but would help me sense any...

My jaw went slack. From the direction of the root cellar, I sensed a trace of ice elf power—potent and vicious in a way I'd never felt before. The ice magic was active, as if someone were preparing to unleash it.

This was a trap.

I darted through the darkness to the square hole in the ground and threw a blast of snow. My magic's light helped me see, but I also got a faint sense of the room below. A few small crates were scattered around. Only three people were down here besides Zidra, but she was surrounded. Ignoring the rickety ladder, I floated down on swirling ice crystals.

"Trap!" I shouted at the same time as Zidra barked, "Ilifir!"

She faced me, her face reddening. "What—oof!" A thin band of metal whipped around her and melded together over her chest, pinning her arms to her sides.

"Zee!" I raced forward in a blast of icy wind, ducking to avoid hanging roots.

The woman who had greeted us jerked away from Zidra's back and looked toward me. Great. I hated fighting metalmages. They tended to break my swords and turn my jewelry against me. Thank Iskyr most of them went into craftsman trades or became guardsmen.

Before I could get to Zidra or the metalmage, one of the other assailants leaped into my path with twin daggers at the ready. His eyes flashed orange in the faint glow of my power. A shifter of some kind, but he probably wouldn't have enough room to shift in this space.

A growl vibrated my bones. Zidra's skin transformed to scales, and my eyes widened. The metalmage swore under her breath. Even my opponent partly turned his back on me.

"Is she out of her mind?" the shifter demanded.

Zidra grew, and the metal banding her chest snapped into pieces. In a blink, she shrank back to her human size and drew her sword. I grinned. Leave it to Zidra to pull off such a rapid and controlled partial shift.

The shifter in front of me snarled and swung one of his blades at my face.

"Whoa!" I parried his blade with a scowl. "Not my face of legendary beauty!"

"Ilifir, you vain fool!" Zidra shouted as she pulled her sword from the woman's torso. Great Iskyr above, sometimes I forgot how fast she could move.

I was too busy deflecting the shifter's rapid strikes and sending tendrils of ice in search of the third combatant to respond beyond a laugh. My magic brushed against other ice magic. I almost cried out at the sensation—far colder than anything I'd felt before, it burned against my power and pulsed with a darkness that made me recoil.

In my distraction, the shifter darted inside my guard and stabbed toward my heart. Cursing myself for leaving

Laedresh without my armor, I formed a shell of ice over my chest. The shifter's curved blade screeched across the ice, then glanced against my arm. I gasped in pain.

"Kyr?" Zidra called, sounding worried.

The fact that she cared renewed my focus. A blast of my cold magic sent my assailant stumbling back. Before I could press my advantage, a sword's blade burst through his chest, then withdrew. The dead shifter crumpled, revealing Zidra.

Our eyes met. A smile broke across my face at the concern in her eyes. "Thank you. See? We're a good team."

She rolled her eyes. "The third one fled, but I want to catch him."

Part of me was tempted to advocate letting the ice elf go, but Zidra would never agree. "All right, but we should be careful—"

I sensed the bolt of icy magic rushing at my back too late to counter it. Instead, I threw myself onto Zidra, knocking her to the ground. She released a pained *oof* as I landed on top of her. The bolt of ice magic crashed into a dirt wall. Its midnight-blue color was unlike anything I'd ever seen.

"Get off me!" Zidra shoved me hard enough I tumbled onto my back next to her.

"Wait—"

As Zidra sat up, another bolt flew through the darkness. This time, it made right for Zidra. I threw up a protective barrier of shimmering ice in front of her and scrambled to my feet. The two magics exploded against each other with a flash. My ice shield exploded into powder with a force that sent me staggering sideways. I blinked dancing spots of light from my eyes.

Zidra stood, her sword at the ready. "Who are you? What do you really want?"

The ice elf glided forward on swishing snow. I loathed the rare instances when I had to fight a fellow ice elf who had chosen a path of lawlessness. Even if we weren't related, it felt like battling family. Not so this time. Something about the twisted power I'd sensed from this ice elf disturbed me. I felt no kinship with him.

He reached into a quiver at his hip and pulled out what looked like an unfletched crossbow bolt, but it was dark blue and pulsed with a wicked light. "To fulfill my mission." He threw out his empty left hand, blasting me with a volley of sharp ice needles. Despite the intensity of his unrelenting attack, I easily blocked it.

"Farewell, rengir." The way he said *rengir* made the word sound like a curse. His hate-filled gaze remained focused on me, even as Zidra growled and sprinted toward the would-be assassin.

He raised the bolt of corrupt magic…

And at the last moment, threw it directly at Zidra.

"Zee!" I punched toward the bolt, sending an arc of ice and snow toward it, but the magic-powered bolt was faster.

Zidra dodged—

Too late. Too slow.

The bolt pierced her right arm.

Her earsplitting scream melded with a dragon roar and shook the cellar. Dirt rained from the ceiling. Her sword slipped from her fingers, and she fell to her knees.

In a haze of fear and fury, I unleashed a blast of power beyond anything I had before at the elf. The *thunk* of icicles embedding in flesh and a strangled cry that cut off in a gurgle confirmed I'd hit my mark.

Zidra collapsed.

"Zee!" I dropped my swords and scrambled to her side. My knees hit the packed dirt.

"It burns," she screamed. Tears streaked her face, glistening in the weak light of the candlestick resting on a nearby crate.

I stumbled over tangled reassurances, hardly knowing what I said. The bolt was embedded in her arm, pulsing with a darkness that chilled my soul. Zidra shivered and curled up like a child trying to get warm.

This was a tainted form of elf magic. I'd never encountered it before, but I'd heard of it. An ice curse. The magic was racing toward Zidra's heart and would freeze her from the inside out.

I coated my hand in pliable ice, then gripped the bolt. Even through my protective layer of magic, the bolt was freezing. I yanked the weapon of pure magic out and threw it aside with furious strength despite how my hands trembled.

Zidra's teeth continued to chatter, and she didn't stop shivering.

Iskyr, how do I help her?

"It's going to be all right; just hold on." I placed my clammy hands over the puncture in her arm. Trying to ignore the slick warmth of her blood, I focused on carefully sending my magic into her.

My magic didn't have to have ice or snow in it, but it was always cold. Would this make things worse? My throat tightened so I could hardly breathe. What if I killed her? My rival, my best friend, my only true equal among the rengiri.

No, I needed to focus. Not imagine my failure and her death before I'd even tried.

I sensed the twisted magic spreading ice through Zidra's veins.

"Iskyr," I prayed aloud. My voice warbled. "Guide me and save her."

I latched onto the dark magic with my own. My scream of pain mingled with Zidra's, but I gritted my teeth and continued. Slowly, bit by bit, I dragged the tainted ice magic away from her heart and back toward the entry point. Sweat ran into my eyes. The curse raged, trying to escape my hold. Every time I neared her wound, the magic not only strengthened but burned against my power, causing both Zidra and me pain.

"I can't—I can't do it." My arms vibrated from the strain. "I can't extract it."

But maybe I didn't need to. Maybe all I needed was to hold it back until we could find a healer.

I couldn't hold this and move her, though. Unless…?

Ice elves could embed magic into almost anything for defensive traps—stone, wood, cloth, metal, trees. Living plants were the most difficult, but I had managed it many times.

This time, I would embed my magic as a barrier to bind the magic poisoning Zidra. I poured my magic into her arm, using the techniques used on plants to ensure I wouldn't cause her frostbite or otherwise harm her.

"Please, Iskyr, make this work."

I withdrew my magic and then released my crushing grip on Zidra's upper arm. My body felt heavy and numb as I sat back. My toes tapped a rhythm on the dirt. I pinched a gemstone earring and rubbed the stone between my fingers.

A relieved sigh eased from Zidra. Her shivers slowed, then stopped, and her teeth ceased chattering.

"Zidra?" I asked hoarsely.

When she didn't respond, I rolled her onto her back. Her eyes were closed, her breath slow and even.

She must have passed out.

I found the thin knife Zidra kept in her right boot in case of emergencies and used it to cut a strip of cloth off the edge of my tunic. After I bandaged her wound, I checked my own injury. The short, shallow cut had already scabbed over. It looked a mess and twinged with certain movements, but it could wait until I had access to clean water and bandages. In the flickering light of the dying candle, I retrieved my swords and returned to Zidra's side.

She was still unconscious. The longer that ice curse and my magic remained in her arm, the greater the risk of something going wrong. She needed to see a healer at once. When an attempt to wake her didn't work, I scooped her into my arms. Her cheek rested against the buckle on one of my baldrics. Murmuring apologies, I jostled her and wiggled until she seemed more comfortably tucked against my chest.

At least my misjudgment in leaving the city ill-prepared meant she could rest against my soft tunic rather than hard armor.

I carried her to the base of the ladder just as the candle sputtered out. My magic lifted us out of the cellar. A glittering slab of ice crystalized beneath my feet, and soon we were flying over the countryside, back toward Laedresh.

Between the imperial palace and Harcos Academy stood Merael's Infirmary and University. Founded five hundred years ago in honor of a great light elf healer, the infirmary was still mostly staffed by elves, but human and shifter healers worked and studied there as well. The best healers in the Laedreshian Empire trained at Merael's, and many of them served there.

The front doors were locked when I arrived. Only moonlight illuminated the sprawling building of white stone, as the lanterns framing the entryway had been extinguished. Unwilling to put Zidra down, I kicked the door.

"Hello! I need help! Is anyone here?" I slammed my boot into the wood, not caring if I damaged the carvings. "Please! We need a healer! It's urgent!"

Zidra stirred in my arms, but instead of waking, she buried her face in my tunic with a groan.

The door shook beneath my persistent kicking. "Is anyone in the infirmary? Please!"

Muffled sounds of shouting filtered through the door.

Something heavy shifted with a scrape and a clang, and then one of the doors swung inward. I blinked against the candle burning in the hand of the petite human woman in the dark entry.

"What's all this—Kyrundar Ilifir?" Her lower jaw went slack.

Oh no. Right now was *not* the time to deal with an admirer.

"Please," I said. "Are you a healer?"

"Yes…well, no." Her bronze skin took on a ruddy hue. "I'm an apprentice."

"Are there any senior healers here?" I demanded. "Preferably an ice elf. Zidra Eilmaris was struck by an ice curse."

The dreamy expression fled the woman's face. She blinked and lowered her gaze, as if she hadn't noticed the unconscious rengir in my arms. "And she's still alive?" Her voice rose to a shout.

"I stopped its progress, but it's too powerful for me to extract—"

"Come in, come!" The apprentice frantically waved us inside. I'd barely cleared the doorway when she set off at a brisk pace. "The senior physician on overnight emergency duty is sleeping, but I'll wake him at once. Through here." She motioned into a room.

I angled through the doorway, careful not to catch Zidra's feet on the frame. Why was she still unconscious? What if I'd failed to save her?

The human scurried around, lighting candles set in

sconces. Golden light spread, illuminating a narrow but unusually tall bed covered in crisp white linens. I eased Zidra onto it, grateful for its height. I brushed curls out of her face, then adjusted her limbs until she looked comfortable. At least, as comfortable as someone could be while wounded and wearing armor.

When I turned to ask the apprentice how long it would take the physician to arrive, she was gone.

A stool stood in the corner opposite the bed next to a narrow table with neatly arranged containers. In the diagonal corner, next to the door, was an upholstered armchair with a blanket tossed over one arm. Instead of taking either, I perched on the edge of the bed near Zidra's feet and waited, praying with all my might that she would live.

FIVE

ZIDRA

I awoke to pain.

Soft fabric greeted my palms rather than packed dirt. Competing emotions tangled inside me, making my head swim—or perhaps that was the pain. Dark spots danced in my vision, and I sat up with a groan. A figure outlined in an orange glow moved abruptly in front of me. On instinct, I reached for my sword, only to find my scabbard empty.

"Zidra?" The anguished male voice snapped my attention up. Kyrundar stood over me, his eyebrows pushing together like they were attempting to merge into one.

Irritated with his face and unwilling to meet his eyes, I continued searching for my weapon. "Where's my sword?" My voice emerged hoarse and indecipherable. I cleared my throat. "Where are we? And where is my sword?"

"Uh…oh. I—erm." He fiddled with an aquamarine on

one of his earrings.

Ignoring a strange surge of embarrassment that Kyrundar should have been feeling, not me, I took in my surroundings. I'd never seen this room before, with its plastered walls, army of candles, and one small bed. A framed embroidery hanging on the wall depicted a crook wreathed in herbs, a symbol of healers.

"You brought me to an infirmary?"

He blinked at me, the fool. "Yes? You were—"

"No!" I grasped my wounded arm. "The people who ambushed me—"

"All dead," Kyrundar interrupted.

"I need to examine their bodies! There could be an indication of who they were, who sent them, if the informant was a deception this entire time or if they killed whoever contacted me! And did you leave my sword behind?" I waved at him. "But you brought yours, I see!"

He edged back a step. "You almost died. I wasn't thinking—"

"Obviously!"

"—clearly." The hurt on Kyrundar's face must have softened my anger, because regret filtered in.

"I need to go back." I sucked in a breath through my teeth and clenched the wound on my arm tighter. "Why does this feel like it's burning and freezing at the same time?"

"That's to be expected with an ice curse," a new, unfamiliar voice said.

My chest tightened. "Ice...curse?"

45

A squat man wearing the close-fitting blue robes of a senior physician slipped around Kyrundar, a tense expression on his ruddy, freckle-dusted face. "Apprentice Banor told me you were struck by an ice curse." He peered up at Kyrundar. "And then you used your magic to keep it from reaching her heart, is that correct?"

Kyrundar made some reply to the physician, but my ears were ringing. Ice curse? They'd taught us about those at Harcos. Rare, dangerous ice magic that took a lot of malice, intention, power, and time to refine into highly volatile bolts. When activated, the curse would seek to smother the closest heat source. As a wyveri with dragon heat in my heart, I'd had nightmares for days after that lecture.

"Rengir Eilmaris?"

I blinked. "Sorry?"

"I was saying, I'm Senior Physician Quillan. I'm a fleshmage, so I'll examine you and see what, if anything, I can do, but I've sent for Physician Mirlanwen as well. She's the ice elf on our staff."

"Is she a senior physician?" Kyrundar asked, his tone causing dismay to spike in my own chest.

Quillan shook his head. "Ice elves don't often study here, and those who do mostly return to Glacori." He held up his forefinger and made a spinning movement. "Would you turn so I can inspect your arm now, Rengir Eilmaris?"

"Oh, right." Heat suffused my skin. I turned so my right arm was facing Quillan and crossed my legs on the bed. "You may call me Zidra."

"Thank you, Zidra." The physician loosened and

unwrapped the fabric binding my arm. Only when he set it aside did I recognize the material from Kyrundar's blue tunic. My gaze cut down to the jagged hem of his clothing, then back up to his face.

The moment our eyes locked, I felt a tug deep in my chest. An odd sensation zinged through me, sending an exhilarating shiver from the top of my head down to my feet; my toes curled in my boots.

Kyrundar's head jerked back. His ice-blue eyes widened, and a bit of pink overtook his pale complexion.

A stab of pain as Quillan did something to my arm broke the unsettling moment, but then Kyrundar hissed in pain at the same instant I did. Curiosity and confusion rose in my chest, but I could now recognize that those weren't *my* feelings—not solely.

They were Kyrundar's.

My jaw fell open. "Oh. No. What did you *do*?"

Quillan hummed and adjusted his hold on my arm. "I only—"

"Not you!" I pointed at Kyrundar. Red tinted my vision. My fangs elongated and my blood heated, and I felt his panic filtering through my emotions. "You used your magic on me. What else did you—"

I cut off with a cry of pain as something cold stabbed at my right arm.

"Zidra!" Quillan cried. "You must control your dragon fire!"

Every breath heaved in my lungs as I glared down Kyrundar.

He held up his hands in a placating gesture. "I don't know! I didn't do anything, Zee."

I leaped to my feet, ignoring Quillan begging me to calm down. "I was unconscious, so *I* didn't do anything, and I don't want this, so *you* must have done something!"

Kyrundar winced, and I hated that I could feel how offended and frustrated he was, but he also had no right to be offended. The icy pain in my arm increased, and Kyrundar grabbed his own arm.

"Zidra!" Quillan shoved against my breastplate, but I didn't budge. "Your dragon fire is burning through Kyrundar's ice magic, which is holding the ice curse in check. You need to calm down, or you will die!"

That shocked me enough that Quillan was able to force me back onto the bed. I willed myself numb, blocking out my own emotions as well as Kyrundar's. Quillan lifted my arm and prodded the wound, then sent a surge of human magic into my skin that tingled in a soothing way.

"Rengir Ilifir," he said, his voice too level. "I need you to block the ice curse again. It's escaping back into her bloodstream, and my magic does not affect it."

Kyrundar stepped forward, but I recoiled involuntarily.

"Zidra," Quillan said softly. He waited until I looked at him to continue. "I don't know what's going on, but Kyrundar Ilifir saved your life, and right now, he's the only one who can save you again."

All of my wyveri pride rankled at the words. I clenched my fists until my fingers ached.

"Will you consent to him treating your wound?"

"Fine," I ground out. "But you better not do anything else."

"What else could I possibly do?" Kyrundar muttered as he switched places with the physician.

Since I didn't actually know, I kept my mouth shut. The worst thing that could possibly happen already had, and it wasn't as if he could make us any more connected than we already were.

Because the emotion sharing, Kyrundar feeling my pain—it could mean only one thing.

Shifters and elves had slightly different magics and so had their own traditions and methods, but both had heart-bonds—strong magic that tied a couple together in body, heart, and soul.

"It's impossible," I whispered to myself. There were prerequisites to these things. Like marriage, being in love, and Iskyr's blessing.

Kyrundar placed his hands on either side of my wound. "This might hurt. I'm sorry."

A new sensation of cold spread into my arm, but this cold wasn't painful. Kyrundar's magic caressed my skin like cool silk on a hot day...until it touched the twisted magic of the curse. I bit my tongue to smother a shout, and Kyrundar grimaced. Sweat beaded along his hairline. Bit by excruciating bit, he wrangled the fingers of frost back toward the wound. When he released my arm, we were both shaking.

The moment Kyrundar stepped back, Quillan moved into his spot at my side. After inspecting my arm and doing something else with his soothing fleshmage healing magic, he looked to Kyrundar.

"Outstanding work. That seems even more stable than before." Quillan turned back to me. "I'm afraid there's very little I can do. I've healed the damage to the surrounding skin and muscle, but closing the wound over the curse would make things worse. For now, I'll clean and reband-age the puncture. Hopefully Mirlanwen can do more."

Suddenly exhausted, I barely managed a half-hearted nod. Quillan cleaned my arm with something that stung, then covered the puncture with gauze and neatly wrapped my arm in a white bandage.

"When will Physician Mirlanwen arrive?" Kyrundar asked.

Quillan lifted a shoulder. "She lives a few streets away, but she might not be at home due to all the Dawning Fes-tival celebrations tonight. The apprentice will have to find her and hope she's in condition to treat a patient."

Kyrundar's lips pursed. "I see. Might I have a moment alone with Zidra?"

Quillan bowed his head. "Actually, I was just going to return to bed, unless either of you require any other medi-cal attention." He indicated Kyrundar's arm. "You appear to have been wounded yourself."

"Oh, it's minor."

I lowered my gaze to my hands, a little ashamed I'd forgotten Kyrundar had been hurt first. A surge of renewed annoyance followed the thought. If that idiot hadn't followed me, interfered with my meeting, jumped into a fight without proper armor, gotten himself hurt, and then been on his knees trying to ward off that ice elf's attack, I wouldn't have been distracted. Without his distraction, surely this ice curse never would have touched me.

"Still," Quillan said, "best to be sure, lest any infection set in." He ushered Kyrundar to the chair in the corner, where he removed the sleeve of Kyrundar's tunic with a pair of shears, much to the vain elf's chagrin.

I shook my head, then lay down and closed my eyes, determined to ignore Kyrundar and the binding.

Ignoring the heartbond proved difficult, as I felt a muted stinging in my arm when Quillan cleansed Kyr's cut, then a tingling sensation as the healer used his fleshmagic to close the wound. Kyr expressed his thanks, and Quillan took his leave.

Before Kyrundar could say anything, I said, "I don't want to talk about it."

"That won't make it go away."

I waved a hand above me. "This ice elf physician will remove the curse, and then you'll remove your magic from me, and then whatever this is will go away."

For a moment, he was silent. Through our unwanted bond, I sensed him sifting through possibilities, as well as a bit of relief.

"I suppose it *could* be simply because I placed my magic in you," he said slowly. "I had to channel magic uncomfortably close to your heart to pull back the curse. Then I had to leave some in you... Yes. I don't know much about how our vastly different magics might interact—"

"Ours are much more tied to our bodies," I interjected. Thinking about Kyrundar's magic traveling through my veins, entangling itself with the dragon fire that allowed me to shift, made me nauseated.

The chair in the corner creaked as Kyrundar moved. "What do you need? Why are you feeling ill?"

I groaned and rolled onto my side so I faced the wall. "Why did you go to the ruins? How did you even know I was there? You know what, unimportant. What matters is that you need to stop doing this!"

"Doing what, exactly? Saving your life?"

"Ruining my life!" I shoved upright and glared at him, unmoved by the shock and hurt coursing through the bond. "If it weren't for you, I wouldn't be in this fire-blasted infirmary!"

"Yes, because you'd be dead in the ruins of Grivolen!"

I bit out a disbelieving laugh. "Please. If you hadn't been there distracting me with your ridiculous craving for glory, I would have been more alert. I would have sensed the trap earlier. I probably wouldn't have even gone into that cellar, because I would have been alone and able to insist they come out to talk to me. I wouldn't have been distracted by you getting yourself hurt, and that ice elf couldn't have tricked me into thinking you were his target. I'd have been more cautious, and I wouldn't have been struck by that ice curse!"

"Craving for glory?"

"Yes! You're so afraid I'll outshine you that you're constantly following me around!"

Kyrundar's eyebrows rose. "Seriously?" He shoved to his feet. "You think I help you because I'm intimidated by you?"

"Why else would you show up and insist on aiding me when I never asked? And I *know* you must be responsible for this 'Kyrmaris' nonsense. Tying our names together and insisting yours come first!"

"First of all, Kyrmaris rolls off the tongue the best! Zidifir is ridiculous, Eilifir is too close to Ilifir, and Zirundar is too long—"

I gasped. "I knew it! You insufferable—"

"But I didn't come up with it! A friend of mine did, but that's beside the point. I accompany you to *help* you! Would anyone know about your greatest feats if I weren't there to see and then tell people about them so the stories spread? We both know you're not as good at public perception. I mean, take your display at the Ceremony. You almost looked angry to achieve your life's ambition! Why are you upset with me after I helped you get what you told me you most wanted?"

My mouth fell open. As much as it had hurt to share that moment receiving the Emperor's Merit with Kyrundar, and as frustrating as it was to believe that he kept following me for his own selfish benefit, this was so much worse. He thought I couldn't earn the Merit on my own? That he was so much better than me that I wouldn't get anywhere without him? For a moment I stared at him, and then I leaped off the bed and pointed at the open door.

"I don't need your help or your pity!" Tears threatened

my eyes, but I refused to cry. "Get out! Leave me alone!" I spun around, hating my own weakness.

"Zidra—"

"Go away." I pressed my eyes closed and willed back the tears. I wanted to shift and either fight him or fly away, but I couldn't do either. If Quillan was right that my dragon fire destroyed Kyrundar's barrier, shifting would kill me.

But the shame cracking through my heart might kill me anyway.

Never good enough.

Kyrundar didn't believe I was capable on my own, and thanks to him and the shared awarding of the Merit to "Kyrmaris," no one else ever would, either. My parents. My siblings. My clan. The wyveri. The entire empire. Maybe I wasn't. What if he was right? I'd thought Kyrundar had ruined my chance at standing on the palace steps alone and receiving the Emperor's Merit, but perhaps if we'd never fought together, I'd have been standing in the crowd with the other rengiri watching Kyrundar receive the Merit.

Everything I had worked for, and it meant *nothing*. I wasn't good enough.

"My parents never told me how confusing a heartbond can be," Kyrundar said quietly. "I know you're feeling hurt and ashamed and disheartened, but I don't understand why."

"Because you've always had sea-foam for brains." I regretted the harsh words the moment they left my lips, and even more so when I felt Kyrundar's hurt through the bond.

A rapid, distant tapping diverted my attention. I tilted my head, listening. Two pairs of rushed footsteps, and someone breathing heavily.

"I want—"

I held up my hand and faced the door. "Someone is coming."

If Iskyr blessed me, it would be the apprentice bringing Physician Mirlanwen, and this ice elf healer would get the ice magic and this heartbond out of me.

SIX

KYRUNDAR

I stepped between Zidra and the door. "Friend or foe?"

"Either way, I don't need your protection," she huffed.

My shoulders tightened. "You can't shift, and you have no sword."

"And whose fault is that? On both counts!"

I clenched my teeth until they ached. Why was she so determined to hate me? And here I was, thinking of her ungrateful dragon hide as a close friend.

"I smell a human and an elf," Zidra said.

"Ice elf?" I inquired without thinking, but quickly added, "I know, we smell the same unless we're actively using magic, sorry." As useful as it was that shifters could usually discern human from elf from shifter by scent, it would be nice if they could tell the differences within those groups.

Based on the impression I was getting of her emotions,

she was probably thinking again that I had sea-foam for brains. Maybe she wasn't wrong.

I kept returning to what she had claimed. *Was* it my fault that her life was in danger from the ice curse? She wasn't entirely wrong that my presence had complicated her meeting and distracted her.

"Stop blocking the doorway," Zidra groused.

Ignoring her, I stepped into the hall. The apprentice was returning, a lantern in hand, and with a spindly ice elf woman at her side. Reassured, I returned to my seat in the corner.

"The ice elf physician, then?"

I nodded, not in the mood to talk to Zidra.

She returned to sit on the bed with her legs dangling off the side. The sight of her feet hanging above the floor almost made me smile. I'd never met any other wyveri, so I didn't know if she was short for her people, but she was short compared to most elves. She'd never appreciated me pointing out how much taller than her I was. Her height did make her easier to carry…although she probably wouldn't see that as a positive.

The glow of the lantern preceded the apprentice and the healer into the room. Mirlanwen bustled around the apprentice and made right for Zidra. Her white hair fell down her back in a braid, and her unwrinkled skin and pink-tinged cheeks indicated she wasn't old. For an elf, that could mean anything from being around my own one hundred fifty-five years to being in her early five hundreds.

"Rengir Eilmaris, I'm Physician Mirlanwen." She bowed,

since her russet physician robes weren't wide enough to accommodate a proper curtsy. "Quillan explained the situation. How are you feeling?"

Zidra lifted her left shoulder in a noncommittal shrug. "The entry site still hurts, but less than it did. It feels like a minor burn, but also cold, in addition to the pinching of the stab wound."

Mirlanwen nodded. "May I remove the bandage and examine it? I will use my magic to probe the wound and the ice magics."

"Of course." Zidra adjusted her position to give the healer easier access.

Since I couldn't get a good view from my chair in the corner, I stood and moved closer. Subtle hints of pale blue swirled around Mirlanwen's fingertips as she felt around the wound. A chill brushed against my own arm at the same moment as Zidra shivered.

Mirlanwen drew her hands back with a frown and then turned to me. "You did well, Rengir Ilifir. To say I am impressed with your work here would be an understatement." She faced Zidra again. "And you, Rengir Eilmaris. I am astounded you are not only alive, but so hale. To look at you, one would assume you'd suffered a far less serious injury. I can sense the traces of the ice curse and Kyrundar Ilifir's magic. They came very near your heart, yet your dragon fire appears strong and unharmed."

Along with the flattered pride coming through the bond, I sensed the physician's words eased a little of Zidra's anger.

"Unfortunately," Mirlanwen continued, "there is nothing I can do." She turned both her hands palm up and dropped them back to her sides. "Rengir Ilifir's power is far stronger than mine." She looked to me. "You were unable to extract the curse?"

I gulped and shook my head. "I tried, but I wasn't even sure how. What I was trying wasn't working, so I did the best I could."

"You did well," she reassured me with a smile. "The problem is, if the curse was too great for your power, and your power is greater than mine, I will be unable to remove it as well. You will need to remove your magic, and a more skilled ice elf healer will have to then remove the curse."

Zidra paled. "I thought Physician Quillan said you were the only ice elf at Merael's?"

"I am." Mirlanwen's expression pinched. "I recommend you find Gautindar Rouven. He was a senior physician—in fact, he was *the* most senior physician on staff until he abruptly retired around six months ago."

"An old man?" I tried and failed to hide my skepticism.

"Rouven is six hundred, yes. But he's still very capable, and he's more powerful and far more experienced than I am. If anyone can extract this corrupted ice magic, it's him."

Zidra took a deep breath. "Where can I find him?"

Mirlanwen grimaced. "I don't actually know."

My breath lodged in my chest, and I wasn't sure if it was my own reaction or Zidra's. "I beg your pardon?"

"When Rouven announced his hasty retirement and that he was leaving Laedresh, he said he didn't want to be bothered. He was always an eccentric old grump, but he loved being a physician. His behavior when he left was odd, to put it mildly. He refused to tell anyone where he was going or why he was leaving. He hails from a noble family, but his relatives in Glacori haven't seen him."

"Is there any other physician that can help whose whereabouts you *do* know?" Zidra demanded.

"I'm sorry, rengiri." Mirlanwen shook her head. "I don't know any other ice elf healers who possess the skill and power required for this task. You could visit them without luck and end up wasting more time than you would simply finding Gautindar Rouven—time you don't have. The potent ice curse and your strong dragon fire are both fighting against Rengir Ilifir's barrier. It won't last forever."

Frost swirled around my fingertips as fear and resolve tangled in my soul. "We'll find him, Zee."

She groaned and lay back on the bed. "This is a nightmare."

"I have contacts," I insisted. "And I'm an ice elf, too. We will have his location within days, I'm sure—"

"Iskyr, give me grace," Zidra mumbled. She turned her head to peer at Mirlanwen. "Are you sure you can't accompany me and remove Ilifir's magic?"

My teeth clicked as I snapped my jaw shut. Of course she didn't want to spend days or weeks with me. Not when she blamed me for this predicament. Or was it not merely that she blamed me, but that I had misinterpreted our relationship all these years? Perhaps she didn't think of me as a friend at all.

Or had she gotten so caught up in her quest to be the best rengir, she'd forgotten our friendship? I'd just have to remind her.

Mirlanwen tilted her head and glanced between us. "Rengir Eilmaris, Kyrundar Ilifir did remarkable work in constraining the ice curse. Right now, his magic—which again, is far more powerful than my own—is the only thing preventing irreversible frostbite. However, it's a temporary treatment, and one that has never been attempted before. You will need him to monitor and adjust the barrier. Besides, I cannot simply leave my post in the infirmary and my teaching position. I apologize that I cannot do more for you."

Zidra sighed. "I understand. Thank you for trying."

"Of course, rengir. It is my oath to serve all in need of healing, my honor to serve rengiri, and my great pride to serve a recipient of the Emperor's Merit." Mirlanwen bowed again. "Can I assist either of you with anything else?"

Zidra shook her head. "No, thank you."

Mirlanwen turned to me, and I shook my head and thanked her as well. She left. Silence fell on the room, smothering us like a wet wool blanket.

After a moment, Zidra stood. She stole one of the candles from a sconce and moved toward the door without acknowledging me.

"Where are you going?"

"Back to the West Quarter Haven to borrow someone's sword. Then back to Castle Grivolen to fetch *my* sword and examine the bodies. Alone."

I exhaled through my nose and followed her. "Zee, someone just tried to murder you, and you want to go back there alone? What if whoever sent the assassins sends someone to check on why they haven't returned? Besides, it's a long way, and I can get you there faster since you can't shift."

The sorrow that crackled through our heartbond threatened my own composure.

"I'm sorry," I murmured. "I could have phrased that more considerately."

"It's true." She continued down the corridor, her movements jerky. "But no, we need to spend time apart. Maybe if we put some distance between us, the heartbond will break."

"Heartbonds don't work like that." At least they didn't for elves. I doubted they did for shifters, either.

"Maybe it's new enough it will!" Zidra's pace increased, and her steps echoed louder against the stone. "Besides, in normal circumstances, bonds aren't accidental. This one might work differently."

I stopped. She was right. Heartbonds were never accidental. As far as I knew, they had to be consensual, too—heartbonds never simply happened between two people who didn't love each other, who weren't devoted to one another.

Granted, heartbonds weren't generally formed when one person threaded their magic through the other person's veins, either. Perhaps she was right, and this one would work differently.

That didn't change the fact that I couldn't let Zidra return to Grivolen on her own.

I jogged to catch up to her. "Fine. I'll return to Riverfront Haven, and we can try being apart for the night—after we return to the ruins." She glared at me, but I spoke again before she could protest. "I forgot your sword, and I brought you here, where they couldn't even do anything. Besides, if we go together, you won't have to detour to the Haven first. You can borrow one of my swords if needed. It's my fault, so let me repay you by taking you back and forth to the ruins faster than you can go on foot."

A muscle along Zidra's jaw ticked. "As long as it doesn't involve you carrying me."

SEVEN

ZIDRA

To my relief, Kyrundar didn't need to touch me to use his magic to transport both of us. We stood on separate floating slabs of ice. Kyrundar moved both slabs at the same pace without requiring that we so much as hold hands. His magic propelled us far faster than I could have run, and I would have tired long before I reached Grivolen.

I refused to acknowledge this, however. Everything that had gone wrong, including our needing to return to the ruins at all, was his fault, and I was not ready to forgive him.

I would eventually. But Kyrundar had turned the best day of my life into the worst day, and I was having difficulty releasing my anger.

When we arrived, we lit a lantern Kyrundar had "borrowed" from Merael's and retraced our steps. The stench assaulted my nose again. Dead grasses rustled in the breeze, and small creatures skittered in the shadows of the ruins.

How had I missed that this was a trap? No, not missed. I'd ignored the warning signs, too eager for a distraction from the debacle of the Emperor's Merit ceremony. Even before that, I had wanted to prove I was right about Magistrate Nevros's death, so I'd followed a lead I shouldn't have.

Fine, Kyrundar didn't deserve all the blame. But if he hadn't intruded, maybe my mind would have been clearer, and I wouldn't have gone into that hole.

This time, I paused at the entrance to the cellar to determine what might await us inside. I detected the tang of drying blood but didn't smell anything else, nor did I hear anyone. I decided not to shift my eyes and risk affecting the ice magic.

Kyrundar held out his hands, and tendrils of minuscule glittering ice crystals swirled through the opening and into the cellar. "Hm."

"What?"

"I don't sense the corpses."

"I'm sorry; *what?*"

He shrugged. "They should still be warm enough my magic could sense them, but I don't. I don't sense anyone living, either, or any latent magic." With that, he leaped down. He always had to be first.

I massaged my temples and followed.

Sure enough, no one was there—not even the bodies. I retrieved my sword, and some of the strain in my shoulders relaxed. "There you are, gorgeous," I whispered while I dug a cloth out of my hip pouch. "I didn't mean to abandon you."

Kyrundar huffed. "And I didn't even get a hello."

I ignored him and cleaned the blood and dirt off the etched blade. With my weapon back where it belonged in the scabbard at my side, I stood and scowled at the cellar.

"Are you certain you killed the ice elf?"

He winced. "Yes."

I turned in a circle. "And I'm sure I killed the metal-mage and the shifter. Someone took them? Already? How long was I unconscious?"

"Not long. You woke up shortly after I laid you on the bed at Merael's."

Why did he have to phrase it like *that*? I wrinkled my nose but moved on, as I didn't care to think about Kyrundar carrying my unconscious body through Laedresh.

"Whoever took them must have been fairly close."

I nodded. As much as I wanted to gripe about having no corpses to inspect, if he hadn't taken me to Merael's and waited for me to awaken, whoever retrieved the bodies might have arrived while I was still unconscious. Perhaps Kyrundar would have handled them as well, but what if there had been too many or he'd been too weakened from helping me? At least we were both alive.

"All right," I said. "Let's see if they dropped anything."

Kyrundar's face twisted. "I'm sure there's a lot of refuse and forgotten items down here. How will we even know if it was theirs?"

"Maybe it will be obvious," I grumbled, already inspecting the dirt around my feet. Searching was probably futile, but

I didn't want to accept another defeat without even trying.

Several minutes of searching turned up nothing of use. I nibbled on my lower lip and surveyed the cellar, as if an answer might be etched into one of the dirt walls.

Kyrundar cleared his throat. "I'm sorry we didn't find anything, Zee. We should leave in case whoever took the bodies returns."

I arched an eyebrow. "Why would they do that?"

"I don't know." He tossed up his free hand, and the lantern juddered in his grip. "They could have someone watching the ruins in case we returned."

That nearly tempted me to stay, but the strain on my body from my wound and all the cold magic I had endured had caught up to me. I needed to rest more than I needed to wait in putrid ruins for someone who might not appear. If I tried to stay, Kyrundar would probably point out that I couldn't shift and my arm was injured. I was ambidextrous, but for someone who usually fought two-handed, still not ideal.

I led the way to the exit. For now, I would return to the Haven and consider what I knew and what to do next.

Kyrundar trailed me out of the cellar and walked at my side back through Castle Grivolen. When we emerged from the ruins, he turned to me.

"To West Quarter Haven, then?"

"No need for you to go out of your way." I'd rather not be seen flying through Laedresh with him any more than necessary. "You can leave me at the gate. I can walk the rest of the way."

He opened and closed his mouth. "Are you sure you don't want to rethink this distance-might-break-the-heartbond theory? What if something happens with the curse in the middle of the night?"

The mention of the heartbond jolted me. "Wait—I haven't felt your emotions in a while." I grinned. "Thank Iskyr! You see? The bond was an accident, and it's already fading!"

Kyrundar didn't look convinced. "My mother and father said that a heartbond is strongest right after it forms and sometimes if one of the couple is in peril. It might be settling in, fading into the background unless we concentrate on it."

I didn't like that possibility. Wyveri didn't usually talk about heartbonds beyond the very basics until the day before the wedding, when they would pass on the knowledge. I had never so much as accepted a token of interest from a man, so I wasn't familiar with the finer details of heartbonds. Even if I had been, shifter and elf bonds were uncommon, and for all I knew, they might differ from elf heartbonds.

"You're displeased and uncertain, and that scares you," Kyrundar said softly. "I'm sorry. I promise I never would have willingly put you in a position to feel like that."

I stiffened. "You guessed that based on my expression."

He glanced heavenward. "Zee, concentrate on me. What am I feeling?"

The thought of spying on Kyrundar's emotions on purpose made me recoil. Who thought these heartbonds were a good idea, anyway?

Sorry, Iskyr. I almost cringed, as if our god might strike me right then and there for doubting his wisdom, even though I knew Iskyr was not so unforgiving and vengeful.

Instead, I directed my unease at Kyrundar. "That feels invasive and rude."

"I give you my permission. Now it isn't invasive."

"All right, fine."

I wasn't entirely certain how to concentrate on Kyrundar's emotions. Did I need to stare at him intently? Imagine his feelings like a rope I could grab? Mentally picture my soul reaching toward him and touching his soul? Or simply think about him and open my heart and mind to his presence?

That would involve letting down the walls of displeasure I had constructed. I had a sensation of humor that I knew wasn't Kyrundar—as if Iskyr were amused with me. *Fine. I forgive Kyr. I don't trust him or like him or want him around, but I forgive him.*

I turned my focus back to him. An emotion filtered into my consciousness, like music so distant and quiet I had to strain to hear it, but the moment I stretched toward the feeling, it swelled.

"Why are you so sad?" The words tumbled out of my mouth without proper consideration.

The corner of Kyrundar's lips tipped upward. "A lot of reasons. None are important right this moment." He turned toward Laedresh and created two floating ice disks. "Come on. I'll take you to the gate. Unless you've changed your mind?"

EIGHT

KYRUNDAR

Zidra tilted her head. "Changed my mind about what, exactly?"

"About me taking you all the way to West Quarter Haven?" I stepped onto my hovering slab of ice. "It's so much faster to fly over the buildings. And it has the added benefit of avoiding awkward conversations with well-wishers."

"Wait!" She gaped at me. "Did you fly over the buildings to Merael's?"

"Yes—"

"So maybe no one saw you holding me while I was unconscious?" At my nod, her shoulders caved like she'd dropped a heavy weight, and the look of relief on her face almost made me laugh.

I wasn't offended. Mostly. After all, I wouldn't be overly keen on Laedresh gossiping about me being unconscious and carried by another rengir, either. Still, I elected not to tell her that I had made such a racket at the entrance to Merael's Infirmary that it was entirely possible people had seen us.

"Why did we fly through the fire-blasted streets on the way here, then?" Zidra's scowl held such fury I was surprised her eyes weren't glowing red.

My face heated. "I didn't want to risk you sliding off. I don't do this often, and you've never traveled by ice disk before, so I thought if you lost your footing or I didn't hold it steady enough, well, best not be twenty feet in the air. But it went so well, I'm not worried about going higher and faster on the way back."

Zidra pursed her lips, but then she shook her head with a sigh and stepped onto the other ice disk. "I suppose that makes sense," she muttered. "And, well...avoiding anyone is compelling."

"Then to West Quarter Haven?"

"All right."

My momentary elation at her agreement died a quick death, as Zidra insisted I drop her off in the back of West Quarter Haven. Apparently she really didn't want *anyone* to see us together. I set down the disks and dispersed them in a glitter of disappearing snow powder.

Unlike Riverfront Haven, with its well-manicured gardens in a walled enclosure, West Quarter Haven offered an overgrown vegetable garden. The sagging picket fence I could only assume was meant to keep out animals, as it certainly wouldn't stop a person.

"I suppose the vegetables are useful, but they're less pretty than flowers."

Zidra cast me an unamused glare, and I had to bite back my mirth. "Tending the vegetables gives the rengiri staying here something to do, but it also gives the poor a way to donate to the rengiri. Many of the people living near here don't have extra money, food, or supplies they can give, but they can give a little time. Tending the garden, helping harvest, and preserving the food are all ways for them to contribute and receive Iskyr's blessings for doing his will. If no rengiri are staying here and the food can't be preserved, it is given to widows and orphans."

That explained why she preferred this Haven. The building was dingy, the streets nearby less clean, the interior not as well furnished…but I had to admit it was a better example of our vows than Riverfront Haven.

Zidra stepped away, following the path of grassy cobblestones. I didn't want to part ways while she was still angry with me. I didn't want to part ways at all, not with that ice curse in her arm. If I wanted to stall her, I needed to say something, anything—well, anything that wasn't about today's events.

"I don't picture you as a gardener."

She stilled. "I don't usually stay here long enough for that, and it seems like every time I have a moment, the garden is already full of people, and I don't want to get in the way… I don't know the first thing about gardens."

A sly smile crept over my face. "Lies. You can tell if strawberries are ripe and pick them. You remember when we went strawberry picking, right?"

She angled toward me and narrowed her eyes. "I remember when you told me a void-tainted beast was attacking farm workers and then when we arrived and there was no monster, you insisted we pick strawberries to 'draw the monster out.'"

My laugh shook my shoulders. "You realized so fast there was no monster." For a few moments, I'd thought she was going to throw her basket of strawberries at me and fly away.

"Besides the lack of evidence of anyone ever having been attacked in that field," she said, "you were enjoying yourself far too much for there to be a looming threat. A child would have realized your scheme."

"Scheme?" My lips twitched. "To trick you into having a relaxing time with pleasant company? You know the holy texts say Iskyr desires that we rest."

"Iskyr also commands that we shun deception," she said, but her tone was more teasing than offended.

I leaned down until she met my gaze. "And you enjoyed it, too. You didn't leave."

Zidra stuck her nose in the air. "You'd already paid those farmers for their field and produce. I wasn't going to turn down fresh strawberries just to spite you. They were good strawberries."

"Were they?" I didn't have to feign my surprise or interest. The strawberries *had* been delicious—the best I'd ever tasted, in fact. Just thinking about them conjured memories of the sweet scent of strawberries and the feeling of

73

dirt under my nails. But… "I didn't see you eat a single one."

"I took the basket with me." She gave me that look again, like she couldn't believe I had the intelligence to be a rengir. Yet when I reached for the heartbond, I sensed more disillusionment than judgment, and most of it felt directed at herself, not me.

"Yes, but after you refused to eat them, I'd wondered if you didn't like strawberries. For all I knew, you gifted them to the first person you saw who looked hungry."

Zidra huffed. "I ate every last one after I washed the dirt off them like a sane person. Now, speaking of *rest*, I'm going to sleep." She took off down the path as if we had nothing left to say to each other.

"Wait!" I reached out to snag her arm, but she was already beyond my reach. She stopped anyway, although she didn't look back. "Shall I return in the morning—"

"No!" She whirled back around and held up her palms as if prepared to push me away. "Just…wait at Riverfront Haven. I'll find you when I'm ready to start searching for Rouven." She hurried around the building.

This time, I let her walk away and leave me standing alone in the garden.

It wasn't the first time I'd watched her walk away. She always walked away. I always let her. After we became rengiri and every time we completed a mission, she walked away.

I don't know if I subconsciously reached for the heartbond or if Zidra's emotions were so strong they filtered through our bond without either of us intending it, but a sense of loss and failure crept into my consciousness. I didn't like leaving her like this. She needed someone to lean on. Part of me hated that I knew she wouldn't open up to me. Another, selfish part of me was relieved that I wouldn't have to figure out how to comfort her without making her angry again.

Maybe I was delusional, thinking that Kyrmaris was a good team. Believing that we were at our best together—encouraging each other, challenging each other. For years, I'd thought Zidra was simply stubborn, shy, or self-conscious about the prejudice some people still held toward wyveri, and that was why she insisted on working alone. She didn't seem keen on a long-term partnership with anyone. I'd certainly never thought she was rejecting me specifically.

Now I wasn't so sure.

All these years, I'd thought we were friends. I'd believed she was warming up to the idea of working together. Most rengiri traveled in pairs. Some even traveled in groups of three or four, but that seemed crowded. I greatly preferred working with one person, and I'd never fit with anyone as well as I did with her.

Zidra, it seemed, didn't feel the same.

In fact, she was incensed by the heartbond. Neither of us wanted it. I just wanted to be her partner, not her husband. Even though Zidra was gorgeous, and talented, and made me better in every way, and sometimes rengiri did marry each other...

I shook my head. What kind of nonsense thoughts

were these? Partners. I wanted to fight and travel together, that was all.

Not that it mattered. She wanted me to leave her alone and would have gone in search of Physician Rouven by herself if she could have.

I looked up at the star-studded sky. "Iskyr." My prayer left my lips in a whisper. "If we aren't meant to be together—as partners or as anything more—why did you allow this bond to form between us?"

Only the chirping of insects answered me.

NINE

ZIDRA

A benefit to staying at West Quarter Haven was that the rengiri who stayed here didn't tend to be late-night revelers. I paused outside the front door and listened. Only quiet met my ears. I eased the door open and crept into the common room. Dying coals in the fireplace provided a dim illumination to empty couches and chairs.

Good. The last thing I wanted to do was tell anyone, least of all Sajen, where I'd been and what had happened.

I didn't even want to think about what had happened.

Weariness dragged down my steps. I passed through the common room and turned down the hallway that ran perpendicular to the front entrance. A half dozen doors lined the back wall, leading to the sleeping quarters. Each small room had a washbasin and changing area hidden behind a dressing screen, and two cots stacked on top of each other on the other side of the room. Even during the Dawning Festival, West Quarter Haven wasn't full. Only four of the rooms had two occupants. All of them were rengiri who traveled together as partners and were used to sharing a room, which thankfully left one of the remaining two rooms for me to have to myself.

None of the candles in the hallway were lit, so I ran my hand along the wall to count doors. When I reached the door on the far end, I went still. The scent of shifter and ale drifted from within, but it wasn't my scent—nor had I drunk any ale. I pressed my ear to the door and heard quiet breathing.

Had an exhausted rengir forgotten which room he was staying in? Or perhaps a rengir had been visiting friends and decided it was too late or she was a little too tipsy to return to whichever Haven she had been staying at?

Or was another assassin lurking in my room?

The slow, even cadence of the intruder's breathing sounded like someone sleeping. Perhaps a good assassin could fake that, though, to fool shifter hearing.

I leaned back and drew my sword, then eased open the door. The hinges creaked.

A grunt and shuffling accompanied someone moving on the bottom cot. My upper lip curled. That was *my* bed.

But then, past the scent of ale, I caught a familiar scent. "Sajen?"

"Zidra?" my friend asked in a groggy rasp. "Why don't you have a light?"

"Didn't think I needed one." I slammed my sword back

into its sheath. "Didn't think there would be someone in my bed."

His hearty laugh reminded me of some of my best days at Harcos. Most of the other students had loved Sajen for his sense of humor and vibrant personality. I'd loved him because he hadn't treated me with suspicion and had taught me more ways to fight from the air, even though wyvern and gryphon anatomy and flight differed. He'd believed in me in a way no one else had—except for maybe Kyrundar, but I didn't want to think about him right now.

"Istraiah came by and brought his cousin. His cousin drank too much and passed out, and Istraiah didn't want to carry him to his home on the other side of the city, so I put them both in my room."

I leaned against the doorframe. "And you're in my bed because?"

"Because I weigh twice what you do. I have a fear of collapsing the top cot and crushing the poor rengir beneath me in the most ignoble death imaginable."

I snorted. It was always difficult to stay upset with Sajen. "How considerate." I pushed off the doorframe and felt my way to the small end table, where I fumbled to find the lamp and light it. "Sorry for waking you."

The lamp flared to life, casting Sajen's deep-brown skin in an orange glow and reflecting in his dark eyes. He sat hunched on the edge of the cot with his elbows on his knees and his fingers laced. His gaze studied my face for a moment before dropping to my bandaged arm.

"I'm glad you did. I've been worried since Kyrundar

came here looking for you and Aigider told him you were meeting someone at the Grivolen ruins."

A rumble of a growl caught in my chest. "So that's how he found me."

Sajen lifted a bushy eyebrow. "Kyr looked troubled when he left." He pointed at my wound. "Seems we were right to be worried. What happened, Zee?"

I winced. Only Kyrundar and Sajen called me that, and Sajen had picked it up from Kyrundar. "Ilifir happened," I muttered. "Look, I'm exhausted, so I'm going to get changed and go to sleep."

"Hm." Sajen closed his eyes and inhaled deeply through his nose before looking at me again. "You reek, wyveri. Like you traipsed through a sewer, used antiseptic, and then cuddled with an ice elf."

"Excuse me?" I exclaimed.

"You smell of ice elf magic. What happened at Grivolen?"

For several long moments, we stared at each other. Me willing him to give up, Sajen returning my glare without budging. Finally, I groaned.

"You're not going to let me sleep until I tell you, are you?"

In response, he just grinned.

"Fine. But I wasn't joking about being exhausted." I snatched up the lamp and went to my pack. While I pulled out my nightclothes and changed behind the dressing screen, I explained the evening as succinctly as possible. Still, I had tucked myself into the top bunk before I finished the awful tale.

"Now I don't know what to do. I should inform the governor about Castle Grivolen being a den of iniquity, and I have to find Gautindar Rouven, but as for the rest... The three attackers, the corpses being retrieved so quickly, it has to mean I was right. Magistrate Nevros's death was no accident. Worse, whoever is behind this must have a long reach. Yet I have nothing solid to go on, and I can't shift until this ice curse is removed. By the time that's done, the trail will be too obscured to follow."

I threw my arm over my eyes. "Will you douse the lamp?"

The cots shook as Sajen got up to put out the lamp and then settled back into bed. "I'll speak to Governor Cline regarding your concerns about Grivolen. If you give me descriptions of your attackers, I can look into it while you and Kyr deal with the ice curse."

I removed my arm from my face. "I can't ask you to—"

"You don't need to ask. I'm offering."

Pressure rose in my chest. "Thank you, but I can't accept. I started this. I can see it through without help."

Sajen was silent for several moments. "Do you need to, though?"

I was so offended I almost sat up, but thankfully I remembered I would hit my head. "What kind of rengir would I be if I didn't?"

"A normal one?" Sajen chuckled. "I've been telling you since Harcos, Zidra. Accepting help doesn't invalidate your hard work."

Of course it did, but I'd never won this argument at the

Academy. I had proof now, though. "If that were true, I wouldn't have been humiliated today."

"Humiliated?" I could hear Sajen's frown. "All of us get hit now and then—"

"At the ceremony."

"The...ceremony." Sajen's bed creaked. "You felt humiliated while receiving the highest honor in the empire because you had to share the moment with Kyr?"

"Not because I had to share!" Well, a little bit, but that wasn't the point. "Kyrundar even told me he doesn't believe I could have earned the Emperor's Merit on my own, well, merit. If I had never allowed Kyrundar to keep attaching himself to me, maybe I would have been awarded the Merit by myself. Or maybe I would have been watching him receive it on his own. Either way, it would have been because that was what I, on my own, deserved. I should fly or fall on my own. Now I'll never know if I'm worthy."

That was the real reason this heartbond couldn't remain. I couldn't live forever in Kyrundar Ilifir's shadow.

"Oh, Zidra," Sajen said with a sigh. "You are worthy of your accomplishment. And working with others is a strength, not a weakness. We all need others. Rengiri were never meant to perform our duty in isolation. Iskyr made all people for friendships and connection, for mutual help and community."

"Rengiri also swear not to burden the Order or the empire," I reminded him. "And Iskyr does not approve of slothfulness."

"Zidra Eilmaris." Sajen's tone took on a warning edge.

"There is a difference between refusing to do a task that you have the ability, opportunity, and calling to do because you simply don't want to do the work, and accepting help with a task you do not have the ability or opportunity to do or have not been called to."

That was logical, I supposed, but I didn't like it.

"Furthermore, there is an independence that comes from resourcefulness and maturity, and there is a stubborn independence born of pride. The first kind accepts help when needed. The second places your own need for validation over Iskyr's will and others' betterment."

He moved again, and the stacked cots vibrated. His decision to take the bottom cot had been wise. "What is the calling of the rengiri?"

"'Forsaking all selfish ambition, we will sacrifice our comfort and, if so called, our lives, to protect those who cannot protect themselves,'" I recited. The words had become rote, but now they tasted bitter on my tongue.

"Which matters more, then: your ability to fly or fall on your own, or protecting the empire? You cannot properly fulfill your rengir warrior duties while injured. 'We see to our needs so that we may have the strength to serve.' Therefore, you must first remove the ice curse. Yet you're right it's also your duty to be concerned about illicit activities and possible assassins. Now, what do our vows say? Do they say 'I' or 'we'?"

"We," I mumbled.

"What is to be our relationship with others in the Order?"

"'We strive together in unity, treating each other as brother and sister, seeking peace amongst ourselves.'"

Perhaps I had gone too long without meditating on my oaths. I believed myself at peace with the rengiri—other than Kyrundar, perhaps—but was traveling and doing my duty alone truly striving *together*? I'd assumed it was enough to be together in spirit. I doubted Sajen would agree with that interpretation, so I didn't voice it.

Sajen hummed approval. "*We* are to protect the people in cooperation. You and I fulfill our vows in aiding each other. I will deal with Grivolen and investigate these attackers until you return. Agreed?"

Everything in me wanted to argue. Yet my mind was too slowed by weariness to find a coherent counterpoint. Nor did a compelling reason to reject Sajen's offer appear to me.

I sighed. "All right. Thank you. But keep the investigation quiet—I don't want to cause a panic when I have no evidence. And the new magistrate might have told me to give up the investigation. I don't want him to accuse the Order of harassment or undermining his authority."

"Why do you love to complicate things, Zee? All right. You have my word, but in return, you must make me a promise."

"What?" I scarcely breathed as I awaited his demands.

"Seek unity, peace, and togetherness with Kyrundar as you travel together. Ask Iskyr to help you. I believe you will find you have misjudged him."

As if. Still, to deny his request would be rude at best, a

denial of my vows at worst. "I promise to do my best to follow your advice."

TEN

KYRUNDAR

A fter I left the borrowed lantern at Merael's, I returned to Riverfront Haven. Music and conversation still carried over the walls. Not in the mood for revelry, I walked in the shadows along the river until the sounds of merrymaking ended, then crept inside. A few rengiri were conversing in the common room, but they were half asleep and didn't notice me slip by.

Riverfront Haven was the fourth-largest Haven in the capital city in terms of beds, but the largest in terms of space. The ground floor held the common room, kitchen, and five bedrooms, and a second floor boasted another ten bedrooms. Every bedroom had one cot—no sharing space, as at many Havens across the empire. I didn't mind sharing when out serving the empire, but I was in Laedresh to relax, and it was a welcome reprieve to not listen to a random acquaintance breathing all night. Plus these rooms all had windows, which wasn't a given at many Havens, either.

Despite my weariness, sleep kept slipping out of my reach. Every time I started to drift off, some terrible moment from the day reappeared in my mind: Zidra's stiffness at the medallion ceremony, seeing that curse hit her arm or her shivering on the floor, her anger when she realized we were heartbonded.

Well, if Zidra wanted to be enemies instead of friends, that was fine. We could get this problem resolved and then never speak again. That didn't bother me.

Lying is an affront to Iskyr, Kyr, I chided myself.

I felt like I had scarcely slept when I awoke to persistent knocking. Sunlight filtered through the thick curtains, giving the room a greenish tint.

With a groan, I rolled out of bed and stumbled over the cool wood floor. As I went, I untangled my hair from the earrings I'd forgotten to remove the night before. The knocking turned to a banging.

"All right! I'm coming!" I wrenched open the door and blinked against the brightness of the sunlight-flooded corridor.

Zidra's eyes widened, and pink tinged her tan skin. Her gaze leaped from my bare chest up to my face. Any hint of being flustered quickly disappeared behind her signature intimidating scowl. "Why aren't you dressed? The sun has been up for hours."

I rested my forearm against the doorframe near my head and leaned into its support. "Didn't sleep well. Nor did I have any idea what time you were coming. Or if you would come today. You said you'd find me 'when you were ready.' You made it sound like you needed time."

"Right. Well." Zidra cleared her throat and angled away from me. "What I need is to get this curse removed as quickly as possible, which means we can't waste time. We need to look for Gautindar Rouven at once. Merael's records indicate that before he moved to Laedresh—"

"Whoa, slow down. If Rouven wanted to disappear, he wouldn't go back home. I have a friend who knows everything, and what she doesn't know, she can learn. We'll start there."

Zidra stiffened.

"Sorry, I mean…is it all right with you if we start there?"

Her mouth puckered, and the tense line of her shoulders beneath her leather armor didn't ease. "Fine. Who is this woman?"

Something about the crisp way Zidra said *woman* caught my attention. I directed my consciousness toward the heartbond. Her irritation pummeled into me with a distinct hint of…

A lopsided smirk stretched my lips. "She's a *friend*, Zee. No need to be jealous."

"I'm not jealous!" Her voice went up a pitch. She winced and glanced down the hallway. "I'm wondering who she is."

"Mmm, you forget I can feel your emotions." I leaned down closer to her and dropped my voice to a husky murmur. "You're jealous."

Zidra's ears turned red. "Do *not* flirt with me. I'm not one of your admirers for you to play games with. And stop spying on my emotions. You're not even interpreting them correctly. Go get dressed so we can meet this person, find Rouven, and get this over with."

Her words and the disgust rippling through our bond made me straighten. My arm dropped back to my side. "Play games with?"

"Please. Unmarried women of an appropriate age— and probably some of an inappropriate age—from here to the corners of the empire throw themselves at you at every opportunity."

I furrowed my brow. "Hyperbolic, but even if they did, how is that my fault?"

"You encourage it!" She tossed her hands up. "With your flashy uses of magic and sensuous voice and all of your winking and smirking and—all of your flirting!"

A door opened down the hall, and another elf poked her head out. Her dark hair fell over half her face, and her visible eye was half closed. "Unless there is an emergency," she said in the forest elf dialect, "there should be no shouting before midafternoon the day after a party." She retreated back into her room without waiting for a response.

Zidra glared at the closed door for a moment before turning back to me. I didn't bother translating—in addition to being fluent in common Laedreshian and Vethalric, the ancestral shifter tongue, she also knew passable Elvish. "Is that why you aren't dressed yet?"

I blinked. "Are you going to accuse me of having slept with her from another room?"

"I meant were you up late partying, but now I'm wondering if you've also been breaking your vow to not have intimate relations outside of marriage." She peered past me as if she suspected me of hiding a woman in my bed.

"I didn't know you thought so little of me," I said through gritted teeth. Leaving the door open so she could observe my empty room, I went and threw open the curtains, then fetched a clean tunic from my things. "Where is your pack?"

"Downstairs. Something was poking into me. I'll go rearrange it while you get ready to leave. Hurry. Please." I glanced over my shoulder at the unexpected *please*, but Zidra was already striding away.

I sighed and glanced at the wooden rafters. "Iskyr, grant me patience."

I rushed through getting dressed and putting on my lightweight leather armor, doing my hair, and getting everything placed back into my travel pack. I almost headed out the door before I remembered to strip the bed, place clean bedding on it, and take the dirty linens to the laundry room, where gracious volunteers would clean them for any rengiri who didn't have time to do the washing themselves. Despite my best efforts, by the time I got downstairs, Zidra was nowhere to be seen. Afen, a panther shifter whose coily hair was woven into rows of tight braids, looked up from mending a stocking and jerked his thumb toward the front entrance.

"Eilmaris left a couple minutes ago. She asked me to tell you to meet her at the cathedral."

"Thank you." If I hurried, I should be able to catch up to her, especially since she would be traveling on foot. The streets were quieter than usual for the hour, but many people were still on holiday—and many were probably still in bed after spending the night carousing. I created a disk of levitating ice and sped off in search of Zidra.

There were three cathedrals and a dozen smaller sanctuaries in Laedresh, but only one was *the* cathedral—Vairdros Cathedral, a short distance away from Harcos Academy. Of the thirty mighty warriors who'd helped Emperor Syrzin defeat Ascadrion, twelve survived the battle and formed the Order of the Rengir. Their general, Alexys Harcos, established the most prestigious military academy in the empire. Clairya Vairdros, the last heir to her noble human family's immense wealth, was elected the Order's first archon, or religious leader, and used her riches to commission the first cathedral in the new capital. Vairdros Cathedral, lovingly referred to as Rengir Cathedral, was where every rengir took their vows, and many of us considered it our spiritual home. No rengir left Laedresh without praying for Iskyr's protection and guidance at Vairdros.

I spotted Zidra's voluminous brown curls and hopped to the ground, letting my ice disk dissipate in a swirl of snowflakes. "Zee!" She didn't pause or look back. I trotted up to her side. "Why did you leave without me?"

Her nose wrinkled, and she didn't break stride. "Afen was asking too many questions about where we're going and why and acting like he suspects we're courting or something." She moved so close our arms brushed, and then she whispered, "It's exceedingly rare, but old wives' tales claim some shifters can sense a heartbond. I doubt Afen can, but I didn't want to risk him getting the wrong idea and spreading that around."

"Thinking we have a heartbond wouldn't be wrong," I said dryly.

Zidra pulled away and glanced around at the few other people on the street. "Shh. I'm sure we won't for long. Once the curse is dealt with, that will go, too."

If that was going to be her attitude about it, I hoped she was right.

As we walked into the long shadow cast by the towering spire-topped structure of Vairdros Cathedral, Zidra's pace increased. Given her shorter legs, I kept pace easily— but I deemed it best not to mention that when she was already on edge.

Wood reliefs carved into the towering double doors of Vairdros depicted Emperor Syrzin and his mighty warriors facing down the hulking dragon Ascadrion on one side, and the warriors kneeling in prayer while Syrzin prophesied about Ascadrion's eventual return on the other. Giant sequoias were carved into the marble doorframe, symbols of Iskyr due to their imposing height and longevity, and because they do not change with the seasons.

As usual, the small door set into the right door, amid the kneeling warriors, was open. I followed Zidra inside, and a sense of peace filled me. The scent of incense from the morning service wafted on the air, tendrils of smoke still drifting amid the beams of the soaring vaulted ceiling. A multitude of candelabras illuminated the nave of the cathedral in a warm glow. At the far end above the chancel, sunlight streamed through a twenty-foot-tall stained-glass scene of children of every race playing in the shade of a sequoia.

Our footsteps echoed as we walked between rows of prayer cushions toward the altar at the chancel. I glanced over at one of the semicircular side chapels, then nudged Zidra with my elbow.

"Remember copying holy texts for hours together in that chapel?" I whispered.

She cast me a flat look. "Yes, I remember your dare getting us both in trouble and our penance of meticulously copying two hundred pages of holy texts that was all your fault." The corner of her mouth twitched, and her steps slowed.

I indulged in a grin. "But a duel on the roof of the dormitory *was* such good practice in balance and environmental awareness."

"And Instructor Kell was wrong." She shrugged. "I have, in fact, had to fight on a roof, and since it had buttresses and spires and gargoyles, I'd have been more likely to cause damage to the building if I'd shifted."

I stumbled. "You fought on a roof?"

Zidra's cheeks reddened. "It's less impressive than it sounds. A vacterin family had built a nest in the attic of a justice hall."

My eyebrows shot up as I pictured Zidra in a rooftop

battle with a horde of sharp-clawed oversized weasels bent on defending their nest. "Perhaps not a particularly glamorous fight, but still impressive. I have a nasty scar on my calf from a vacterin." Old superstitions associated them with death and misfortune, so rengiri were often called upon to get rid of them.

The shy smile she sent me felt like a victory.

We reached the front of the nave and knelt before the altar. In unison, we fell into the familiar rhythm of the rengir litany, our voices mingling as we recited short prayers of praise and intercession for our upcoming mission. After the last prayer, we fell silent but remained kneeling on the cold stone to offer our personal prayers.

I lifted my head to stare at the stained-glass window. A forest elf girl skipped toward a boy with scales on his arms—an artistic representation of a wyveri. A surprising inclusion given how many people mistrusted the wyveri even now, let alone when the window was commissioned. My gaze rose to the sprawling branches of the sequoia.

Iskyr, I don't even know what it is I want. The tug of my awareness toward the woman at my side argued otherwise. Unable to recall an appropriate prayer or put my knotted feelings into words, I simply sent a plea for help. After all, those holy texts I'd copied said Iskyr didn't require grand words to hear the honest cry of a faithful heart.

Zidra stood, and I followed suit. As she turned toward the entrance, a dark shape moving in my periphery caught my attention.

ELEVEN

ZIDRA

Prayer usually instilled in me a fresh sense of calm and clarity, but not today. The sense that something unidentifiable was wrong had haunted me since I'd awoken that morning. As I rose to my feet, that feeling did not abate. There was something I had forgotten, or was overlooking, or a mistake I had made that was going to cause a problem at any moment, or…I didn't know what. I just knew that agitation vibrated through every inch of my body.

I reached tentatively for the heartbond, which confirmed that Iskyr had not granted my request to remove it, either. No reassurances about Iskyr having plans above our comprehension could make me feel better about the current situation.

This heartbond was a problem. Kyrundar's face had haunted my dreams. I couldn't recall what had happened in those dreams, but he'd been there. When he'd opened the door to his room this morning, a sense of *rightness* had flowed through me—and then I'd seen his toned chest with its faint scars from past battles. I didn't know how to describe the heat that had rushed to my cheeks or the flurry of confused feelings the sight had stirred.

Why had his state of undress affected me so? I'd seen him and other men without a shirt before. Such things were unavoidable sometimes when men and women trained together or shared sleeping accommodations at the Havens. I'd always averted my eyes and not paid much heed.

But just thinking about Kyrundar leaning against the doorframe, his muscular form looming over me and his bare torso so close to my face... Heat flamed over my face again.

No. I wasn't going to fall victim to his seductive ways.

"Rengiri, welcome." The sudden emergence of the deep voice off to the side, past Kyrundar on my left, made me jolt.

I smothered my surprise and turned to face the approaching priest. "Greetings, Respected Brother," we said in unison.

The priest smiled. "Greetings, my brother and sister." His unadorned black robes swished around his sandaled feet as he approached and then stopped in front of us. Candlelight gleamed on the dark skin of his shaved head, marking him as a member of the studious Allantine Order. "It is always an honor to welcome rengiri, but an extra honor to welcome recipients of the Emperor's Merit."

Annoyance and a twinge of shame went through me. What did everyone truly think of me? The second wyveri member in the history of the Order of the Rengir, and I couldn't earn recognition without the aid of an elf.

"It's delightful to see the two of you here together, saying your prayers in unison before setting out on a new shared mission. Do you have any intercession requests?"

"We need to find someone," Kyrundar said. "Urgently. And we have very little information to guide us."

The priest nodded gravely. "May Iskyr be your guide, then." He looked to me. "I feel that Iskyr is prompting me to give you a word of advice. Do not lightly shun his good gifts."

All I could manage in response was a sharp nod.

Kyrundar looked at me out of the corner of his eye, one eyebrow raised, and then he inclined his head to the priest. "Thank you, Respected Brother."

"Thanks be to Iskyr for his wisdom."

"Iskyr, we thank you," Kyrundar and I said by long-practiced habit.

The priest continued on his way.

Kyrundar turned to me, the look on his face somewhere between smug and amused.

I shook my head and started back down the nave. "He could have meant any gift. Including a gift we haven't received yet."

"I suppose that could be," he said, but his tone betrayed his skepticism.

Electing to ignore Kyrundar's nonsense, I focused on

leaving the cathedral. Once we were outside, I reluctantly turned to him. "Where are we going?"

"Ravensburgh. I'll fly us, so we should get there around…" He frowned at the sky. "Close to dusk." He smiled apologetically. "I know you would do it faster if you could take us."

I adjusted my pack on my shoulders. "This works better, anyway. If we went separately, I'd be bored waiting for you; it would be too far to carry you in my claws, and no one rides on my back."

Kyrundar's blue eyes twinkled. "I'm going to convince you to change your mind about that someday."

"It's a good thing gambling goes against our vows." I sniffed. "I don't need to warn you not to stake any money on such a ridiculous claim."

"I don't have any money, anyway. Spent it all on Dawning Festival feasting."

I shook my head. "Of course you did."

"What?" he asked with exaggerated innocence. "The holy texts mandate holidays with music and dancing and speak of Iskyr hosting feasts for his people. I think he approves of throwing a celebration now and then."

Since I couldn't argue with that, I continued down the road. Kyrundar chuckled, as if knowing he had won, and fell into step beside me.

To my relief, he didn't insist on keeping up a stream of conversation. It was awkward enough having to smile and nod to the people who shouted "Kyrmaris!" at us as we walked to the southern gate.

Crowds of people leaving Laedresh clogged the gate with bodies, carts, wagons, carriages, horses, and pack mules. I slowed as we approached the hubbub. My stomach churned. I hated tight crowds—all of the bumping into me, the conversations on every side pressing in on my hearing, the vast array of scents from every direction mingling together. The overburdening of my senses always left me anxious and exhausted. And that was only half the problem.

I rubbed the insignia pinned to my chest. Even if I stowed it in my hip bag, someone might recognize us. Recognition in a crowd of that size, where we would get trapped in the press of people leaving, would mean questions, scrutiny, unsolicited speculation, and women batting their eyelashes at Kyrundar. Normally I'd fly over the wall to avoid the bottleneck at the gates—one of the special privileges granted to rengiri.

Kyrundar leaned down and murmured, "Not in the mood to be the center of attention while waiting to exit?"

I lifted an eyebrow and peered up at him. "Are you saying you can get us over the wall? It's taller than the roofs we flew over last night."

"Of course I can." He squared his shoulders. "I only went through the gate last night because it's harder to judge the height in the dark. In fact, I could get over the wall faster than you could shift and get over." He sighed. "A shame we can't race."

"Oh, no, you're not getting out of that claim so easily." I folded my arms over my chest. "Next time we're both in

Laedresh, we'll test who is faster."

Kyrundar's smile looked entirely too pleased. "Deal. Now, we don't have time to waste." He held out his hands, and glittering snowflakes cascaded from his fingers. Two hovering disks of ice grew before us. I waited for him to step onto his before I stepped up onto mine.

"Look!" someone in the crowd shouted. "It's Kyrmaris!"

I clenched my jaw.

"Here we go," Kyrundar warned. The disks rushed forward and up, but not fast enough for my sensitive hearing to evade all the comments.

"Why is Zidra traveling by ice magic and not flying?"

"They've been sighted together more often lately. Are they courting yet?"

Heat rushed to my face.

Then we soared over the wall—Kyrundar went far higher than necessary to clear the stone and guards, the show-off—and left the voices behind. He took us past the heavy traffic on the roads near the gate. Once the crowds thinned, he lowered the disks until we flew along only a few feet above the ground.

The wind on my face and in my hair felt good. A touch cold, but decidedly different from flying as a wyvern, where my scales were less affected by the wind. That was a good thing, of course. At wyvern flight speeds, the wind would no longer be pleasant. But this was more enjoyable than I'd ever admit to Kyrundar.

Above the rushing wind in my ears, I detected a strange sound, like a sharp *crack* distorted by our speed. Was it coming from in front of us or—

Ahead of us, a towering pine swayed and fell toward the road.

"Kyr!"

The ice disks slammed to a stop, and I teetered forward. Kyrundar grabbed my upper arm and steadied me. With a crash, the tree hit the road. Pine needles and dust burst into the air.

Amid the strong smells of pine sap and freshly cut wood, I caught another scent.

I pointed toward the side of the road. "Shifter—"

A snarling wolf as tall as I was and an even larger black panther leaped out of the tree line. Dragon heat stirred in my veins.

Kyrundar's grip on my arm tightened. "Don't shift!"

"I know!" I snapped, ignoring that I *had* almost shifted instinctively. In my wyvern state, I'd be twice the size of the panthera, and I'd have plenty of room to maneuver on this quiet stretch of road. I could subdue both shifters in moments.

Instead, thanks to this infernal ice curse, I would have to face them with nothing but my sword—

The ice disks lurched upward, taking us high above the approaching shifters, who snarled and yowled in response.

"They can't run as fast as I can fly us out of here," Kyrundar said, but our magical conveyance continued to hover high above the circling predators.

He was waiting for me to make the call to engage or not. The realization prompted a warm stirring in my chest.

I shook my head. "A second assassination attempt? I need to know who they are and why they're targeting me—or us." Whichever it was, I needed answers.

"Then let the hunt begin." He drew his twin swords.

I allowed myself a small grin and removed my pack, then drew my own sword. He navigated our ice disks away from the shifters and then descended. The shifters didn't wait for us to touch ground to run toward us, so I didn't, either. I jumped and landed in a crouch with my sword extended point-first in front of me.

The panthera growled and turned aside, avoiding running straight into my blade. A flash of Kyrundar's glittering magic raced toward the wolvus, so I focused on my own opponent.

I might not have been able to access the full power of my wyveri blood, but my senses and strength were still heightened compared to a human's or even an elf's. Every time the panther's paws hit the ground, they caused a subtle vibration in the packed dirt. My eyes tracked every twitch of powerful muscles beneath its dark rosette-patterned fur and the telltale movement of its golden eyes.

I pivoted to keep facing my opponent. Slowly, I rose to my feet and pulled my sword in close. The panther's tail twitched. I eased one foot back. *Steady...*

When the panthera leaped, I ran a step to the side and slid forward, parallel to the great cat. I slashed my sword down the panther's side. My boots cast up a cloud of dust, and my back hit the ground hard.

The panther yowled, but I didn't have time to assess

my strike. I rolled away and jumped to my feet, already swinging again. My blade clipped the panther's upper leg as it tried to swipe huge claws at me. It limped back a step and growled.

I held my ground, waiting.

With another ear-splitting yowl, the panther pounced. This time, I took a risk and lowered my sword, instead rushing forward between the grasping paws to tackle my opponent. The force of our collision nearly knocked the breath out of me, but I threw all my strength forward. My blood heated, and I willed my shifter magic to settle.

I crashed to the ground on top of the panther. It whimpered beneath me. Before it had a chance to recover, I brought up my sword and laid the edge against its throat.

"Maki'elle!" I shouted in Vethalric, the native tongue of the shifter clans. *Reveal your true self.*

The panthera bared its teeth in a snarl.

I frowned. Conversing in our non-animal forms was a sign of mutual respect, as it put all shifters, regardless of clan, size, and strength, on relatively equal footing. It was also considered respectful to fight another shifter only in baik'eth, "same form"—both animals, or both humans— and the honorable thing was to start any fight in di'ora.

"I cannot shift," I said. The panther squirmed, and with its greater strength and flexibility, it could easily throw me off. I pressed my blade harder against its throat.

"Our archon thought that might be the case." In his animal form, the panthera had a raspy, indistinct voice.

My lips parted. "And you still chose to attack in di'yar?"

"Rengiri do not deserve the respect of di'ora."

Outrage sparked in my veins, and I took a deep breath to cool my dragon fire. "Why are you targeting me? Who is your archon? Which order are you part of?"

"Not any order that answers to your pathetic god." The panther swiped with all four paws and twisted beneath me, trying to throw me aside. Long claws scraped against my armor. I drew back my sword, but too late.

The panther's thrashing had caused its throat to shove against my blade.

Its claws retracted, and then its oversized paws fell heavily. I stumbled to my feet. Blood dripped from my weapon. The panthera twitched. As it choked out a last breath and its magic died along with it, its form morphed and shrank until I stood over a man with dark-brown skin and curly hair. Blood from his neck stained the edge of his chainmail.

My shoulders slumped. I turned to see how Kyrundar fared and found him standing beside a kneeling, pale young woman with brown hair. Her orange eyes flashed over a gag of ice, and ice bound her arms to her sides. I could deal with the wolvus in a moment.

Turning back to the dead panthera, I adjusted my sword so I held it in my right fist with the point down, then held my fist in front of my heart. I closed my eyes, bowed my head, and said, "Iskyr have mercy upon this man's soul, and upon me for having brought death to one of your people." In Vethalric, I added, "May the honor with which you lived your life be the honor with which you are welcomed into the next, brother."

Sorrow pressed upon me. If our brief interaction was any indication, this distant shifter cousin had not lived a life of honor. But even the outcast wyveri would follow thousands of years of shifter tradition that called for honor and respect among tribes, including in battle and victory. It would be to my shame to return his dishonor with equal dishonor.

I used a cloth from my hip bag to clean my blade and then marched over to Kyrundar and the wolvus woman. Before I said a word, the ice gag dissipated.

She snarled, her canines flashing in the bright morning sun. "You pretend to have honor, rengir, but we know the truth—how you oppress us, keeping secret knowledge and power for yourselves!"

I blinked and looked to Kyrundar. He shrugged, his wide eyes reflecting equal bewilderment.

"Who is 'we'?"

The wolvus tilted up her chin. "No torture can make me tell you anything. And I have failed to complete my mission and kill you. You might as well kill me."

"Why are you trying to kill me?"

"And is Zidra your target and I'm collateral damage?" Kyrundar asked. By his tone, I wasn't sure if he was offended or curious.

A novel idea occurred to me, and I willingly sought the heartbond. An impression of anger snapped across the bond—but it didn't seem to be wounded pride. He was furious that…someone would try to harm me? I slammed the door on the bond.

"Eilmaris was our target, but now that Kyrmaris is working together on this, you're both on the league's list."

My ears perked up. "League? What league? Working together on…Magistrate Nevros's death? This league killed him?"

The wolvus's eyes glowed golden, and she strained against the magical ice binding her, then threw herself to the side. The ice cracked but did not break.

Kyrundar rolled his eyes and added more ice. "You already tried to shift, lady. You aren't winning this one."

She growled in response. This was getting us nowhere. We didn't have time to wait for her to decide to talk, and rengiri did not stoop to torture.

"Can you bring her with us to Ravensburgh?" I asked. "We can turn her over to the local authorities to interrogate and punish her."

"I won't tell your corrupted officials anything, either!" The wolvus growled. Gray fur spread over her face, neck, and hands. The ice groaned and cracked.

"Certainly." Kyrundar's face pinched. A sheen of sweat showed on his forehead, and glittering ice crystals fell from his fingertips. "Although we'll need to knock her unconscious first."

I sighed and drew my sword, holding the pommel down. Somehow, the woman rolled aside, snarling. Some instinct raised the hair on my arms. I ducked and turned my face away. "Kyr, watch out!"

Before I finished speaking, echoing pops and cracks of breaking ice sounded, and then ice chunks pelted my back.

I waited only a moment before spinning around, sword at the ready.

Back in her di'yar, she lunged for me, her attention focused on my throat. I stumbled back and swung. Just as my sword sliced into the gigantic wolf's chest, an ice spear pierced her side.

The wolvus collapsed and shrank back to her true form. By the time I crouched at her side, the life had left her. Wearily, I stood and, once again, said the rengir and shifter blessings. This time, Kyrundar joined me in asking Iskyr for mercy for the wolvus and his own soul.

After I wiped and sheathed my sword, I turned to Kyrundar. "Maybe—you're bleeding!" I strode over to him and turned his chin to get a closer look at the blood drying on the side of his neck, just above the edge of his leather breastplate and pauldron.

"It's not bad—"

"Why didn't I feel it?" I frowned as I gently rubbed away flakes of dried blood with my thumb. Kyrundar stiffened, so I stopped. "Sorry. I didn't feel that, either."

"That didn't hurt." He cleared his throat and took a step back. "Why would you feel it?"

I worked my jaw, not wanting to speak of it. "The…you know. You felt my pain at the infirmary."

"Oh." Kyrundar grinned weakly. "I don't think feeling each other's pain is a normal part of a heartbond. That would be incredibly distracting in battle, and I know of a few married rengiri with heartbonds. Maybe it was because it was new and so strong? Just like how we were sharing emotions without meaning to, but then that went away. Or maybe it was just because my magic tangling with the curse isn't…pleasant."

"Oh. Good." I brushed some dirt off my gauntlet. "Still, a scratch from a claw—"

He waved his hand with an amused smile. "It really is just a scratch. I'll clean it, though, so you can stop looking so anxious."

"I'm not anxious," I muttered, then crouched beside the corpse. "Anyway, I'm going to search their clothing. Maybe there's something on one of them that can give us more information."

After he washed his injury—which, with the blood gone, I could see really was minor—he assisted me in searching the corpses. The assassins were no fools, though. They carried no letters or documents, and their clothing bore no symbols or crests.

"I suppose you're going to insist we bury them," Kyrundar said.

"It is the rengir way." I turned around, searching for my pack. We both carried small shovels with folding handles—all rengiri did. Usually we used them for things like building fire pits or makeshift shelters as, thanks be to Iskyr, we seldom had to take a person's life. I spotted my discarded pack and shuffled over to it.

Kyrundar kicked a pebble. "They fought without honor. I heard that panthera say they knew you might not be able to shift. And this was not a battle, but an assassination attempt! That woman slandered the character of all rengiri. They deserve no honor."

I opened my mouth, but he held up his hand.

"I know. 'None deserve honor, except that Iskyr has granted us honor as his people. Therefore treat one another with integrity.'" His mouth pulled to the side. "But...this 'league' might collect the bodies themselves. They took the other ones."

I paused in rummaging through my sack. "We don't know how long that might take. We can't leave the bodies until then."

"Then can we dig shallow graves?"

"All right." I didn't mention that I agreed so readily because I was more tired than I should have been after such a short fight. Nor did I mention the slight chill and low-level pain in my arm.

I wasn't about to let Kyrundar fuss over me on the side of the road. I'd probably recover by the time we reached Ravensburgh, anyway.

TWELVE

KYRUNDAR

After we buried the corpses, I turned to Zidra. "How is your arm feeling?"

Her snapped "fine" came too quickly. "We should continue if we want to reach Ravensburgh before dark." A pout twisted her lips. "If I could shift..." Her fingers strayed to the bandage tied around her arm.

"Are you certain your wound is all right?" I pressed. It had to have been difficult for her, fighting the urge to face the panther and wolf shifters in her wyvern form as would have been proper. Not to mention shifters usually used some of the energy of their magic to heighten their strength and speed during a fight in their true form. "Your dragon fire didn't—"

"I'm fine, Ilifir." Zidra crossed her arms. "We need to talk to this *friend* of yours as soon as possible, so—"

"Oh, we won't be able to visit her tonight."

She blinked. "I beg your pardon?"

"We'll meet her tomorrow. It'll be better."

"Better? How is waiting better?"

"It's more polite." I didn't expound. It'd be much more fun for it to be a surprise. She was going to be upset, but a chance to relax would do her so much good. "Besides, you just said your arm is fine, so it's not as if there's any new urgency."

She blew a long breath out her nose that probably would have been smoke-tainted if she hadn't been keeping her dragon fire at bay. "It's your contact, so fine. We'll do it your way."

I grinned and created two ice disks. Only after we set off did I risk reaching out along the heartbond to check if she was being honest. A simmering annoyance overlay a constant hum of worry. I glanced toward her, but her face was set in a stony mask. She *did* have an ice curse stuck in her arm, after all. It was fair to be worried.

Still, I couldn't shake the feeling that there was more to her concern than that.

We reached Ravensburgh after dark, but oddly, Zidra seemed more relieved than irritated by our lateness. As we walked to the Ravensburgh Haven, she kept to the edges of the streets and favored the shadows. Was she seriously that averse to being seen with me?

Iskyr, give me patience.

Voices, light, and the scent of baking spilled out of the rows of windows lining the front of the three-story wood building that was the Ravensburgh Haven. Zidra stopped so abruptly in front of the clothier's shop next to the Haven that I bumped into her pack.

I stepped around to stand at her side. "Zee?"

She groaned. "I didn't think about all the rengiri leaving Laedresh. There's going to be so many of them here!" Shaking her head, she began to retreat. "I'll sleep outside the city—"

I seized her arm. "I doubt it's so full they have no beds—"

"I don't want to face them!"

Something about the quaver in her voice that she tried to hide made me discard my initial intention of saying something dismissive or teasing. I eased my grip on her arm. "Why?"

Her face flushed and she ducked her head. "You wouldn't understand."

I took a breath to cool my frustration. "I can't if you don't tell me what's going on."

After an agonizing moment of silence, Zidra raised her head. She yanked her arm free of my grip. "It doesn't matter. I'm fine. Let's go." With her jaw set, she took off toward the Haven.

I watched her go, unsure of what to do. Perhaps I should let her enter by herself, but I didn't think this was about not wanting to be seen with me. When I reached out toward the heartbond, I felt more shame and fear than mere embarrassment. If she didn't want to face our rengir brothers and sisters, even if I didn't understand why, I wouldn't make her face them alone.

Zidra entered the Haven several steps ahead of me and let the door swing shut behind her, but it didn't latch. The murmur of conversations hushed, and then a woman called, "Zidra! Congratulations on receiving the Merit!"

I still had our bond open. Her discomfort heightened further, and the sorrow I sensed confused me.

"Thank you, Samina."

Understanding bowed my head. If it was the Samina I knew, she was a panther shifter—like the man Zidra had killed today.

I pushed open the door and then made sure it latched behind me.

"And Kyrundar!" Samina bounded to her feet, her smile widening. The thick twists of her black hair bounced around her shoulders. "How good to see you as well."

"Always a pleasure, Samina," I said as I moved to stand at Zee's side.

Aside from Samina, four rengiri lounged on the plush cushions spread over the rug on the floor of the common room that took up most of the ground floor. The kitchen, pantry, laundry, and a large supply closet made up the rest.

Maybe only because I was standing so close to her, Zidra's gulp was audible. A wave of anguish pummeled me so hard through the bond, I almost pulled her into my arms and asked what was wrong—but that would only make her angry.

"Are there any beds left?" Zee asked tightly.

Another rengir, Euan, nodded with a lopsided smile

that pulled at his thick red beard. "The west-facing room at the south end of the third floor is empty. Obviously Kyrmaris won't mind sharing."

A few of the other rengiri laughed quietly. My eyebrows drew together. Had word gotten around? Did they know about the heartbond? Surely not. How could they know?

"No more than I'd mind sharing with any other rengir," Zidra said lightly, but by her roiling emotions, she was not as unfazed as she was trying to appear. "I wish I could socialize, but I've had a long day and must retire." She gave a curt nod and strode past the others toward the stairwell in the back corner.

Samina sashayed over to me with feline grace. "You'll join us, won't you, Kyr?"

I smiled apologetically. "I'm afraid not. It's been a long day for me as well."

"There must be a story there," Euan said. He motioned me over. "You love to tell a good story, and we'd love to be the first to hear a new Kyrmaris tale."

Chuckling, I shook my head. "I think this particular tale is just getting started. I should save the telling for when I know the ending. Good night." I nodded and followed Zidra upstairs.

She must have nearly run, because by the time I reached the room, she already had her armor halfway removed. While she finished, I took out my teardrop and chain earrings and set them on the nightstand that was tucked into the corner between the heads of two cots. At least these rooms were large enough the beds weren't stacked. I didn't care for stacked bunks. Too great a risk of whacking one's head.

Zidra picked up her pack and moved to go behind the dressing screen across from the cots.

"Wait." I pointed to one of the beds. "Let me check your arm."

She drew back and opened her mouth, but then her shoulders caved. Her gaze avoided mine as she moved to sit on the bed without a word. Lips pursed, I sat next to her and untied the bandage.

The wound looked worse, and I had to work to keep my expression neutral. I'd done my best to use my magic to keep the cold from touching Zidra's skin, but the edges of the puncture wound had taken on a patchy blueish tinge. Frostbite would kill her skin, and the longer it affected her, the harder it would be for any healer to fix the damage.

"It's worse." Zidra's whisper wasn't a question. "It's been getting colder since the fight."

I jerked my head up to glare at her, but she wasn't looking at me. "Why didn't you say anything?"

"Anyone could have seen you tending me on the side of the road. It would have raised questions I don't want to answer."

I contained my eye roll with effort. "I know you're displeased about the heartbond, but no one is going to guess at that if they discover my magic is in your arm."

"This isn't about the bond!" Zidra stood, and her arm slipped from my loose grip. "That panthera—he mentioned an archon, but then he said he wasn't a member of any

115

order that worshiped Iskyr."

I frowned, disturbed at the thought. There were few restrictions on how people in the empire worshiped or what exactly they believed, but not honoring the creator god at all? It was incredibly rare.

"He said their archon thought I might not be able to shift. They suspected I couldn't shift, and they attacked in di'yar anyway. They saw I did not shift, which doubtless confirmed their theory, and yet they did not shift to di'ora."

Indignation on her behalf made my skin prickle. "They dishonored you—"

"It was more than dishonor!" She whirled to face me. "Don't you see? They saw me as weak. Not worth honoring. Perhaps they are right. If I were wise enough, I wouldn't have been ambushed. If I were fast enough, I would not have been struck by the ice curse. If I were strong enough, I could have burned it out myself. And now...now I can't shift. It could be argued I dishonored *them* by not shifting."

"But you couldn't—"

"Exactly! I am half a wyveri. Less than that, as that fight..." She angled away, and her head sagged forward. "It was harder than it should have been." Her jaw worked. "I don't want anyone to know. I can't afford for anyone to know."

I tried to understand her fear and shame. Certainly, if I found myself unable to wield my magic, it would be a blow, but I could still fight. And... "You're acting as if it's your fault. You acted in good faith at Grivolen, and with reason.

I distracted you; you said that yourself. You were caught by surprise by the curse because you thought he was attacking me. Your inability to shift is no more your fault than catching a cold. No one will blame you."

Zidra laughed, a hollow, empty sound. "You're not wyveri. How could you understand?" She went to the other bed and sank onto the edge of it. Her fingers curled around the edge of the mattress as she leaned forward. "Your people were not exiled off the continent for the actions of a king so heinous his line was eradicated and his name was wiped from history. Your people do not still mostly keep to their islands, even though the banishment was lifted after only a century, because of how much everyone else distrusts your kind. If they aren't buying wyvern scales or hunting dogs from us, they want nothing to do with us. An ice elf can't understand the thin line between respect and fear and how it both isolates and protects us on the continent. A wyveri who can't shift is no longer the strongest and most feared of the shifters. The derision and suspicion some feel for my people...it is their fear that stops them from acting upon it. I am not merely weak; I am little more than a magicless human."

I nodded slowly. I'd never admit it, of course, but the first time I saw Zidra as a wyvern, I almost hid behind another student. She was terrifying and spectacular. I'd certainly never choose to fight a wyvern, shifter or not. Another thought occurred to me—if Zidra had been able to access her wyvern form, would the shifters have fled? Would they have dared take on a creature larger and stronger than themselves, with armored scales and the ability to breathe fire and carry her foes into the sky? Such considerations would only reinforce her fears, however.

"If people know…" She gulped. "What if more people than just assassins want to come for me?"

"No." I shook my head fiercely. "Zidra, you are a beloved member of the Order. People respect you not merely for your powerful wyvern form, but because you are a model rengir. People cheer for you and tell stories of you and part with their precious gold for things you might have touched. Iskyr knows how I pray for a quarter of your humility and tireless dedication."

She whipped her head up to stare at me. "You what?"

My face heated, but I raised a shoulder in feigned nonchalance. "I admire you, Zidra. Always have. Sometimes with a heaping side of envy, and that admiration also drove me to try to one-up you as a student, but you're a good rengir, and a good person." I smiled self-deprecatingly. "I know, because when I volunteered to help the Brothers of Beneficence serve the destitute while we were studying at Harcos, I was competing with you. The perfect model of an aspiring rengir. You helped the Sisters because you wanted to."

Instead of looking reassured or smug, Zidra hunched. "I didn't volunteer with the Sisters of Beneficence for altruistic reasons—although I'll admit, by the time I finished, the Sisters' eagerness to serve in even the most ignoble capacity had made a deep impression on me. But I did that as penance."

"Penance?" I sat up straighter. "Whatever for?"

"Erm…" She cleared her throat. "You kept beating me at footraces and obstacle courses, and I was embarrassed and angry, so I…put that ribbon snake in your bed."

My eyes nearly bulged out of my head, and then I broke down in laughter. "That was *you*?" I flopped back on the bed, tears leaking from my eyes. "Perfect little Zidra Eilmaris put a snake in my bed!"

"You didn't think it was funny then. I heard your scream all the way down the hall. Which was gratifying until I went to chapel and naturally the passage from the holy text was on living in unity and peace." She wrapped a curl around her forefinger. "Of course, did I apologize or truly put aside our rivalry? No, although I did try, for a while." She glared at me, although it held no heat, and I swear the corner of her mouth tipped up. "You're simply too infuriating to let win."

I shook my head and snickered. When I checked on the heartbond, I was pleased to find her mood had lightened. "Well, come back here and let me see what I can do about you not listening to the physician's orders."

Zidra huffed. "You try fighting without accessing your magic even a little bit." But she sat next to me and offered her arm.

"Apologies if this hurts."

"If you can take it, I can."

My gaze snapped from the wound to her eyes, but she quickly glanced away.

"You mentioned it hurts you, too." Her voice quieted.

"I haven't... I should have... Thank you."

Two little words, and maybe I should have been annoyed it had taken her so long and been so difficult for her to say, but instead, the whispered gratitude warmed me. Maybe because I knew I couldn't fully understand how terrifying this all was for her. On top of being unable to access her magic, she had let me work ice magic inside her, where it hurt her and could clash with her dragon heat. In my frustration with her stubbornness, I hadn't considered the immense trust this must take for her.

"Thank you for trusting me to do this."

"I don't have much choice." But her words lacked the bitterness I'd expected.

I focused on the puncture mark. Once again, the unnatural and aggressive cold of the curse burned and warred against my own magic. If I concentrated, I could also feel Zidra's dragon fire simmering in the background. Perhaps she, consciously or unconsciously, was holding it back. Or maybe it had something to do with our heartbond, so the magics recognized each other? An interesting possibility, but not worth mentioning.

The ice curse had spread, but thankfully not much. I pulled it back as close around the injury as I could without passing out from the strain and pain—if I fainted, I'd lose control, and Zidra would die. It didn't take long to ensure my magic was once again shielding her and locked tightly around the curse, but it felt like a lengthy battle. I released her arm and leaned back.

"Done."

"Thank you."

Despite my concern over how the curse had spread, I smiled at her sincere acknowledgment. "I know it's hard, but you need to make sure you keep your dragon fire moored as much as possible. We'll need to avoid any excitement or fighting until we find Rouven."

Zidra snorted. "That may be difficult with a league of assassins hunting me." She bit her lip and glanced toward the door.

"No one is crazy enough to attack a Haven full of rengiri," I reassured her.

"I suppose." She focused on her hands folded in her lap. "But you've already gotten caught in the middle of this twice. What if they send more assassins and other people get hurt, or worse?"

"Please." I put on my most confident, winning grin. "We're Kyrmaris! Recipients of the Emperor's Merit! No assassins stand a chance. They've failed twice. They've probably given up already anyway."

That had been the wrong thing to say based on how Zidra wordlessly went behind the screen to change into a loose, flowy shirt and pair of trousers. She didn't acknowledge me as she climbed into the other cot and settled in facing the wall.

My spirits fell, and I resisted the urge to reach for the heartbond again. She wouldn't appreciate me spying on her emotions so often.

I changed into a pair of linen sleeping trousers, and then I blew out the candle mounted on the wall and felt my way to my own cot. After a moment's hesitation, I whispered, "Good night, Zidra."

Several heartbeats passed in silence. I smothered my hurt and closed my eyes.

Then, so quiet I almost didn't hear it…

"Good night, Kyr."

Thirteen

Zidra

Kyrundar was still sleeping when I woke. Only a hint of light showed in the sky through the window over his cot. Even after I dressed, he still slept, sprawled over his narrow bed with one foot hanging off the edge. His silvery-white hair spread out over his pillow like a halo, and I had the oddest impulse to stroke it.

Instead, I clenched my fist at my side.

This heartbond must be doing something strange to my head. That was enough to reignite the frustration with my situation that had faded with his gentleness and reassurance the night before. Of course, if the heartbond was getting stronger, that was my own fault. I shouldn't have accessed it last night to check his sincerity. I couldn't imagine using the bond would make it any easier to break, and we had to break it.

Even if spending this much time with Kyrundar had reminded me that between all the rivalry, we had been friends.

Even if I couldn't deny his kindness in saving my life, sharing words of reassurance, and putting up with my fears and irritability.

Even if his whispered *good night* had soothed me in a way I couldn't explain.

I was a wyveri and he was an ice elf, and it didn't matter that intermarriages were not unheard of. I knew a few off-spring of such unions, in fact.

The bond still had to be broken. Wyveri rarely married outside the clan. As demonstrated last night, Kyrundar didn't understand what yoking himself to a wyveri meant, not really. And marrying an elf? One with a light elf mother, too, like the light elf king-turned-emperor who had banished my people to the islands? I might as well sur-render all pretense of ever making my family proud.

This fretting and growing anger did me no good. The story about the snake and my time volunteering with the Sisters of Beneficence had chastened me. If I had a prayer of getting this curse out of my arm and breaking the heart-bond, all without failing in my piety and rengir vows, it would take just that—prayer.

I slipped out the door and made my way through the dawn light to the Ravensburgh Sanctuary. The public house of worship in Ravensburgh, the Sanctuary was also attached to a monastery, and the abbot was just leading the monks in a sunrise liturgy. I sneaked into the back row of low benches and knelt on a cushion, adding my low voice to the refrain of the monks.

Kyrundar had once admitted he struggled with the memorization and repetitions of such traditions. I'd judged him for it at the time, but later I'd had to acknowledge his faith wasn't any less sincere, and at times I was tempted to envy how easily and without pretense he could speak to Iskyr. For my part, though, the rituals helped steady the fire in my chest and clarify my thoughts and supplications.

When the abbot finished, I added my own traditional prayers and recitation of holy texts asking for guidance, provision, protection, and endurance, and then I crept out before any of the brothers noticed me.

With the sun up, the streets bustled with activity. People pushed market carts or opened doors to shops, calling out their wares. A girl hurried past me, corralling a flock of geese, and a boy tugged on the lead of a stubborn pig. A man with tattoos covering his muscular arms—likely a human, as few shifters or elves cared for tattoos—walked by carrying a barrel on his shoulder. I caught a few curious glances at my sword and was glad I'd stowed my Order insignia in my hip bag. Even though the time in the sanctuary had helped, I still wasn't in the mood for extra attention.

When I returned to our room in the Haven, Kyrundar was dressed—thank Iskyr—and braiding back the sides of his hair. For a brief moment, I watched in fascination as his deft fingers flew through weaving together the thin strands, but then he turned his head to see me.

"Where did you go?" He raised a brow and leaned to

the side. "And what are you hiding behind your back?"

"Sanctuary." I pulled my hands in front of me, revealing two warm, glazed buns with dried currants. "And a baker was leaving as I returned. She'd donated some fresh baked goods. I was glad I was able to thank her before she returned to her bakery. I wasn't sure if you'd still be asleep, so I thought I should grab one for you before the others get up and they're all devoured."

He grinned. "I appreciate it. Let me finish this, if you don't mind."

"Braiding your hair with sticky fingers would be unwise," I agreed.

I waited until we'd both finished our buns to ask the question burning at the back of my throat. "Can we meet your friend now?"

Kyrundar looked up from his sticky fingertips and glanced out the window before shaking his head. "Not yet. I don't want to inconvenience her."

If asking a few questions was an inconvenience, his contact must not be overly friendly. The idea that he truly wasn't that close with this woman pleased me, and I decided not to examine why.

"How is your arm?"

I shrugged. "The same." Which included a glimmer of cold pain every time I made an abrupt movement or bumped the spot, but that would worry him for no reason. He'd done all he could.

Kyrundar nodded. "Want to walk around town until it's time to meet my friend?"

As that seemed preferable to sitting in the Haven, I readily agreed.

About an hour later, as I was wondering whether I risked sounding like a petulant child if I asked again when we would meet this mysterious woman, Kyrundar changed course. He switched from an aimless stroll to jaunty strides as he left my side to approach a long building.

The ground floor was made of limestone, while the upper two stories were built of timber-framed wattle and daub. Wood shingles covered the steep gables of the uppermost rooms. A sign jutting out from the second floor over the busy thoroughfare depicted a steaming teapot, and red letters painted over the door declared THE BLOOMING LOTUS TEAHOUSE.

I caught his sleeve and brought us to a halt. "What is this?"

"It's a tea parlor."

"I can see that." I crossed my arms, ignoring the icy twinge of my wound. "Why are we here?"

"To have tea, obviously." Kyrundar's wide smile made me want to singe off his ridiculously silky hair. "The Blooming Lotus not only serves the best tea on this side of the continent, it also observes the ancient tea ceremony from Shuallang as a practice of pursuing calm, releasing worries, and treasuring the blessings of the present moment."

Just saying all of that took too long. "We don't have time for—"

"My contact is the proprietor." He waved toward the front door. "It would be terribly impolite to ask her for a favor without first giving her our business, now wouldn't it?"

I narrowed my eyes. "You said she was your friend."

"So she is," Kyrundar agreed far too cheerfully. "And I like to support my friends."

"You said you spent all your money."

"I suppose you'll have to pay, then. But a rengir's money is never truly her own." He winked. "Come on. An hour won't delay us that much, and it will be good for you to remember it's all right to rest now and then." He headed inside.

An hour. On top of the night spent at the Haven and the hour spent milling about Ravensburgh... I groaned and followed him. It wasn't as if I had any leads of my own.

A bell behind the door jingled as we entered. The interior was surprisingly airy. Tables with two to six chairs around them, depending on size, were spaced throughout the room, with wide aisles between them. Only a few of them were occupied by men and women drinking tea or eating finger food. Perhaps the establishment didn't get much business, since they didn't feel the need to cram in seating. Green organza curtains draped from the ceiling, tied back to the staggered support beams. A long wall along the back was broken by a curtained door in the center, which doubtless led to the kitchen. A staircase occupied one back corner, and in the opposite corner stood a curious, empty square room that could be no more than four feet wide.

The curtain moved, and then a diminutive elf woman

emerged—no, not short.

An elf woman in a wicker chair with wheels. A braid of golden hair fell over her maroon dress down to her waist, and she had a rosy flush in her cheeks beneath her light-beige complexion. Gold hoops and chains and dangling rubies dripped from her ears from lobes to pointed tips. Her ears weren't as long as Kyrundar's, though, and her earthy-brown eyes were unusually dark for a light elf. Her gaze landed on Kyrundar, and she waved with a wide grin, then returned her hands to the wheels and propelled herself forward.

"Kyr, you rascal! Six months without seeing you is entirely too long, and I was most offended you didn't stop by on your way to the Dawning Festival."

Kyrundar's shoulders hitched up toward his ears. "I do apologize, Sylathria. I was traveling in the wolf clan's lands and would have been late to Laedresh if I'd come so far out of my way." As she stopped in front of him, he leaned down, placed his hands on both of her shoulders, and lightly kissed the top of her head. "How are you feeling today?" he asked, far quieter.

Sylathria waved dismissively. "My bad leg collapsed this morning, but the pain isn't bad. It's just too weak today for the crutch, clearly. Hulfson tried to talk me into taking the day off, but there will be people coming through leaving Laedresh, and I can't miss out on all that excitement." She looked to me, and the corner of her lips curved up. "No need to stand there looking so self-conscious. Injuries happen. Sometimes they don't heal."

She looked pointedly at my arm. I started to reach for the bandage, as if to hide it, and decided that would look more suspicious.

But rather than asking invasive questions, she looked back to Kyrundar. "Congratulations on the Emperor's Merit, Kyr! It's well deserved. And would I be correct in assuming this is Zidra?"

"Goodness, yes, forgive me." Kyrundar ducked his head, causing his silver earrings to sway. "Sylathria Graystone, this is Zidra Eilmaris. Zidra, my dear friend Sylathria."

I inclined my head. "It's a pleasure to meet you."

"The pleasure is mine, having the honor of serving not only two rengiri, but the co-recipients of the Merit!" Somehow, when she said it with that sincere tone and warm smile, being a co-recipient didn't sound as much like an insult. "What will you be having? Your preferred private tea room is available, Kyr, if you like."

"Excellent. We'll take…" He turned to me. "How much coin do you have?"

With Sylathria watching, I couldn't berate Kyrundar like I wanted to. And with Iskyr watching, I couldn't lie. "Two crowns, four half-crowns, and a few copper pence."

"Then we'll have the full ceremonial tea and some light desserts," Kyrundar declared. "I know the way, so don't worry. We'll seat ourselves."

Only after we were on the way up the stairs and safely out of earshot did I dare ask how she would have shown us to a room upstairs.

"Oh, the little room on the opposite side from the

stairs is actually an empty shaft that opens onto all three levels," he said. "Syl uses her plant magic to manipulate vines to carry her up and down so she doesn't have to use the stairs. It's big enough she can move her wheeled chair up and down as well. She lives in the rooms on the third floor with her husband—that's Hulfson Graystone. He's a human, from Neaston."

The revelation that Kyrundar's friend was *married* almost made me trip. The scoundrel had teased me about being jealous, all the while knowing she was married? I would have scolded him, except that would only prove that I *had* been jealous, and he would doubtless love that. Infuriating elvish rogue.

He led the way to a room decorated with blue organza dripping with green tassels. Blue cushions were arranged around a low table. A painting of an emerald sea surrounded by blue-toned mountains covered most of one wall. I had to admit, the atmosphere was relaxing.

Kyrundar dropped onto one of the cushions. "Syl's father was Shuallangian," he said, confirming my theory she was half-human. "She lived the first fifty years of her life there, which is why she loves their teas and traditions. Then her father's eyesight failed, and he had to retire from being a stone carver, so they moved to Bryluthia. Obviously that's where we met. Syl inherited human magecraft with an affinity for stone from her father, but her plant magic is much stronger. She mostly uses it to get around and check the quality of tea leaves. She started this teahouse while I was still at Harcos. It's close enough to the capital that it's lively and gets a variety of visitors, but it isn't as crowded and chaotic as Laedresh—"

"Is any of this relevant to how she can help us?" I settled onto a cushion on the opposite side of the table.

"I suppose, in a way." Kyrundar's happy expression faded into something almost sulky. "Sylathria knows everything, and I mean *everything*. If we could gamble, I'd bet that she has heard something about Rouven. The Blooming Lotus is well known and has a wide variety of clientèle. People pass through from all over the empire. In the evenings, she hires bards and storytellers and other performers. The Blooming Lotus is an excellent locus for both disseminating and gleaning information, and Sylathria or her staff have heard every noteworthy story, whether fact or rumor."

"Disseminating stories?" My posture went rigid. "Like tales of Kyrmaris?"

"Ye…" Pink spotted his pale cheeks, and he abruptly was very interested in unbuckling and removing the swords strapped to his back.

I crossed my arms. "So you *have* been following me around and then selling stories to bards!"

"Don't be ridiculous." Kyrundar smiled, but it was more guilty than confident. "I don't ask for payment. Oh, come on, don't look at me like that. Most rengiri tell stories about themselves. Every story I've told is completely true, and anyway, the bards mostly ask for additional details. They prefer the tales about events that other people have witnessed. If only one troubadour tells a story, people think it's fabricated. But if she has extra, never-before-told details on a story many bards are telling, people will pay more for that. I'm helping entertainers make better wages."

Before I could argue, Sylathria rolled into the room with a large tray balanced across the arms of her wheeled chair. It felt wrong to let her manage by herself, but Kyrundar knew her better, and he made no move to get up, so I remained seated. I didn't want to insult her by offering help that wasn't needed, or worse, try to help and instead make her task more difficult by interfering with her process.

Sylathria set down the tray. "Your desserts should be up by the time you've finished the tea ceremony."

"Thank you," we said in unison.

Her knowing expression as she glanced between us made me hot under the collar of my tunic and leather breastplate. She backed away in her chair before turning in a circle and rolling out.

I frowned at the items on the tray. How many cups and pots did two people need? There were two handleless teacups, oddly small given that tea drinking was meant to be the main attraction. A teapot and a large kettle sat on either side of another teacup, but this one was larger and had a lid. The tea leaves waited in a miniature oval trencher. An empty bowl to the side further confused me.

"I'll serve," Kyrundar said, as if there were a chance I had any idea what to do with everything arranged on the tray. He picked up the kettle, his movements slow and measured. "You know how I struggle with the recitations and some of the rituals in the sanctuaries?"

I nodded.

"Well, something about this tea ritual…it calms me. Perhaps because I know I get delicious tea at the end of it." He chuckled. "Maybe because of how Sylathria explained it to me. She said every step demonstrates that you value the gift of the tea, that you appreciate the access to the implements of the ceremony, and most importantly, that you honor and are grateful for the friendship of your guest."

As he spoke, he poured steaming water out of the kettle into the teapot, then into the teacup with the lid, then into both smaller teacups.

Admittedly, it was harder to be upset with Kyrundar for wasting our time with ritualized water pouring when he claimed it was symbolic of gratitude and honoring our friendship.

To my growing confusion, he poured the water out of the teapot and the teacup with the lid into the empty bowl. "Did you forget the tea?" I asked with a raised eyebrow.

Kyrundar grinned. "No, that was to warm the dishes."

He carefully poured the tea leaves from the trencher into the empty teapot…and replaced the lid. I resisted the urge to drum my fingers on the tabletop as, instead of pouring the hot water, he gently shook the teapot, removed the lid, and then lifted the teapot, closed his eyes, and smelled the leaves.

With a sound of contentment, he held out the teapot to me.

I looked at him flatly over the vessel. "We could have

drunk tea by now—"

"It's not about the tea. Not only." He lowered the pot, his expression thoughtful. "Why do *you* drink tea, Zidra?"

I kept my impatience off my face with effort. "For refreshment, as the body needs hydration. Perhaps for the little bit of added energy it provides, or the heat on a cold day; otherwise, I would simply drink water."

"Ah, so you drink tea to aid your productivity." His tone was gently teasing. "I don't know why I'm surprised."

I shrugged as if that would disguise my blushing. "Essentially. This"—I indicated the ceremony implements—"serves no purpose. It could be achieved faster, with less waste and effort."

"That's true." He waved the teapot. "Smell the tea, Zee."

"Only to get you to move on." I didn't lean as close to the teapot as he had. With my shifter senses, I could already catch a hint of the complex, nutty leaves. I inhaled deeply through my nose and refused to let my face or words admit the soothing quality of the rich, earthy, and slightly floral aroma.

Satisfied, Kyrundar placed the little teapot in front of himself again. At last, he poured hot water over the leaves and replaced the lid.

"Purpose is an interesting concept," he mused as he methodically discarded the hot water from the teacups. "I don't believe there's value only in things that have a practical, material application. We can't solely do things that help us earn coin, fulfill a duty, or increase our glory, right?"

"I'm not only concerned with glory," I protested, bristling.

"No, I know that." He removed the lid of the larger teacup. Into this he poured the entire batch of tea, and then he replaced the lid. "Is your main concern your image, then? Your need to prove to your family, the citizens of the empire, and yourself that you are a good rengir, a good person?" He glanced up. "Which you are, by the way. You don't need to prove it."

I nudged my teacup with my forefinger until it was centered in front of me. "I do, though. I need to prove I'm not like the ancient wyveri king, and I need to prove I made the right choice in becoming a rengir."

His mouth twisted to the side. "Anyone who spends more than a few moments with you can see both of those things are true." He used the lid on the large cup as a strainer to catch any escaped leaves as he poured the tea into my teacup and then his own. "Why do you seem to think something is valuable only if it's, I don't know, productive? Including yourself? That your value is contingent on your being useful in some way, like...um...a sword?" Setting down the cup, he motioned toward my sword.

I reached for the tea, thankful for the excuse not to answer, but Kyrundar held up his hand. "The second steep will taste better."

To my horror, he took my teacup and dumped the contents into the waste bowl, then did the same with his teacup and the entire contents of the cup with the lid.

"This is insanity," I declared.

Kyrundar smirked. "No, it has a practical purpose—I promise it really will taste better."

"Not that I can compare them," I muttered.

"Or you could say its purpose is teaching patience." He winked. Once again, he poured hot water over the tea leaves and replaced the lid on the teapot.

"Fine, I will admit it has marginal value." My attempted joke felt brittle even to me.

"Only marginal if you're discounting less practical value. Things like...hm." Kyrundar set down the kettle and looked around the room, his eyes brightening as they landed on the painting. "Elves believe art's purpose is to be beautiful, to inspire joy and wonder. That's not practical, but it's valuable, right?"

He spoke faster and leaned forward, like a child describing his favorite subject. "I love this room because the painting and the colors remind me of winters in Glacori. Décor making me sentimental isn't strictly useful, but it brings me joy. What is a world without beauty, without reasons to smile, without things that leave you in awe and take your breath away? These things aren't lesser. Perhaps you can't eat beauty or use art as a defense against a blade or slay a monster with wonder, but they're still necessary for life if we want to truly live. These things feed and heal our souls. They are gifts from Iskyr and remind us of divine beauty and awe and goodness as well."

His words caused my heart to swell. I dug my fingers into my leg beneath the table, refusing to get caught up in Kyrundar's useless elven philosophizing.

"Anyway. Tea!" For the third time, he poured the liquid from the teapot into the large cup. Setting the lid at a slight angle, he carefully poured tea into first my cup and then his own. After he set down the cup, he gracefully turned his palm up and motioned toward my cup.

"First, smell the tea," he instructed. "This is the ritual. You like rituals, come on."

I sighed, half faking my exasperation, and breathed in the tea's pleasant aroma.

"Now we admire the color. Then sip, savoring the tea. In this way, we acknowledge the tea's value, and we give ourselves time to properly thank Iskyr for his gift of pleasing tea."

I obliged. The pale amber tea was far more flavorful and less astringent than any I'd tasted before. Silently, I thanked Iskyr for pleasant tea, even though I had mixed opinions on how *valuable* both tea and this elaborate ritual truly were. Across from me, Kyrundar held his free hand in front of the teacup, as if hiding his imbibing. I'd seen Shuallangians do the same before, so it must have been a practice he'd picked up from Sylathria.

He refilled our teacups. "This tea ceremony reminds me why I fight in the first place. Why I wander the empire."

"*How?*" I asked, baffled. "Wait—you aren't saying you became a rengir to drink tea across the empire, are you?"

Kyrundar laughed. "No, no. Our goal as rengiri is serving Iskyr, specifically protecting his people. Therefore, the whole reason there's value in protecting Iskyr's people is because there's value in those people, right?"

He waited for me to nod, then continued. "Then the way I see it, there must be value in the good things they create. Art. Songs. Stories. Delicious tea. If those things are good, then there's also—perhaps even more so—value in friends to enjoy those things with. Enjoyment isn't bad simply because it isn't productive, right?"

I wasn't sure I was following, so I sat quietly while Kyrundar squinted at the ceiling.

"Iskyr could have given us a purely utilitarian world," he continued slowly, as if still piecing his thoughts together. "We *could* have been made to exist on our own, like tigers who keep to their own territory. Instead we have a world of beauty and emotions and relationships." He grinned. "That's the point!"

I blinked. "The point of what?"

"Of the slow, ritual steps of the tea ceremony. We can miss the blessing of relationships and creativity and emotions if we do not take the time to appreciate them." Kyrundar held up his teacup. "This is only tea. The highest quality tea, but still only tea. In spending time and care in its preparation and consumption, we acknowledge the value it has, without asking it to be anything more or labeling it as inferior for not being something else."

I did not move to drink my second cup. Where was he going with this? My skin prickled, and my pulse increased, but there was no threat for me to face. Only this ridiculous ice elf, peering at me over his teacup with a strange glimmer in his eyes.

"Don't undervalue the tea because it can't become a

sword, Zidra," Kyrundar murmured.

My spine stiffened. There it was.

I'd been fool enough to trust him with my fears about being unable to shift, and this was how he handled my vulnerability?

FOURTEEN

KYRUNDAR

Based on the steely expression that slid over Zidra's face, I'd said the wrong thing again.

"So I'm as useless as tea because I can't shift," she said flatly.

My face drained of color. "That's not what I meant." I set down my empty teacup with more haste than was appropriate for a tea ceremony. "I wanted to explain why I enjoy the tea parlor and point out the benefit of including things in your life that aren't only work or worry! I also hate seeing you undervalue yourself. I don't care if you can't shift or if your fighting is compromised—"

"Of course you don't care," Zidra snapped. Her eyes flickered red.

I didn't dare remind her to control her dragon fire

when I'd already stupidly bungled my words of affirmation into an offense.

"It gives you more of a chance to be the hero, right? I'm sure you'll have great stories about how you saved and took care of me after this. Everyone will see more clearly that poor Zidra Eilmaris never would have earned the Emperor's Merit without Kyrundar Ilifir's help."

My mouth went dry. "What?"

She laughed, the sound acidic. "You know, I used to think you always followed me and inserted yourself into my missions because you wanted to leverage my talent for your own victories, but it's pity. You think I can't achieve anything without you, so you magnanimously help me and share our stories together so you can be the benevolent ice elf who helped the graceless wyveri. All the better that I can't shift now, right? In one fell swoop, my reputation can be destroyed and yours exalted even further."

"That—that's what you think of me?" I struggled to get the words out. "Zidra, you're my friend, and I would never—"

"Spend more time and effort on me than I deserve, like useless tea?"

"No." I shook my head, frantically searching for the right words to fix this. "You're not tea, it's just that similar to tea, you have unique value. Maybe that was a bad metaphor, but my point is your value doesn't change if you can't fight or shift because that isn't what makes you worthy."

"Then what does?" More emotion bled into Zidra's harsh query than I imagined she'd intended. "Of what use am I if I'm—I'm broken?"

"A broken plate may be discarded," a quiet voice said from the entrance to the room. I jerked my head around to see Sylathria stopped in the doorway, a tray of desserts across her lap. "A person is not a plate. A person doesn't have one function that they must fulfill in a specific way or be tossed out. A difference does not make you useless, even if perhaps your role might change."

I glanced toward Zidra, but she was staring down at her teacup.

Sylathria wheeled over and slid the tray onto the table. "I was gored by an armored hog and then trapped in a ravine when I was a child. By the time I saw a fleshmage, it was too late to fully repair the damage. As I grew, it worsened. There are many things I cannot do. I realized long ago I'd rather focus on what I can do, yet there are days I am in too much pain to even leave my bed. Does my value change on those days? How can a person's value vary from day to day? To assign value based on pragmatic measures of usefulness is illogical and hurts more than just yourself. The holy texts tell us Iskyr has formed us all and loves each of his people with a love that cannot be broken or removed by any known force of people or nature. Will you dare to assign less value to yourself than the god you swore to serve does? Or if you fear what other rengiri or the citizens of the empire will think, do you mean then to elevate the opinion of created beings over the opinion of their creator?"

Zidra lifted her teacup with shaking hands. Tea sloshed onto her fingers, and she set the cup back down. Her gaze didn't lift from the table. "I am a warrior and a wyveri. Without that, I have nothing."

"There is always something new," I said quickly. "And you have me. Besides, it is too early to give up hope."

"And you have Iskyr," Sylathria added. "Even if you leave the Order, Iskyr keeps you in his hand. Or do you believe Iskyr's care is only for those in holy orders, and not for those they serve?"

Zidra's shoulders hunched. Ignoring how much it felt like a violation of her privacy, I reached for the heartbond. A torrent of aching emotion rushed through like a scream—shame, conviction, fear, anger, confusion. Guilt-ily, I closed the connection. She wasn't in any frame of mind for a rational conversation about her feelings, her identity, how much I wanted her to lean on and trust me, nor for me to ask more about her false belief that I was using her to feel better about myself.

I adjusted my position on my cushion to face Sylathria and cleared my throat. "Since we have you here, Syl, we actually had another purpose besides tea."

Zidra looked up, and though her face was unnaturally pale, the tension in her jawline eased.

Sylathria narrowed her eyes but then accepted the change of subject. "Gossip hunting again?"

My forced chuckle sounded more like a cough. "Yes. Have you heard of Gautindar Rouven? He was the head physician at Merael's until about six months ago."

"Rouven…" Sylathria rubbed her ruby drop earring. "Recently retired… Ah, yes. Elderly ice elf? A bit grouchy?"

"That sounds like him," I said.

Across the table, Zidra perked up. "He came through here?"

"Yes, I suppose right after he retired." Sylathria frowned. "I remember, because he complained about the 'noise' from the musicians who were performing and was annoyed that all the private tea rooms were taken. One of my poor serving staff came to get me because he didn't know how to appease the man. Not terribly uncommon, unfortunately. I often calm down cantankerous customers by stroking their egos—that is, I get them to talk about themselves. I learn interesting things, and they feel important."

"I don't suppose one of the interesting things you learned from Rouven was where he is living now?"

She gave me an apologetic frown. "Not exactly. He mentioned he was looking forward to getting away from people. I did overhear him asking another ice elf if any new roads had been built through the Ithemorca Mountains or if taking a ship remained the best way to access the inlets along the Glacorian coast. Let me think."

While Sylathria considered, I snuck a glance at Zidra. She looked calmer, but she was good at hiding her emotions. I wished I knew what to say that would make her stop undervaluing herself—without overstepping and offending her.

"This might help," Sylathria said. "Rouven had expensive tastes. He ordered the best of everything and asked if we had any Nyksian mead, and he was incensed that we didn't. If you can find anyone delivering Nyksian mead to a Glacorian inlet, you might find Rouven."

I nodded. The night elves made a mead from the honey of nocturnal bees that collected nectar only from a flower that blooms at night in the Kingdom of Nyksia, and petals from the sweet flower were also used to flavor the mead. It was a uniquely delicious concoction, and incredibly rare outside the night elves' homeland.

"I'm sorry I don't know anything more," she said.

"At least we have a starting place." Barely, but I donned a smile anyway. "Any information is helpful, so thank you!"

Zidra changed positions to access her hip bag and pulled out a drawstring pouch. "How much for the food and drink?"

"For the recipients of the Emperor's Merit? Discounted price of four half-crowns." Sylathria grinned at me. "Only because I know you'll fight me if I try to make it complimentary."

Zidra counted out four silver coins and passed them to Sylathria with murmured gratitude.

"Thank you." Sylathria focused on Zidra. "May Iskyr show you the way, be your fortress, and grant you peace."

"May it be so," I said at the same time as Zidra, and I wondered how much of her reply was a faithful agreement and how much was a rote response to a benediction.

Sylathria turned back to me and narrowed her eyes. She wagged her finger in my face. "Don't be so long a stranger this time, Kyr."

I chuckled abashedly. "You know I can make no promises, Syl. I go where the prompting of Iskyr leads."

"Mmm." She raised one eyebrow. "Remarkable how often that prompting leads you to Zidra."

Heat flamed over my face. Across from me, Zidra pursed her lips, raised her eyebrows, and inclined her head in silent, accusatory agreement.

"Er…" I cleared my throat. "A fortunate coincidence."

"Mm-hmmm." Sylathria's knowing smile was unfairly smug. I'd have wondered whether she knew about the heartbond if I hadn't known that was impossible. "Enjoy the desserts, both of you." With that, she departed, leaving Zidra and me in strained silence.

We ate the desserts without a word. When the last jam-filled cookie was gone, Zidra started to rise.

"Wait."

To my relief, she settled back onto her cushion, although she didn't meet my eyes.

"What you said—that I'm helping you out of pity or using you to bolster my own reputation or feel good about myself or for any other reason. It's not true. I certainly don't pity you, Zee. You're the most incredible, awe-inspiring, and terrifying person I know. You deserved the Merit and didn't need my help to get it, and I'm not friends with you only for glory or recognition. I follow you because we're friends, because we fight well together, and because I thought we both had a better chance of achieving everything we dreamed of by working together."

I fiddled with my teacup to give my hands something to do. "But I haven't thought about how you might interpret my actions. I never asked if you wanted me around. Looking back…"

The words lodged in my throat, and I opened and closed my mouth several times before I could make myself say it.

"I ignored signals you didn't want my assistance. I thought you were just not used to having people around and supporting you and would get more comfortable over time. Or at times I believed you were putting on your prickly and unapproachable act but were secretly glad I was there, because we *do* fight so well together, and you never said otherwise—but that's not an excuse. If anything, maybe it makes you right, in a way. I did think I was helping you, by giving you friendship and fighting at your side, but I didn't ask if you wanted friendship or aid, and perhaps it was…I don't know. Proud or foolish of me to assume you'd want my friendship. I never intended to hurt you, but I did, and I'm sorry."

Silence greeted my declaration. I couldn't make myself look at her. I didn't dare access the heartbond, afraid of what I might find. My shoulders slumped.

"And if you don't want to be friends anymore, if you want me to leave you alone after we find Rouven"—I gulped—"I understand."

After several tense moments, Zidra still hadn't spoken, so I lifted my gaze from my empty teacup. She hunched over the table and rubbed her thumbnail. As if feeling my eyes on her, she glanced up and immediately looked away.

"Thank you," she said, her voice as thin as the organza

hangings. She stood. "We should collect our things from the Haven and start for Klavon's Port in Gamnica. That's the most likely place from which to charter passage along the Glacorian coast."

Smothering my disappointment at her lack of acknowledgment of my apology and attempt to make amends, I dragged myself to my feet.

"And thank you for the tea, Kyr."

My head jerked up and my lips parted, but she was already marching out of the room.

FIFTEEN

ZIDRA

After we retrieved our packs and replaced our bedding—regretfully leaving the washing for someone else to deal with—I requested we detour to Ravensburgh's messenger guild. While Kyrundar waited outside, I wrote a brief letter to Sajen explaining the attack by the wolvus and panthera, describing their mention of a 'league' ruled by an archon, and warning him to be careful. I considered telling him to stop investigating for his own safety, but I doubted he would listen.

After I paid for the letter to be delivered, Kyrundar and I bought some dried jerky and hardtack with my dwindling supply of coin and headed north. Restless and needing more movement than flying on Kyrundar's hovering ice disks afforded, I requested that we walk for a while. To my relief, he didn't argue. If he'd pointed out time was important, I wouldn't have been able to disagree. Also a relief, he didn't insist on filling the silence with more shaky analogies or apologies I didn't know what to do with.

Maybe I had judged him too harshly. While he was correct that he hadn't considered my feelings or desires, the thought kept pushing into my mind that I hadn't asked him his intentions, either.

And why did everyone think I needed friends? Sajen, Kyrundar... Perhaps two people wasn't actually *everyone*, but it felt like I was being attacked from all sides.

Two are better than one.

The words came from a memory of a teaching on Iskyr's gift of community and commands that we help each other, but it wasn't merely a memory. Not often did I feel—or hear—Iskyr's prompting so clearly.

Guilt pricked me, not least because despite my claiming that I had forgiven Kyrundar, my outburst at the Blooming Lotus indicated otherwise. Certainly, I had heard before that forgiveness is often an ongoing practice, but I'd not had to actually, well, practice that before.

Were Sajen and Kyrundar right? Did I need to let other people help me more often than I did? Which, admittedly, was almost never, unless someone forced their assistance on me, like Kyrundar.

I glanced toward him. Sunlight highlighted his white hair and glinted on his silver earrings. The chains and dangling gems swung with his steps. The baldrics crossing his chest and the cut of his dark-blue tunic emphasized his lean, muscular frame. Had he always been so attractive? Or was the heartbond tampering with my perception? Surely I'd need to be using the heartbond for it to affect me.

Right?

Using the bond. What was a heartbond's function, anyway? I didn't dare voice my question. Besides not caring to admit I was thinking about the bond, I didn't want Kyrundar to give me some ridiculous answer about it being like art or sunsets that are colorful for no practical reason.

"You know," Kyrundar said, "I am getting the strangest sensations through the heartbond."

I recoiled. "Stop accessing it, then."

"I'm not." He cast a smirk my way. "But I was getting the distinct impression you were thinking about me. Dare I say it—positively."

My face burned like it had been enveloped in dragon fire. Clearly the purpose of the heartbond was to humiliate me.

A faint sense of displeasure rippled through me, but I knew it wasn't from the elf.

No, Iskyr. I know you wouldn't give couples a heartbond to hurt them. Not when your prophets taught that all relationships, especially marriage, should be founded on love that puts others first and does not harm.

Thankfully, Kyrundar and I had no relationship.

That was a weak excuse, but he had hurt me first.

Unwilling to let this line of thought continue, I forced a shrug. "I was thinking I've had enough exercise and am ready to continue this journey at a faster pace."

"Oh, excellent!" He did a little jump, and snowflakes

danced around his feet. "I've been struggling to keep my worries in check. The sooner we find Rouven, the sooner we can destroy that ice curse, and I'm not going to feel at ease until then."

Because until then he was stuck with me? Or because he cared about me? Or was he just pretending he cared since I'd said he might like it if my shifting powers never returned? I found I didn't actually believe it could be the last option.

Within moments, we were rushing through the air. I thought about sitting down, but if that were an option, surely Kyrundar would do it himself. Perhaps that would be too cold. My feet were colder than the rest of me, after all, although not enough to cause concern.

Some time in the early afternoon, we stopped in a village and bought small hand pies for lunch, saving the dried beef for when food wouldn't be available to purchase. I frowned as I counted the few coins left in my pouch. We would have to count on charitable goodwill to get us passage on a ship unless something drastic happened before then.

Night fell before we reached the next town, so we stopped and looked for a place to make camp. Often I would sleep as a wyvern if I had to sleep by myself in the wilds. Not only was it safer, but it kept me warmer, too. It rankled that shifting wasn't an option. I had a cloak rolled up in my pack that could double as a light blanket, and this late in the spring, the nights weren't too cold. A few clouds drifted overhead, but none looked like they held rain.

While I dug my cloak and the hardtack out of my pack, Kyrundar set about building himself a snow shelter. I ignored him, trying not to feel the sting of knowing my magic couldn't contribute anything. In my di'yar, I could breathe fire. Not that we needed a fire.

My fingers brushed against the flint in my pack, and a sardonic smile tugged at my mouth. I could light a fire in my di'ora, too, just as any elf or human could, even if flint and friction were less impressive. And, I supposed, if I had to be trapped in one state, at least it was in my true form. As discouraging as it was to be unable to shift, being trapped as a wyvern would be far more difficult. I'd probably have no choice but to return home, defeated and ashamed. At least in di'ora, I could blend in as a human.

"There," Kyrundar announced. "Done! That should be sufficient space."

I closed my pack and twisted around, still crouched, to peer at his snow shelter. It looked larger than others I'd seen him make before.

"Don't look all confused. You always refuse to share, but that was when you could turn into a wyvern." He waved toward the small entrance to the domed snow structure. "This will protect you from any wind or rain that comes up, and it'll be warmer than out here—the nights are still chilly, don't argue. You can't afford to get cold with an ice curse in you. Most importantly, I won't have to worry about whether you're safe. Not in a self-important way, just…as a friend looking out for an injured friend."

I glanced between him and the dome of ice. It looked

cold, but he'd explained before that the packed snow trapped heat. His magic not only kept the snow from melting, it regulated the temperature inside and would alert him if anyone or anything tried to enter. But being inside would involve being in close proximity to him all night, with nothing between us. That felt different than sleeping on separate cots in the same room. More…intimate.

Besides which, a part of me still bristled at the thought of accepting his help. Whether because of my own stubborn pride or because I didn't believe his sincerity, I wasn't certain.

I stood to face him. Carefully, as if he might detect it, I reached for the heartbond. Once I had a sense of his emotions—currently mostly embarrassment and impatience with a simmering note of hopefulness—I posed my question.

"Did you mean it when you said we work well together? And about wanting to help me, not trying to use my skill to increase your own glory and not seeing me as an opportunity for self-righteous posturing?"

Kyrundar stepped closer, urgency in his ice-blue eyes. "I swear on Emperor Syrzin's grave, my help was not given for selfish reasons. Not entirely, at least. I won't pretend I didn't also think we could bolster each other's reputation. Maybe that's selfish, but I promise I didn't want to better myself at your expense."

His resolve and honesty poured through the heartbond with crackling intensity.

"I'm sorry I overstepped in wanting to save you from perceived loneliness," he continued. "I've never come to your aid or joined you on a mission or saved your life because I considered myself better than you. You're worth my efforts, Zidra. You're my friend. Honestly, I owe you my aid. Our friendly rivalry is the only reason I graduated from Harcos with honors. Possibly the only reason I was initiated into the Order of the Rengir at all." His thoughtful expression broke into a grin. "Admittedly, our competition is also why I had to do extra homework to make up for disciplinary marks, but still."

I snorted and rolled my eyes. "You would have found trouble without me. For example, I never hosted parties that caused half the academy to be caught out of bed after curfew."

"Parties you never attended," he said with a dramatic sigh. Then his eyes widened. "Wait, did you report us?"

I couldn't help my snicker. "No. It felt unsporting to take such an easy victory, and you were always caught and ended up in trouble anyway."

I found myself smiling. If there was anything good about the heartbond, it was that I was sure neither of us could fool it. The bond showed me Kyrundar's true emotions as surely as it revealed feelings to him I would never have shared.

The heartbond said he had told the truth.

Had I been so caught up in my own pride and fear of how others perceived me that I'd never realized even Kyrundar's competition had been an offer of friendship? Was I so terrible at accepting help that I alone had poisoned our friendship?

If Kyrundar could apologize, surely I could. "I misjudged you. I have treated you poorly, believing the worst of you instead of respecting you as a brother-in-arms, and I am sorry."

"Apology accepted, even if I'm unsure I deserve it." He rubbed the back of his neck and smiled, looking more sheepish than I'd ever seen him. "So…is that an agreement to share the shelter?"

I shuffled back a step. "I'd rather sleep out here. Wyveri like open skies."

"You don't sleep in houses in the Wyveri Islands?"

I winced at the stupidity of my excuse. "Of course we do—but in stone houses on the hills and cliffs. It's different."

Kyrundar opened his mouth, then closed it. "I'm sorry. I thought it was like sharing a room in a Haven, but I've made you uncomfortable. Do…you want your own snow shelter? I can make you one—"

"No, it's fine." I held up my hands to stop his protests. "Maybe some other time."

"All right." He blew out a breath. "I am sorry. Syl has told me many times I need to get better at reading women."

I choked on a laugh. "You? The seductive rengir who enchants women like a snake charmer hypnotizes a serpent?"

Kyrundar's jaw went slack, and something about the wounded look in his eyes silenced me. "I don't… That is, I don't mean to… No, this is ridiculous. You said something like this before, but where are you coming up with this slander? When have I ever seduced or even flirted with someone?"

I faltered. "Women are always flirting with you. Like Samina—"

"That isn't the same thing!" He flung his arms wide. "I can't control—wait, Samina was flirting with me?"

"Are you blind?" I tried not to let it bother me that Kyrundar appeared tantalized by Samina's interest. "Women practically throw themselves at you."

He shook his head. "I have admirers, yes. In honesty there are times I enjoy their attentions. However, I don't purposefully flirt back, and I do my best to not give any lady a false impression. I certainly have never *seduced* anyone. I've never even kissed a woman!"

We stared at each other, the red creeping over Kyrundar's cheeks mirroring the heat in my own face.

"In hindsight," he continued, "I suppose Samina has been trying to get my attention for a while. If I've encouraged her, it was unintentional."

Unwilling to accept that once again, my mental image of Kyrundar was completely skewed, I crossed my arms. "So of all these women who admire and flirt with you, you've never wanted one of them?"

"No. Not seriously."

"Why not?"

"They're not—" Kyrundar cut himself off with a click of his teeth. His eyebrows knit together. Even though I wasn't trying to sense the bond, a mixture of confusion and shock rippled from him.

"Not what?"

His lips parted as he searched for words. "They're not who I want."

The unspoken implication hung in the air, more terrifying than any monster I'd ever faced.

Finally, Kyrundar stepped back, his expression shuttering. "Good night, Zidra."

He retreated into his shelter, leaving me with an unwanted fluttering in my chest and the lonely call of an owl in the dark.

Sixteen

Kyrundar

I swear my heart physically ached as I retreated into my snow shelter like a scolded puppy. Not until the words almost escaped my mouth had I realized the truth.

I was in love with Zidra.

And she didn't feel the same.

I wanted to scream my heartbreak to the stars and Iskyr's ears, but even if I closed off the entrance to my shelter, snow didn't insulate sound that well. So instead, I poured out my bruised emotions in silence while I prepared to sleep. My appetite had fled, so I didn't bother with dinner. After removing my earrings and changing into a pair of loose sleeping trousers, I pulled my blanket over me and prayed.

The holy texts promised Iskyr would understand even that which we could not express in words, which was good, because words had deserted me. Other than *why*, my prayer was more internal sighs and groans than any coherent complaint or request.

What was Zidra doing? Was she warm enough? Would she be safe out there by herself, unable to shift?

I was being paranoid. She was a capable warrior, and she was a rengir. Iskyr would watch over her.

All the same, I tossed and turned on the grass-covered ground under my shelter. Finally, against my better judgment, I reached for the heartbond.

It lacked the faint heat I'd come to associate with Zidra's dragon fire. Instead it felt like touching steel.

Was she blocking me? Was that possible?

I was about to pull back when a hint of her emotions bled through. She wasn't blocking *me*. She was trying to ignore her own feelings.

But the truth was there, beneath the hardness of her denial.

Zidra was as restless as I was—and hurting, too, although I couldn't imagine why. She wasn't the one who had been wordlessly rejected. The mental wall prevented me from getting a clear read on her, but there was sorrow and shame and a confusion of competing emotions. Despite my own hurt, I ached at the pain I sensed in her. I didn't understand, but how I wished I could soothe her.

The idea intrigued me. *Could* I? Could the troublesome bond do something good?

Would she even want that?

Maybe she wouldn't notice, or wouldn't realize it was me.

As subtly as possible, I sent calm, comforting impressions through the heartbond. I had no idea if it worked, but I held lightly to the heartbond as I finally drifted to sleep.

When I awoke the next morning, it was still dark inside my shelter. I poked my head outside to see Zidra moving through a series of stretches in the pink-tinted light of dawn. After getting dressed, I left my shelter. With a wave of my hand, it burst into snowflakes that swirled away into the forest and would soon melt.

But Zidra was gone.

My heart lodged in my throat. Desperately, I seized the heartbond. It was there, and calm—she was fine. But why would she leave, and without a word?

A shudder of annoyance echoed through the bond. I could almost picture her rolling her eyes and telling me to relax. Was that real or my imagination? Closing my eyes, I focused on the magic binding us. There! I spun around. Somehow, as if the heartbond had become a string connecting us, I knew she was in that direction. She had wandered off into the woods, away from the road. Why would she do that?

The connection was fragile. The moment I stopped fully concentrating on it, I lost it. I found the sense of her location again and took a step forward.

Wait.

What if she was simply relieving herself? Heat burned my ears.

I took care of my own business and then ate a breakfast of dried berries, stale biscuit, and leather-like dried meat.

Birds twittered and fluttered through the trees, and squirrels argued with each other. The sun lifted above the horizon, driving away the chill of the night. I started muttering prayers of protection under my breath.

Still Zidra did not return.

She'd left her pack behind, and every time I accessed the heartbond, I felt no distress. If she had decided to continue without me, she would have taken her pack. If she had been kidnapped or attacked, surely she wouldn't feel so unworried.

At the same time, she was gone, and I could think of no reason why. What if she felt calm because she was unconscious? I didn't know who would have the nerve or ability to kidnap a rengir, though. Whatever league was hunting her, they wanted her dead, so it couldn't be them.

Then where under Iskyr's great sky was she?

I had just determined to go find her, even if she would be angry with me, when I glimpsed movement through the forest. Tensing, I eased forward, then leaned heavily against a tree as I spotted Zidra's tan face and bouncy curls. She angled forward, struggling with dragging a brown mass behind her—a deer. A large one, too.

When she reached me, she dropped the deer's leg with a grunt. "Hunting deer in this form is frustrating," she muttered. "I can smell them, I can follow them, I can hunt them as humans do—and elves, I suppose. But it's so much easier to swoop down and catch one in my claws. Easier to carry it back, too."

"You were *hunting*?" I demanded. "Why didn't you tell

me?"

At least she had the decency to look embarrassed. "I caught the scent and hurried after them. I didn't want to lose the scent, and I didn't think it would take so long." Her face screwed up in a scowl. "It's been years since I hunted without shifting. Deer are so heavy." Abruptly she looked at me. "And however you were sending sensations through the heartbond without me accessing it, stop it. Your worrying was distracting."

"Oh, forgive me for being concerned that you vanished! At least thanks to the heartbond, I knew you weren't dead or in imminent danger."

Zidra rolled her eyes, so exactly like I'd earlier imagined that I almost laughed. Shaking her head, she knelt beside the deer. "Then why were you worried? Making me rush back for no reason. I need to field dress it still, then we can depart. Can you transport it on another ice disk?"

I huffed. "Of course I can. But I don't know if it will keep all day, even with my ice to keep it cold."

"I don't need it to keep all day, just long enough for someone to buy it."

"Ah, it's for coin, not food."

"Of course. Coin is much easier to transport and doesn't spoil."

Zidra made quick work of removing the deer's innards, and soon we were off again. Once my agitation abated, I was glad things seemed normal between us. My vague admission last night hadn't ruined our friendship, and the turbulent emotions we'd both felt had faded with the night.

Still, I couldn't deny that even if our external relationship remained the same, something had changed inside me. I was more aware of Zidra than ever. Of her practicality, quick-thinking capability, and range of skills, yes. But also of her presence, of the heartbond tying us together…and of how wildly attractive she was.

Not long after we started north, we stopped at the edge of a mixed human and elf village comprising a cluster of wood and wattle-and-daub houses and shops. While Zidra negotiated the deer's price with a villager, I stood back and watched because it gave me a chance to admire her while she was distracted.

I'd always thought Zidra was beautiful, but now as I took in her lean, curvy figure, full curls, and tan skin, I couldn't believe I'd never stopped before to think about how alluring she was. Perfect from head to toe, even in her scuffed boots, dusty fitted trousers, and leather breastplate, with a sword at her hip, a bag strapped to her thigh, and a traveling pack on her back. She looked capable, dangerous, and gorgeous.

No, I had to stop thinking like this. She wasn't interested, so we would stay friends. Or become strangers, if that was what she wanted.

Even if what I wanted was to put a ring on her finger and never part ways with her again. Although right that moment, all I wanted was to wrap my arms around her, draw her close, and kiss her like my life depended on it.

"Kyrundar?"

I blinked, startled out of the pleasant daydream of her

lips pressed against mine. I cleared my throat. "Ready to depart, then?"

She gave me an odd look but nodded.

We'd been traveling for less than half an hour when a strange sight caused me to slow. Ahead of us on the road, a lone man raced in our direction on foot. Sunlight glistened on the sweat dripping from his brown forehead, and dark patches of perspiration marked the front of his plain shirt.

"Something is amiss," Zidra said, just as the man started shouting.

"Help! Help! You there! Help!"

I frowned, trying to decide how to phrase this. "I'll take care of whatever this is. You're not—"

"My current condition does not negate my oaths," she said hotly. "Put us down. It looks like we may have a mission."

The only mission we officially had, and the one that concerned me most, was finding Rouven and saving Zidra's life. Still, I couldn't turn aside from a person in need, and I'd only waste time trying to convince Zidra to stand aside—something that went not only against her vows but against her very nature.

I brought us down in front of the man, who stumbled to a halt, breathing hard. Short, sweat-slicked dark hair parted around his rounded ears, and he was on foot. Most likely a magicless human.

"Please," the man said between gasping breaths, "with your magic, you can travel much faster than I…" His eyes bulged, focused on the insignia pinned to my chest. "Rengiri!" He collapsed to his knees and held up clasped hands. "Thanks be to Iskyr!"

"What's your name?" Zidra handed the man her water flask. "And what has happened?"

"Allinde." After several gulps of water, he pointed back down the road. "My village—void wolf. We've no mages and only two light elves with little training. Sent a runner to Baslune for rengir assistance, but I was going to Deersfield village to ask for men to help hold the village."

My heart fell. "How many so far?" I whispered.

"Some livestock. My nephew." His voice cracked. "He was six. Old man Vigon distracted the monster so us runners could escape. I fear..." He shook his head.

"I am sorry," Zidra said, her quiet tone tight with emotion. "May Iskyr grant their spirits peace and give you and their families and friends comfort."

"May it be so," I agreed solemnly. "I grieve for your loss. We will take care of the monster."

"Thank you!" Tears ran down Allinde's cheeks, mingling with his perspiration.

I fashioned three ice disks and stepped onto one. Zidra immediately stepped onto the second. I motioned to the third. "If you wish, you may return with us, and then you can ensure we find your village quickly."

He eyed the disk, hovering inches above the ground.

"I won't let you fall," I reassured him.

"All right. Thank you." Allinde's legs shook as he moved from kneeling on the ground to sitting on the disk.

167

As we flew to the village, I steeled myself for the upcoming fight.

Void-tainted creatures were difficult to take down. While some beasts caused harm because they were hungry or were protecting their territory, themselves, or their young, monsters were driven by Ascadrion's malice. Energy from the void-between-worlds twisted by the Earth-Shaker's rage at his banishment sometimes escaped through weak places and invisible tears in the barrier between the void and our world. Animals that came in contact with the leaked malicious energy turned into monsters. Void taint warped beasts' appearance, made them fiercer and stronger, and drove them mad so they attacked any living thing they saw.

Thankfully, if people came in contact with void energy, which was rare, it only made them ill for several days.

"That's it!" Allinde pointed to a cluster of old buildings scattered among gardens and animal pens and surrounded by fields of grain. Not a person or animal moved between the structures.

I turned toward the village and began descending.

"Stop," Zidra shouted.

I complied so abruptly that she stumbled half a step forward and Allinde yelped.

No, I'd been wrong. Something *did* move between the buildings.

A wolf with an uneven gait prowled around the corner of a house. It had grown far larger than most wolves, perhaps half my height at its shoulders, but it hadn't grown uniformly. One grotesquely large back leg dragged a little as it walked. Lumps where its spine had grown pushed up, creating a line of bumps down its back. It threw itself against the closed wood shutters, which rattled but did not give.

"We need to lure it away from the village," Zidra said at the same moment I said, "We should get it to come to us outside the village."

Our eyes met, and despite the situation, the corner of my mouth curved up. If it hadn't been for Allinde, I might have actually said, "See, we *are* a great team."

Moments later, we had a plan. Actually, as usual, Zidra had a plan. She could see how things might play out in a fight better than I could, strategizing and planning ahead while I tended to act more on instinct and impulse. I sent Zidra's ice disk close to the ground and then to the far side of town, to a fallow field where little could be damaged. The void wolf caught sight of her and gave chase, and even though everything in me screamed to go to her aid at once, I stuck to the plan.

Allinde landed next to the closest house, one far from where I was sending Zidra and the wolf. As soon as the occupants unbarred the door and pulled Allinde inside, I zipped over the rooftops.

Seventeen

Zidra

The void wolf released an unnatural warbling howl and bounded after me. Even though I trusted Kyrundar to move the ice under my feet fast enough that the wolf couldn't catch up, watching it gain on me made my breath come faster. I drew my sword and purposefully slowed my breath, summoning years of practice remaining calm during a fight.

The ice disk reached the field and continued, but slower. Braying with triumph, the wolf stretched its misshapen legs longer. This close, I noted the red and black of its void-tainted eyes and the blood splattered over its legs, sides, and snout.

Unlike the shifters we had faced, this monster would cause me no remorse when it fell.

At least it was only one. If I could shift, I'd grab this

single monster in my long talons, and the fight would be over quickly.

No use in wallowing over what couldn't be changed.

With a growl of my own, I jumped off the ice and brought my sword down in a powerful arc toward the creature. Although the wolf turned, my blade still struck its side.

As expected, the cut didn't go deep. The transformation had thickened the wolf's hide into leather-like armor. Still, some of its gray fur fell to the ground, and blood dripped from my sword.

I whirled to face the monster. It crouched to leap, but a blast of sharp icicles pelted its side. Some bounced off the tough skin; others pierced it, but not deeply. The icy assault was enough to send the wolf stumbling sideways.

Kyrundar marched closer, a sword in each hand, blue eyes glowing. He held his left sword in front of him, two fingers raised off the grip as he concentrated his magic into pushing the icicles that had stuck in the monster even deeper.

Senseless and enraged, the wolf turned away from me to charge at the new threat. I swung and sliced deep into its gnarled back leg. My blade stuck in the bone.

I muttered a curse and yanked hard.

Snarling, the monster twisted to swipe toward me with elongated claws. My heart rammed against my ribs. With another fierce tug, my blade came free, and I stumbled out of the reach of its paw just as Kyrundar slashed both of his swords across the wolf's side.

The monster howled as if it still felt some pain. Jaws snapping, it lunged toward Kyrundar, but its back leg collapsed, and he easily stepped out of its reach. I stabbed at the base of its skull, but it moved at the last moment. My blade grazed the side of its neck and thudded into the dirt.

This time, I freed my weapon in moments.

Kyrundar encased the beast's head and front legs in solid ice. Its back legs, even the half-severed one, thrashed and tried to kick off the ice. He raised the ice, pulling the overgrown wolf with it, and slammed it back down, this time on its side with its underbelly toward me.

I thrust my sword through its ribs and into its heart.

After a moment, the monster went still. I withdrew my sword with some effort, and then Kyrundar melted the ice.

A cheer mixed with relieved weeping went up behind us. We turned to find the villagers—men, women, and children—running toward us. I sent Kyrundar a dry look and he returned it, neither of us needing to voice our thoughts.

Why was it so hard for people to stay safely in their homes? But no, they always had to come out and watch the rengiri work, forgetting they were putting themselves in harm's way and thereby making our job harder.

Ah, well. This one had held little danger as far as monster fights went.

I pulled on the pleasant smile I'd learned to use to reassure fearful citizens and ensure that grateful citizens didn't misinterpret my usual serious expression as disregard or boredom.

"Thank you, and praise be to Iskyr!" Allinde said,

standing a little in front of the others. Apparently the village had deemed him the spokesperson since he had found us. "Please, what are your names so we can give thanks for you and ask Iskyr's blessings upon you?" His shoulders hitched up toward his ears as he smiled. "I'd thought perhaps you were Kyrmaris themselves, but I suppose you're not a wyvern shifter, lady rengir."

My smile froze awkwardly on my lips, brittle as charcoal. Lying went against my vows, at least unless someone's life was in danger—but only my pride was at risk.

"We're humbled you recognized us," Kyrundar said, sounding far too jolly. "A single void wolf isn't too much of a threat to a rengir, so this was a perfect opportunity for Zidra to keep her sword skills in top form. She's far too talented a warrior to need to bring out her wyvern form for every fight."

None of that was a lie, but it skirted the truth so well it felt like one. I discreetly bumped my elbow against his side, but he just grinned at me.

The confirmation of our identities sent the villagers into a further tizzy. Several pushed in close to touch us. I worked to keep my smile in place, hoping it didn't look too much like a grimace, and tried not to panic or shove the flailing hands away. They didn't mean any harm. Some likely hoped touching a Merit recipient might bring Iskyr's blessing.

But I wasn't a miracle-working prophetess. I was a rengir who wouldn't be so well known if it weren't for the ice elf at my side. I was a wyveri who couldn't shift because she'd gotten distracted during a fight and gotten cursed as a result. The smell of people crowding around combined with the void-tainted blood of the monster behind us, the cacophony of voices thanking us, blessing us, inviting us into their homes, or asking for our prayers, and the sensation of fingers brushing against or clasping at my armor and clothing made me want to scream. Or fly away.

My breaths came shorter and faster.

Snowflakes in an icy wind swirled around me and Kyrundar. People drew back from the cold, affording us a little space.

"Good people, we accept your thanks, but regretfully, we must depart," he said, his effortless smile mocking the way my hands were starting to shake. "Zidra and I are your humble servants, merely doing Iskyr's will to protect your village, and now we must continue, for we need to be elsewhere."

"Here, take this!" An older woman shoved a small pouch toward Kyrundar.

Kyrundar shook his head and softened his smile. "We do not need and will not accept payment. Our duty is to protect the people, and our reward is Iskyr's approval and blessings now and in the afterlife. We desire no reward."

Except the Emperor's Merit. My already fraying mental state cracked further.

Had I forgotten my calling and vows and made the Merit my true goal, rather than pleasing Iskyr and protecting people for the sake of those people? If the emperor or anyone else never saw my value, shouldn't that bother me

174

less than whether I did what was right—and for the right reasons?

The old woman pushed the bag into Kyrundar's hands. "Not a reward or payment. A thank offering to Iskyr and a donation to the Order of the Rengir, so that you may have what you need to help others in the future."

Kyrundar bowed over the little bag in his hands. "Iskyr smiles upon your generous heart, and Zidra Eilmaris and I thank you for your kindness." He turned to me and held out his hand.

Trusting he had a plan to get us out of there, I took his hand in mine. Although we couldn't leave, not yet.

"The corpse—burn," was all I managed to get out. A truly illuminating instruction.

"Ah, yes, right. As Zidra says, burn the corpse until nothing is left but ash. Do not eat the meat or let any animals do so," Kyrundar warned.

The villagers agreed, and someone started giving orders for a bonfire to be prepared.

"Until Iskyr wills that we meet again." Kyrundar stepped backward, tugging me with him. The ground beneath my boots changed from dark, loose dirt to slick ice.

Finally, with more space between the villagers and me and an odd calm spreading in my chest, I had the presence of mind to tell the villagers, "Iskyr guide you."

"And you," they chorused back.

Kyrundar released my hand to wave, and then the ice disks rose into the air. He must have been preoccupied, because we moved far slower than usual. I released my pent-up breath as we hovered around the village and back toward the road. Even though wanting to be loved, not feared, had been one of the reasons I became a rengir, I hadn't realized how much of being a rengir would involve being in close proximity to people and trying to find the right things to say.

I would never be the greatest rengir. I could be the best combatant in the Order and slay the most monsters, I could keep my vows better than anyone else, I could pray more regularly and memorize more liturgies, I could travel further. I could do all of that, and I wouldn't truly be the best rengir, because I'd never be as good with people as Kyrundar was.

"Earn the Emperor's Merit," Kyrundar said, intruding on my melancholy thoughts, "and suddenly you're not a person who is deserving of common decency anymore. Who wants to be crowded and pawed at like livestock at auction? They'd crowd an ox less, to be honest. Are you all right?"

"Fine. It bothered you, too?"

Kyrundar adjusted his footing. "A little. Not as much as you."

Despite the cool air whipping back my hair, my face warmed. I wrapped my arms around my middle. "I under-stand why they—"

"It's all right that it bothered you," he said gently. "And you handled it well, even if I could tell you were uncom-fortable before I accessed the heartbond. I'm just sorry I didn't get you out of that situation faster." He crossed his arms and drummed his fingers against his upper arm. "People are going to keep wanting to be close to you, though. You were already revered before you were awarded the Merit, and clearly word spread quickly. We'll need to think of something else people can do to feel close to you without overwhelming your senses."

"Wait, you used your magic to nudge them back and insisted we leave for...me?"

The tips of his ears turned pink. "Rengiri don't only watch each other's backs in a fight. You can do the strategizing, and I can handle people." He smiled, warm and soft in a way that melted my insides even more than his confident, flirty smirking. "I keep telling you we make a good team."

My dragon fire danced in my chest as it never had before. Unable to refute his claim but afraid to voice my agreement, I fell silent.

After a moment, Kyrundar said, "I've been meaning to ask you. At full strength, of course, you versus a real wyvern—who do you think would win?"

If this was his attempt to get my mind off my discomfort, it wasn't working. "How about after we find Rouven, I'll shift into a wyvern and fire-blast you, and then you can tell me again how I'm a fake wyvern."

Kyrundar chuckled awkwardly. "You know what I mean. A regular wyvern."

On second thought, the opportunity to lean into old bickering was *exactly* what I needed. "Now I sound like an abnormal wyvern. I think that's more insulting."

This time his laugh was more genuine. "All right, then. How about an ordinary wyvern? That would imply you're extraordinary. And don't you dare argue that you're not extraordinary."

I blushed. "We just call them wyverns. We're wyveri, they're wyverns. Our di'yar is a wyvern, they're…just wyverns. It's not that complicated."

"And you knew what I meant but still chose to argue," he teased. "Is it because you think you'd lose against a wyvern and hoped to distract me from repeating my question?"

I bristled. "No."

"No you didn't hope to distract me, or no you don't think you'd lose?"

"Mostly the second, I suppose."

He looked over with an impressed expression. "You'd win against a wyvern?"

"Yes."

"That readily? Don't get me wrong, confidence looks good on you."

My face heated again, and I wasn't sure how I felt about the fact that his words were having that effect.

"How are you so sure? Wyveri aren't bigger than wyverns, right?"

"No. The one I killed was bigger than me."

"The one…"

The ice disks jerked to an abrupt stop, and I stumbled forward, nearly losing my footing. But Kyrundar's boot slid off the edge of his disk. Without thinking, I stretched across the small space between us and grabbed his shoulder to steady him. Magic already swirled around his boot and gave him a boost back to level footing. He looked from my hand grasping the fabric of his tunic up to my face with a slow smile.

"I really don't want to bandage your face if you face-plant on the road." I released his arm and resolutely faced straight ahead.

"Because it would be a shame to cover up all this handsomeness?"

I snorted but couldn't come up with a good response while I was stuck on the fact that he *was* unfairly handsome.

"When did you kill a wyvern, and how do I not know about it?"

"Why would you know everything I do?"

"Because everyone knows everything you do. I don't know if you know this, but you're famous."

"Ha ha." I waved ahead of us. "Are we going to start moving again?"

"Not until you tell me the story."

That wasn't an idle threat. Kyrundar could be as stubborn as I was. "Fine. I was still in the Academy. It wasn't an official mission—"

He gasped and moved his ice disk so he was hovering directly in front of me. "You broke a rule! Zidra, I've never been so impressed."

I made a face. "I was going home over a holiday break and took a scenic route through the unpopulated areas of the Avorn Mountains."

"Why?" Kyrundar scrunched his face like he couldn't imagine any possible reason for doing something so unnecessary.

"I didn't want to go home to my unwelcoming family," I said as carelessly as possible. "I didn't realize I had trespassed into a wyvern's territory until it was too late. It took offense, naturally, but wasn't content with me simply leaving. It was male and unusually aggressive. I think it must have been protecting a family, probably a hatchling too young to fly." I shrugged. "I did what I had to in order to survive, but I don't consider it a story worth telling. Taking some hatchling's father."

We remained there, hovering on the ice disks and staring at each other in silence for several moments.

"You're amazing, you know that?" Kyrundar murmured. The soft look in his eyes threatened to undo me. "Indomitable, humble, inspiring, kind. You're…" He shook his head. "Amazing."

My skin itched under the praise. "Not amazing enough to avoid getting an ice curse embedded in my arm."

"Amazing enough to survive it."

Only thanks to Kyrundar's intervention, but instead I said, "Not if we don't find Rouven soon."

His shoulders drooped. "Right. Yes. We need to get moving. Of course."

Yet as we sped down the road, the wind whistling past my ears, I regretted a little that we could no longer converse.

I wanted to get to Gamnica quickly, but that would

mean parting ways with Kyrundar…wait. I wrapped my arms around my middle, tucking my suddenly cold hands under my arms.

Did I actually *want* to spend more time with the ice elf I had resented for so long?

The truth trickled in like water finding the cracks in my mental walls.

I didn't want to leave him.

And that thought scared me more than any void-tainted creature.

EIGHTEEN

KYRUNDAR

When we stopped to eat, I checked on Zidra's arm despite her feeble protests. Thankfully, she had kept her dragon fire reined in while slaying the void wolf. Still, I didn't like the blue tint to the skin surrounding the puncture. Having any amount of ice magic embedded in her body for so long was dangerous. Silently, I prayed that we would not encounter any more people in need of help. Zidra would cut her arm off before she refused aid to anyone—although if it came to that, I'd encase her in ice and carry her away no matter how much she hated me for it.

That night we reached a small town with a Haven, if the austere single-room cottage with three mats on the floor could be called a Haven. But it was warm and dry and better than the ground, and we had the place to ourselves.

Zidra kept tossing and turning on her mat. Absently, I reached for the heartbond. Once again, I met a wall, as if she were trying to lock away whatever was troubling her. The barrier felt weaker. Maybe if I'd pushed I could have broken through, but I didn't know if she might sense that, and I didn't want to intrude. So instead, I focused on sending soothing, caring sensations her way. Soon she stilled. Her breathing deepened to sleep, and I quickly followed.

By some miracle, I woke before Zidra. Sunlight from the one dingy window fell over her mat, and she'd rolled over to put her back to the light, which put her face toward me. She looked younger while asleep, maybe because the prickly defensiveness and iron self-sufficiency she usually wore had fallen away. Her dark eyelashes nearly brushed her high cheekbones. I had the urge to run my fingertip over the gentle bow of her pink lips, bury my hands in her curls, and kiss the slope of her neck.

I turned away and got dressed with my back to Zidra, then went to the outhouse. I wasn't gone long, but when I returned, she was dressed and rearranging her pack. The door groaned as I closed it behind me. She glanced over, and her cheeks reddened before she bent over her pack, her curls hiding her face.

I looked down at myself but couldn't find any reason for that reaction. Unless perhaps she was angry with me? Ah, of course. I'd disappeared without saying anything, the exact thing I had berated her for doing.

"Sorry," I said. "I was around back—"

"I know. Did you eat yet?"

I shook my head. I wasn't looking forward to more travel rations.

"We should stop by the bakery on our way out," Zidra said. "Save the preserved foods for the road. Maybe they have those iced cinnamon buns you love."

I stared at her as she tied off her pack and stood. "You remember my favorite pastry?" Then I grinned. "And I thought you didn't care."

She waved her hand. "You're incredibly vocal about how much you love them. Everyone who has met you probably knows you love cinnamon buns."

Still grinning, I strode past her to my own pack and set about shoving items into it. "Well, maybe the bakery will also have those flaky, buttery apple turnovers you love so much."

Zidra was quiet. When I turned toward her, she was watching me with a curious expression.

"What? You're allowed to make note of my favorite, but I'm not allowed to notice that's what you always pick if they're available?"

"I never thought you were paying attention. To anything other than yourself, really."

I clamped down on my tongue, holding back my affronted argument. *Maybe Iskyr allowed this heartbond simply to teach me some awareness I didn't even know I was lacking.* The thought brought a sardonic smile to my lips, which I quickly morphed into a teasing smirk. "I pay attention to a great many things, but to you most of all."

Her eyes narrowed.

So I rose to the challenge. Abandoning my pack, I took a step closer and counted on my fingers. "You prefer the bottom cot of stacked beds. You don't like mushrooms and always leave them on your plate if you can get away with it without causing insult. You prefer red meat to white meat. You have the sharpest senses of any shifter I know, and sometimes your senses overwhelm you and give you a headache, especially in crowded spaces. If you were to buy yourself a gown, you'd get one in dark red, because you think you look good in it. You—"

"How do you know that?" she demanded.

More than once, I had watched her linger over dark-red fabric or choose dark red when she purchased a scarf. One time I'd caught her holding a dark-red cloak over her armor and admiring her reflection in a tiny mirror before reluctantly putting it back. She hadn't realized I was there.

"Like I said. I pay attention." I set about dealing with the bedding I'd used, and Zidra did likewise with her cot. That taken care of, I strapped on my swords, then fastened my pack and looped it over my shoulders. "Ready to go?"

After we bought cinnamon buns and flaky apple turnovers for breakfast, we continued on our way. The sound of whooshing air made conversation difficult, but we still spoke occasionally. To my surprise, Zidra usually initiated, making some observation on the landscape or recalling a story from Harcos. It was the most pleasant day of travel we'd had so far.

As we traveled north, settlements became smaller and

less frequent, and trees thinned from thick forests to copses tucked amid rolling hills of grasslands and cereal fields. When night fell and we made camp in a glen, the sound of bleating sheep carried faintly on the breeze.

This time, I didn't bother making the snow shelter large enough for both of us. I'd learned my lesson. Still, when Zidra said "good night" as I bent to enter my shelter, I considered asking if she was sure she didn't want to share. Not wanting to lose the more friendly interactions we'd achieved today, I instead wished her good night and went inside.

Without consciously thinking about it, I reached for the heartbond as I lay down. Zidra felt restless, but there was much less resistance. Perhaps she had worked through whatever emotions she'd been trying to bury. I recited a prayer of protection and rest over us both and let myself fall into sleep, holding the heartbond like a child might hold a stuffed bear toy.

Something jerked me back to consciousness.

I had no idea how long I had slept, but a panicked energy coursed through me. I opened my eyes to blackness and rolled over, reaching blindly for my swords. The moment my fingers brushed a leather sheath, I seized the weapons.

As I sat up, my brow furrowed. It wasn't dark only inside. Past my feet, where there should have been light from the stars and moon illuminating the world beyond the low door, there was nothing. As if I were inside not a snow shelter, but a tomb.

Another spike of panic shot through me, and something deep in my soul urged me to go outside.

Zidra was in danger.

I had no time to question how I knew that or what it meant, or even whether the door to my shelter was truly gone. Zidra needed help. I drew my swords and sent my magic ahead of me as I moved toward where the entrance should have been. Sure enough, it was there, but my magic tangled with the energy of another elf's magic. I burst through the opening into an inky murkiness. Brisk air brushed over my face and bare chest and teased the ends of my hair, but I couldn't see a thing.

Night elf.

"Iskyr aid me," I breathed.

Trusting the guidance of the heartbond, I raced in Zidra's direction, sending waves of whirling, glowing ice in front of and above me. My magic drove back the night elf's shadow magic, allowing moonlight to shine through. My jaw clenched as I caught sight of the nearly full moon. Night elves were strongest at night, and the light of the moon and stars fed their magic.

A faint scuffling sounded ahead, and the heartbond wavered.

"Zee!" Where was she?

I increased the swirling snowflakes until a miniature blizzard localized around me. The shadows in the night elf's control pushed back.

I hated fighting night elves, and I'd never had the ill luck of facing one outside of training bouts. They wielded shadows, growing them, giving them form, using them like grasping and crushing tentacles. They could hide themselves in shadows, moving at night unseen, and while our magics could battle, the only sure way to defeat a night elf was to find and incapacitate the elf.

A choked gasp came from the tangling shadow and ice magics, and then a tan hand shot upward and grabbed onto a tendril of darkness. The glow of my ice crystals illuminated the outline of a dark, writhing mass.

Zidra was at the center of that web of suffocating magic.

With a battle cry, I blasted ice at the enveloping shadows, directing it to avoid hurting her. I slid to my knees and dropped my swords. They did little against magic, and I'd need all my strength to beat back the night elf's power.

Fingers spread wide, I reached out until my palms bumped into the night elf's corporeal shadows—an odd sensation, like passing through thickening mist and then hitting something solid. With a growl, I unleashed a pulse of raging cold into the seething darkness.

The shadows retreated before my onslaught, revealing Zidra's arm and thigh. Her movement slowed, and through the heartbond, I sensed her resistance fading.

"No!" My pulse pounded faster. "Release her!"

As soon as her head and a shoulder emerged, I pulled her toward me. Ice magic still swirled from my other hand. In the back of my mind, I diverted ice away from us into the shadowed glen in search of the attacker.

No longer suffocating, Zidra gasped down air. She

shoved and kicked at the grasping shadows. The heartbond heated, and Zidra's eyes glowed red.

My grasp on her shoulder tightened. "Don't shift!"

I hadn't saved her from a night elf assassin to lose her to the ice curse.

She hissed her displeasure, but the glow faded from her eyes. She lunged forward and grabbed the hilt of her sword, yanking it free of the sheath without any indication she'd barely escaped death.

"Can you find the infernal elf?" Zidra ground out.

From the trees beyond our makeshift camp sounded a hiss of pain right as my magical sense indicated the presence of a person. A vengeful grin pulled at my mouth.

"Indeed. Follow me." I seized my own swords and surged to my feet. A cyclone of ice kept the grasping fingers of shadow from reaching us as we sprinted toward the opening of the glen.

I concentrated on my magic that surrounded the assassin. Using my magical sense, I pinned the struggling elf to the ground with manacles of ice.

Grunting and muttered curses in a male voice carried through the night. I slowed and decreased my protective snow magic so I could see. A few strides in front of us, the pale blue glow of my magic warred with the night elf's shadows.

With my eyes closed to better rely on my magical sense, I pulled back my sword. If I missed my target, I'd bury my sword in the hard dirt and lose precious moments.

There.

If I was right, I'd strike the elf in the shoulder. The wound shouldn't be fatal.

Yet I hesitated. I might kill the elf, and with both our magics between us, the assassin likely couldn't see me, either. I'd be killing a bound, sightless opponent.

Iskyr, guide my blade, and forgive me should I kill unjustly.

I stabbed downward.

Nineteen

Zidra

Just as Kyrundar slammed the point of his sword downward, a vine of shadow whipped out of the churning maelstrom and collided with his chest. He flew backward and skidded across the ground. My entire body went cold. I should have been focused on the assassin, but instead I took a faltering step toward Kyrundar. His swords lay beside him.

He wasn't moving.

It would take more than a single hit to take down Kyrundar Ilifir. Even as I told myself that, I couldn't take my eyes off his still form sprawled over the grass.

If Kyrundar was dead, forget the curse. I would shift and the assassin would be dead before the curse took me down. It would be worth it.

The heartbond!

I seized the bond, and a gasp wrenched out of me as I realized it was still there—*he* was still there. Kyrundar yet lived.

The assassin would not be so fortunate.

Snarling, I spun back to our attacker.

Moonlight shone on trampled grass and provided dim illumination to the sloping sides of the glen. No unnatural shadows amassed nearby, nor did ice magic wrestle with the night elf's any longer.

The assassin had fled.

Perhaps I should have been relieved, even pleased. Instead, I smothered my dragon fire once more and swung my sword uselessly at the grass. The assassin should not live to hurt anyone else.

Had I been able to shift, I could have hunted him down. Even now, I could smell him, so I could track him. But night elves could use the shadows to help themselves travel faster, and their natural elf agility and speed was increased by moonlight and starlight. Without at least a partial shift, I'd never catch up with him.

Feeling useless, I stomped over to Kyrundar and knelt beside him. Before I spoke, he groaned and sat up. Rubbing the back of his head, he looked around, then focused on me.

"Did you defeat him?"

I looked away. "He escaped."

Kyrundar muttered an imprecation. "Not entirely surprised. He's strong."

"Unusually strong?" I tilted my head.

"Perhaps not." He shrugged. "None of the other elf-kind like to admit it, but our night elf brethren have the most powerful magic, at least at night. Rumor says they make formidable assassins, but the night elves keep to themselves and mostly stay within the borders of Nyksia. I haven't heard of a night elf assassin in my lifetime." He frowned. "Do you think he's a member of the league the shifters mentioned? Or perhaps someone they hired?"

"I wish I could ask him."

He winced. "I'm sorry—"

"Whatever for?" I tightened my hold on the grip of my sword to hide how my hands were shaking. "If you hadn't emerged from your shelter when you did, I'd be dead."

Yet that wasn't the reason for my trembling hands.

I'd been prepared to shift, fully aware of the consequences, just so I could burn the assassin to avenge Kyrundar. Thoughts of enacting justice, protecting the empire, honoring my vows, saving myself—they had all fled, replaced by the frantic need to see to it that the person who had taken Kyrundar's life would never take another.

Just like at Grivolen, caring about Kyrundar had affected my judgment in battle. First I'd lost the ability to shift. Then I'd let an assassin escape. All because I'd been more concerned about Kyrundar than my enemy. While in the past I'd have argued I was worried because I didn't trust or believe in him, the lie no longer carried much weight.

It didn't matter what I told myself, my reaction told the truth. I cared about Kyrundar, more than I did about

193

anyone else, and I had for some time. More than I should. Perhaps I even…

Loved him?

I startled as Kyrundar placed a pale hand over mine on the hilt of my sword.

"It's all right. You're safe now." His expression hardened. "From now on, if we must sleep outside, you're staying in my shelter with me. No magic or person can enter without me sensing it. I'll put an enchanted threshold on the door of any Haven we stay at as well. I don't want to count on the heartbond awakening me in time again."

"The heartbond?"

He nodded. "I was awoken by a sense that you were in danger. I'm sure it was because of the heartbond." For a moment it seemed like he might say something more, but then he closed his mouth.

So the heartbond had some usefulness. Hating something that had saved my life was more difficult than hating something that caused only discomfort.

Well, not only. The last few nights, the heartbond had felt oddly comforting. Safe, in a way.

"In fact"—Kyrundar picked up his swords—"we should go inside my shelter in case the assassin returns." He stood and started back in the direction of camp. "I'll need to make it larger first, though…" He kept mumbling something half to himself as I trailed after him.

It didn't take him long to enlarge the shelter. While he did that, I returned my sword to its scabbard and gathered up my cloak and pack. As soon as Kyrundar announced the shelter was ready, I ducked inside. By the look he gave me, he'd expected me to argue. But with my throat and lungs still aching and bruises covering my body, I was more than ready to accept some reassurance that I wouldn't awaken again to slithering shadows wrapping me in a crushing embrace of death.

I felt my way through the darkness inside the shelter and sat near a wall, listening to Kyrundar move past me and fumble for something in his pack.

"Where is it...ah-ha."

A golden-hued light flared to life, and he placed a glowing stone the size of his fist on the ground. The light elf magic cast a warm illumination over the spacious interior. Next he pulled on a thin white shirt, then retrieved a roll of bandages and a knife. He moved to my side and reached for my arm.

"You started to shift, so I need to check on this. Don't argue."

I cast him a flat glare. "I wasn't going to."

"Oh. Good." He unwrapped the bandage. Soon I felt the gentle coolness of his magic prodding around the aching wound. "I don't think the curse has spread, but my barrier is weakened. I'll have to strengthen it again."

"Understood." I didn't meet his eyes as I added, "Thank you."

Either I was getting used to the pain, or it wasn't as bad. Perhaps because Kyrundar didn't have to pull the ice curse back through my veins this time. His expression still tightened with discomfort, but it was over quickly.

"We need to travel faster," he muttered. "Do you feel that?"

"What?" I looked down to see his fingertips pressing against the discolored edges of the dark-red puncture mark.

Kyrundar sighed and started wrapping my arm in a fresh bandage. "You're losing sensation around the affected skin. The cold is likely killing your flesh. I'm trying to slow it, but the curse itself needs to come out. It needed to come out days ago," he added under his breath.

"Thank you for doing what you can," I said.

His eyes locked with mine. "You're welcome."

The warmth of his sincerity crackled through the heartbond. I cleared my throat and stared across the shelter at the curved wall of packed snow. "I didn't know the heartbond could be sensed while you're asleep."

His hands slowed, but then he tied off and trimmed the bandage. He moved to sit with his back to the wall beside me. "It might be because I fell asleep while...I don't know. Holding it? Concentrating on it might be a better way to explain it."

"Why would you do that?"

He wriggled as if getting more comfortable. "You've seemed restless. I hoped somehow I could put you at ease. Help you calm your emotions enough to sleep."

A lump caught in my throat. That was why the last few nights the heartbond had felt so...cozy? Kyrundar was doing that? On *purpose*?

I didn't know what to make of it.

That wasn't true. I knew why he would do that; I even

knew why I might like it.

But I didn't want to admit that I'd realized he liked me, and I certainly didn't want to admit I liked him as well. These feelings were a ridiculous and passing side effect of the heartbond.

After all, what did he see in me?

I knew what every woman who had ever swooned over Kyrundar Ilifir saw. I saw it, too. He was the most attractive man I'd ever met—tall, muscular enough to be striking but not so much that he seemed uncomfortably chiseled out of rock, with a sharp jaw, high cheekbones, and those ice-blue eyes and silken, white-blond hair like a waterfall over his shoulders. But Kyrundar was so much more than that. His confidence sometimes grated, but perhaps that was because I envied his self-assurance. Despite being an ice elf, he had an inviting, exuberant smile that could melt a glacier's heart. He had a way of drawing people in, making them feel included, and inciting celebration amid the most mundane gatherings.

And he had swooning female fans the empire over, constantly foiled my plans, never took anything seriously enough, and was a distraction in battle. This newfound attraction wouldn't last, so I shouldn't entertain it.

So I did what any fearless rengir would do.

I changed the subject.

"I shouldn't have let myself get distracted and allow the night elf to escape." I tore off a blade of stiff grass and started tying it in knots. "We need more answers than what the panthera and wolvus provided. I should also warn Sajen.

I should have already told him to abandon it, but I'd hoped this would go away—or perhaps that he'd find something."

"What does Sajen have to do with anything?"

I leaned my head back against the domed shelter. It was cool, but not freezing. "I let him talk me into allowing him to help me," I grumbled. "He was going to ask around about the attackers at Grivolen. If this night elf is associated with whatever the league is, they are serious about keeping their secrets. What if Sajen is in danger because of me?" I grunted and tossed aside the knotted grass. "This is why I don't ask for help! I stand alone, and I fall alone."

If assassins harmed Sajen because of me, I wouldn't forgive myself easily.

"Don't be ridiculous." Kyrundar stretched out his legs. "We're rengiri. We're meant to stand together."

"Easy for you to say."

"What's that supposed to mean?"

I shook my head. He would never understand. "I'm going to sleep."

But Kyrundar's hand on my shoulder stopped me. Not by force. His touch was light, undemanding and easily escaped. Still, his hand arrested my movement.

"Zee," he said softly. "Do you push me away because of me, or because of you?"

"Both," I blurted. What did it matter? He might be able to sense the truth through the heartbond he kept accessing, anyway. "How am I supposed to prove myself with you or anyone else interfering? How will I know if the outcome, positive or negative, would have been the same without interference? If I do something on my own, I'll know I earned the results, good or bad—and so will my family. You know wyveri are matriarchal, right?"

He nodded and released my shoulder. "Ever since the wyveri king died after summoning Ascadrion. You have clans, right? Each ruled by a family with the matriarch at the head, and they answer to a queen?"

"Basically, although it's more like the queen answers to the matriarchs except to judge disputes between the clans." I buried my fingers in the grass beside me. "My mother is the matriarch of our clan."

Kyrundar was silent for a moment, and when he spoke, the question wasn't what I expected, although it made sense. "Is your sister older or younger?"

"Younger."

The word hung in the muffled quiet.

"You left your role as the next matriarch to be a rengir," he said. There was no judgment in his tone, simply a gentle observation.

His acceptance crumbled the last of my reticence, and words flowed from my mouth.

"My decision to go to Harcos simultaneously enraged and pleased my mother and sister. I'm not sure my older brother cared much either way." I moved my fingers around in the grass, tangling them in grass blades. "Wyveri value strength and self-sufficiency. Well, we say we value self-control, honor, humility, wisdom, and intelligence, in part because we fear being known only for our capacity for de-struction. But we don't tend to be very good at supporting each other in those goals. We're supposed to be honorable and discerning and to exercise self-control on our own, just like we fly on our own."

Kyrundar snorted. "Wyveri have wings. Of course you fly on your own."

I pursed my lips. "I mean as children."

He straightened. "Are you talking about learning to fly? I've heard some birds push their young out of the nest, but surely wyveri don't—"

"Essentially. Once we can shift reliably and our wings are deemed strong enough, we leap off a cliff over the rocky coast into the strong winds off the sea, and we either fly or we die."

"What!" I winced at his loud voice so close to my ear. "Sorry. But, what? How old were you? And how old would an elf be?"

"Usually around eight, so that would be the same for an elf." Humans, shifters, and elves had similar development until around age twelve, but after that, shifter aging slowed to less than one-third the rate of a human, and elves' aging to nearly one-ninth. That was why, despite Kyrundar being one hundred and fifty-five while I was seventy, we were roughly the same age relative to our lifespans.

"How many wyveri die doing this?" he demanded.

"Death is rare, although severe injuries aren't uncommon. Many clans and families are doing away with the practice, but not my mother." I chewed on my lower lip. "She was so proud of how young I learned to shift, how well I did on my first flight, how powerful my di'yar is. She used to say my dragon fire burns hotter than average."

"Used to?" Kyrundar moved to sit in front of me, watching me intently. "Why did she stop?"

My head drooped forward as I avoided his gaze. "I didn't have her control. Her patience. My prodigy in shifting became a liability, as I shifted too quickly, too frequently, and with too much energy in my di'yar. I had to work hard to develop the icy control a wyveri matriarch is supposed to have."

His snort interrupted me, and I snapped my head back up to scowl at him.

"Sorry." Kyrundar's lips twitched. "It's just…I once complained to Syl that I might be an ice elf, but you are an ice queen. All cold control and condescension."

I stared straight ahead at the packed snow wall. "I am what a wyveri must be. Unfortunately, I never became what a clan matriarch must be."

"Which is?"

"Hospitable, gracious, both respected and liked. A humble yet confident leader who can spend all day sitting and listening and visiting people in their homes, who knows everyone in the village and remembers their names. Someone who can mediate a dispute with such equity and gentleness that the ruling is honored without damaging the matriarch's relationship with either party. You've said it yourself: I'm not good with people." I sighed. "I wasn't meant to be a matriarch, and the entire village whispered about it."

"So why did you choose the Order? I imagine there were

many other things you could have done."

I lifted a shoulder. "Not really. I needed an option that took me away from the islands, and things like becoming a merchant, clerk, or priestess didn't suit me. By the time I was fifty-two, my lack of direction was becoming embarrassing. So I joined a merchant's caravan as a guard for a trip, as a trial. I told my mother it was temporary and that the experience would teach me skills that would help me be a better matriarch. That's when I realized how many people on the mainland still hate and fear wyveri."

"I'm sorry," he whispered.

What did he have to apologize for? He wasn't responsible for the prejudices of other people. "It wasn't all bad," I added quickly. "It was also the first time I met Nakirosha."

"Nakirosha Tulyerin? My cousin?"

I gaped at him. "Your what?"

"Well, my...fourth or fifth cousin or something on my mother's side, and she's three hundred years older than me, but yes."

"All three of us have been at the same Haven together twice, and that didn't come up?"

Kyrundar made a face. "Why would it? We're all rengiri, and honestly, that's a closer connection than distant cousins. And what about you? Neither of you mentioned knowing each other."

"I don't think she remembered me," I admitted, hoping I wasn't blushing. "She came to our caravan's aid when we stumbled upon a nest of void-tainted rekaras. I was still so young, and it was dark, and we spoke only for a moment.

But she was spectacular. She didn't care that we were wyveri, only that we were people who needed help. She was confident and assured and knew her worth, her purpose. She was respected and admired. That was what I wanted. I dreamed that I could change people's minds about wyveri—and about me."

Kyrundar smiled. "So you applied to Harcos?"

I shook my head. "Not yet. When we returned home, I went to our village's chapel to pray for guidance. The priest and priestess were out when I arrived, and I have no idea how long I'd been kneeling before the altar when they entered. The priestess seemed surprised, almost confused, and a little saddened. Then she told me she felt Iskyr had told her to give something to the next supplicant she saw kneeling before the altar. She handed me a sprig of blue harbell flowers. On the Wyveri Islands, harbells are given to bless a large change in someone's life, particularly moving to a new place or a new role. That was when I applied, but I didn't tell my parents until I received the letter inviting me to take the in-person tests. They discouraged me from going, and when I wrote to tell them I'd been accepted, I received a one-word reply: understood."

"By the void." He shook his head. "I decided I wanted to be a rengir when I was five. My parents thought I would grow out of it, but I never did. They were supportive when I applied and was accepted at Harcos, though, even if my mother cried about how little she would see me if I made it into the Order. She still complains about it every time I visit home. But then, she isn't wrong. Those visits *are* rare.

Still, most parents are honored to have children among the rengiri, not disappointed or even opposed to it."

"I suppose we're special," I quipped.

Kyrundar went still, and his ice-blue gaze locked with mine. "You certainly are," he said, his voice oddly husky.

I swallowed hard. "Anyway. That's why I need to do things on my own."

Kyrundar's jaw tightened, and his upper lip curled. "Forget your ridiculous mother and sister and your entire clan. They don't know what they lost when they lost you, and you have nothing to prove to them. If they can't see how amazing you are simply because Iskyr gave you a different calling than the one they envisioned, that's their problem. As surely as he hung the stars in the night sky, Iskyr made you to be a rengir, Zidra."

I didn't consciously reach for the heartbond, but the complete confidence with which he said the words rushed through me. His emotions burned with the ferocity of defiance and a deeper, more tender passion that warmed me from the inside out. The part of me that usually whispered any affirmation was a lie, that either the speaker was secretly mocking me or I didn't deserve their honest praise, was silenced by the strength of unwavering belief and deep affection I heard in his voice, saw in his eyes, and sensed in my soul through the bond. For a moment, I borrowed his confidence and let myself rest in the belief that I didn't have anything to prove to anyone.

Maybe the heartbond—and Kyrundar himself—wasn't so bad.

TWENTY

KYRUNDAR

Z idra and I gazed into each other's eyes. I swayed toward her, as if drawn by her magnetism. My gaze dropped to her lips before flicking back to her golden-brown irises.

"You asked why I've never wanted any of the women who flirt with me," I murmured.

Zidra's breath caught, and she went still as a frozen lake. For a brief moment, I doubted what I was about to say. But then she leaned ever so subtly closer.

"None of them seemed right. I didn't realize why until a few nights ago." I gulped as I placed my heart at her mercy. "None of them are you. I want *you*, Zidra."

Her eyes widened. I couldn't read her expression, and the hints of emotion I felt through the heartbond were frantic and tangled. A good sign? Or a terrible one? I purposefully released the bond so I could focus on what I wanted to say without overanalyzing her emotions.

"I'm in love with you." My throat was so tight that my voice came out low and hoarse. "I think I've loved you since before we graduated; I've just been too much of an idiot to see it. You're my dearest friend, my inspiration, the only person I've ever wanted constantly at my side, and I love you."

Every word squeezed my heart. Something inside me cracked as Zidra gawked at me, her parted lips and pinched expression hardly joyful acceptance and certainly not amorous in return.

Confessing my feelings had been a terrible idea. I'd known that. Yet I was tired of lying to her and to myself.

I almost reached for the heartbond but was too much of a coward.

"Zee?" The nickname sounded like a broken plea on my lips.

For several excruciating heartbeats, she was silent. When she spoke, her voice was a stoic whisper. "Was the heartbond an accident, Ilifir?"

The use of my surname struck me like a physical blow. "I swear it wasn't a conscious choice. I didn't know it would happen, and I didn't intend…" I trailed off, hearing my constant refrain yet again. *I didn't intend.*

I hadn't intended to use Zidra to elevate myself, but that had been the result.

I hadn't intended to ever hurt her, but I had.

I hadn't intended to come across as a womanizer, but I had.

I hadn't intended to create a heartbond that tied Zidra and me together, but I had.

"I'm sorry," I murmured. "Tying us together wasn't intentional. I wasn't aware of my own feelings yet. But it might have been my fault, and for that, I'm sorry."

As if she would believe that. What kind of fool doesn't realize they're in love?

With my hands clasped in my lap, I leaned back and dropped my gaze. The silence dragged on.

"I'm sorry," I repeated with a sigh. I forced myself to look at her before I continued. "You were just attacked, it's the middle of the night, and you've made it clear—"

My words cut off in a muffled cry of surprise as Zidra darted forward and pressed her lips to mine with such intensity we bumped together harder than was romantic or comfortable.

She winced and started to pull away. "Sorry—"

This time, I interrupted her apology. I tucked one arm behind her and pulled her close while I slipped my hand under her curls to cradle the side of her neck. Zidra inhaled sharply, but then she relaxed as our lips met. My eyes drifted closed. Her warm hands moved up my arms, and then she wrapped her arms around my neck and shoulders.

The sensation of her fingers toying with my hair while her lips moved against mine sent tingles of lightning through my veins. Needing her closer, I released her neck, grabbed her waist, and pulled her onto my lap. My palms slid against the fabric of her shirt as I pressed against her back and deepened the kiss. Zee made a soft sound of pleasure that made my breathing go ragged. She turned her face away, breaking off the kiss, but her arms tightened around my shoulders. I placed featherlight kisses along her jaw, marveling at how right it felt to finally have her in my arms.

"Kyr," she panted.

"Zee," I breathed against her cheek. I moved, searching for her lips once more.

She gulped audibly. "Kyrundar, stop."

Even though I longed to continue kissing her, I immediately heeded her quiet request. Dropping my arms to my sides, I pulled back and opened my eyes.

Zidra's entire face was flushed, and her chest heaved as she slowly backed off my lap and sat on the beaten-down grass. Eternal icicles, she was gorgeous. But her wide-eyed gaze darted around the shelter, not meeting mine. Had I misinterpreted that? Made her do something she didn't want?

I'd never forgive myself if I had.

Half afraid of what I'd find, I reached for the heartbond—and immediately released it, but not fast enough to stop my mischievous grin.

She'd enjoyed that at *least* as much as I had.

"I—we—we shouldn't have done that." Zidra ran her fingers through her hair, tangling them in her curls. "What if we don't love each other and it's just the heartbond—"

"Are you saying you love me?" My pleased smile probably made me look like an exuberant puppy, but I didn't care.

"I don't know!" Zidra tossed up her hands. "I thought maybe if I kissed you, I'd know if I care about you as a friend or if my feelings are romantic, but I can't think about anything while doing that! At least not anything appropriate," she added under her breath.

I lifted an eyebrow, but before I could say anything, she held up her hand.

"A heartbond is not a marriage, Ilifir."

Normally her use of my last name would quell me, but something about the melodramatically put-out way she said it only made me bolder. "We took no vows against kissing outside of matrimony."

She rolled her eyes. "Good to know you wouldn't think it's cheating if you kissed someone else."

"I wasn't talking about kissing anyone else." I leaned forward and dropped my voice to what I hoped was a seductive register. "If you'll have me, I vow to kiss only you, Zidra Eilmaris."

Her lower lip went slack, and an odd squeak caught in her throat. I chuckled, but then she shoved me back. "And you expect me to believe you're not a flirt."

"May my insignia be revoked if I've ever said something so flirtatious or kissed a woman before tonight."

Zidra side-eyed me, and her lips twisted to the side. "You'll be the death of me."

I might have laughed again if her tone hadn't been so

deadly serious and if the bandage tied around her arm weren't mocking me.

"We can't have that." I shrugged, fighting another smirk. "We'll have to train together more so we can build trust. Perhaps utilize the heartbond more, since it seems it can warn us if the other is in immediate mortal peril. Then we can go into fights confident in each other's ability to handle their side of the fight on their own."

She looked ready to argue, so I added, "The emperor didn't give us both the Merit because we're pretty faces. We're formidable on our own and together. We were top graduates from Harcos Academy. The top one percent of the top fifty percent who even graduate, and two of the three students in our class who were accepted into the Order. If anyone can have each other's backs in a fight and work out any problems with coordination and trust, it's us."

"Hm." Zee wrinkled her nose, looking unconvinced, but she didn't argue.

"We should sleep." I moved my things over, making more space for her, and lay down. After a moment, I heard her move around and then settle down, leaving plenty of space between us. I tapped on the enchanted stone, and the shelter went dark.

"Good night, Zee."

Her answering "Good night, Kyr" was soft, yet it set my heart racing once again.

Sleep. I needed to sleep.

I closed my eyes and tried to ignore the hushed sound

of her breathing, tried to forget I could roll over and draw her into my arms. I stifled a snort. Zidra had been right. Sharing a snow shelter *was* more intimate than sharing a room in a Haven.

"Kyr?" Zidra whispered.

I held my breath. "Yes?"

"Can you do it again?" I was about to be elated she'd changed her mind about kissing when she rushed to add, "The thing with the heartbond? Where you make it feel safe?"

Safe? That hadn't exactly been my intent, but I supposed it was good that the sensations I'd tried to send had felt safe. Instead of answering with words, I mentally laid hold of the heartbond and focused on flooding it with all the warmth, comfort, and happiness I felt. Zidra hummed a relaxed sigh.

I closed my eyes and rolled onto my side.

Thank you, Iskyr.

When I awoke, the snow dome above me glowed a faint yellow, and the grassy, vibrant green of the glen was visible through the opening. I stretched, then froze when the back of my hand bumped into something firm and warm. Carefully, I wiggled onto my side, and my breath caught.

During the night, both Zidra and I had migrated to the middle of the shelter. She lay on her side facing me, one arm tucked up under her head. Mere inches separated us. She probably wouldn't appreciate me staring, but she looked so ethereal and peaceful. I wanted to hold her close.

The urge to kiss her forehead tormented me, but not right now. Not when she'd pulled back after our delicious kisses last night. I wouldn't rush her and risk killing our tender new romance as surely as a late frost would wilt a flower bud.

Zidra sucked in a deeper breath and then groaned. Her eyes fluttered open and met mine. I blushed even though I hadn't done anything wrong.

"Good morning," I murmured.

Without replying, Zidra sprang upright and looked around. "It must be so late! Why didn't you wake me?"

"I only awoke a few moments ago myself."

Frowning, she looked around the shelter. "I suppose I can't entirely blame you for our current position, as we both moved."

"Perhaps we were cold and moved toward each other's warmth."

"Can ice elves even get cold?"

I laughed. "Of course we can. Our magic helps insulate us naturally, and in freezing weather we can draw on our magic to keep ourselves warm, but that takes a lot of energy and is difficult to keep up while sleeping. We still like warm, cozy places." I waved at the snow dome above our heads. "Hence the shelter to trap in heat."

"Right." Zidra stretched her arms over her head, avoiding looking at me. "We should leave. I'd like to get this curse out of my arm before it does any more damage—and preferably before someone attempts to assassinate me again."

Guilt pricked me. I'd gotten too distracted by thoughts

of kisses and embraces when I should have been focused on the growing urgency of our quest. "How's your sense of direction?"

At last, she faced me and cocked her head. "I'm wyveri. It's excellent—better when I'm shifted, but still good."

"You probably noticed yesterday that the road here curves a lot between the hills and glens, but there's few forests in Bryluthia, so we could cut across the countryside directly north. However, my sense of direction isn't strong enough for that."

"I can let you know if you're going off course," Zidra said, nodding.

With that settled, we packed up, ate some salted meat, and set off.

TWENTY-ONE

ZIDRA

The memory of kissing Kyrundar burned like a fire—warm, compelling, but also potentially dangerous. Perhaps some reckless wyveri impulse had prompted me to kiss him, but I'd enjoyed the movement of his lips against mine far more than I ever would have guessed. More than I should have.

I could talk to some of the married rengiri. Surely they would have advice on how to navigate life as a rengir and a spouse and, most importantly, how to not let your spouse be a liability in a fight.

Still, a persistent voice said all of this was a mistake. The heartbond, the kiss, the growing attraction—it was all a misstep. None of it fit with my plan to prove myself or win my family's and clan's respect.

"We're drifting too far west," I shouted. The rushing

air seemed louder and colder today, as if Kyrundar were going as fast as possible.

"What?" he yelled back.

With the wind snatching our voices, trying to course correct had been a headache all day. If only I could speak directly into his mind.

Wait.

I'd never heard of a heartbond working that way, but Kyrundar had sent sensations through the bond. Could I send a specific enough feeling he would understand without words?

It was worth a try.

I visualized bumping us to turn a bit more to the east and sent that thought along the heartbond. Kyrundar looked over, his face pinched, and turned his palms upward.

I tried again, picturing shoving him in the right direction over and over. He tilted his head. After a moment, he nodded slowly. The ice disks adjusted course. I grinned and nodded.

I could imagine Iskyr chuckling and saying, *See, the heartbond isn't useless.*

The rest of the day passed far smoother than previous days. Whenever we drifted off course, I nudged Kyrundar in the right direction through the heartbond. If I needed to stop, I managed to communicate that through the heartbond as well. By sundown, the expanse of the Aizurgon Sea glittered on the horizon. I pointed a little to the east. With his keen elf eyesight, Kyrundar spotted the same thing I did—a cluster of dark shapes on the shoreline.

We continued into the night. As lamps and fires were lit in the coastal town, Kyrundar no longer needed my assistance with navigation. Most people slept by the time we reached the city of Gamnica.

Once a small fishing village, Gamnica had grown since the founding of the Empire of Laedresh into a thriving center of civilization. One of the imperial mints was in Gamnica, as were some of the most respected trade guilds and the most prestigious university on the continent, and a few major trade routes connected here.

Thus, like Laedresh, Gamnica boasted several cathedrals and sanctuaries and a few Havens. Kyrundar led us along the cobblestone streets to Lighthouse Haven. Technically, it wasn't a lighthouse anymore, although it still had the small tower attached to a spacious manor. As larger ships frequented the harbor, a far larger lighthouse had been built on a shoal. The story went that a shipwright had purchased and expanded the abandoned lighthouse with the intent of living there. One day his son was caught on the sea in a storm, and the man had promised Iskyr that if his son returned alive, he would gift the lighthouse to a religious house. After his son survived, he turned the lighthouse into Gamnica's first Haven. His descendants still paid for its upkeep.

A couple of the rooms were taken, marked by closed doors with sea monsters carved into the wood. I strode through the first open door I saw, ready to sleep in a bed. Kyrundar sat on one of the three cots with a contented sigh.

"Mm, I thank the wealthy citizens of Gamnica for keeping this Haven outfitted with the softest linens and the most comfortable feather mattresses."

"The life of a rengir isn't meant to be one of gentle comforts." I shook my head, fighting a smile. After our rough night in the countryside, I was grateful that some people chose to provide for the Havens as their offering to Iskyr.

Kyrundar snorted. "Just because we vow not to own anything we cannot carry and disavow greed doesn't mean we can't enjoy quality and comfortable things. We aren't members of the Pachissian Order who think Iskyr is best served by asceticism." His nose wrinkled.

"Good thing, too, or we'd have broken our vows last night, since they swear to abstain from all physical pleasures and passions."

I immediately regretted the words. Our vows *did* include honoring the other holy brotherhoods and sisterhoods, but the Pachissian monks were so irritating. They tended to believe every other order was inferior, and as staunch pacifists, they often declared rengiri shouldn't be allowed to fight people, only beasts and monsters.

Mostly I wished I hadn't let the words slip free because Kyrundar looked up from removing his boots and pinned me with his gaze. The subtle upward slant of the corner of his lips, the slight tilt of his head, and the fire smoldering in his piercing blue eyes all sent blood rushing to my face.

"I'm going to change." I darted behind the dressing screen in the corner.

"I...am going to do my best not to think about that."

"Kyr!" I stuck my head past the edge of the screen and scowled at him.

He laughed. "Meanwhile, *I* am going to change over here. So stop peeking."

I had to be red as a fire salamander. I fled behind the marginal safety of the dressing screen, wishing I could vanish. Or at least stop thinking about Kyrundar coming to my rescue in just his linen sleeping trousers with the moonlight highlighting his muscles...

Why did he have to be so stupidly attractive?

To give both of us time to cool down, I changed slowly. My clothes really needed to be washed, but that meant letting them dry, and we didn't have time for that. Finally, I took a steadying breath and emerged from behind the screen.

Kyrundar was already nestled under the blanket on his cot, which was both a relief and a disappointment. I hurried to my cot and crawled inside. My nose twitched. It was chilly near the sea, but it didn't seem right that I smelled snow.

"Are you using your magic?"

"I put a line of magicked ice across the threshold and around the window," he confirmed. "No person or magic should be able to enter the room without it waking me. Sleep well, Zee."

"Good night, Kyr."

Warmth filled the heartbond. I smiled in the dim light shining through the windowpanes and surrendered to sleep.

Knocking woke me when the pinks of sunrise still tinted the sky. I groaned and rolled out of bed. With my sword in hand, I stumbled to the door.

"Who's there?"

"Sajen," called a familiar voice.

I wrenched open the door and blinked at the burly gryphoni. "Sajen?"

"Is Kyrundar awake? I can sense this line of ice is enchanted, but I don't know if that means it's going to attack me if I cross it."

I looked over my shoulder. Kyrundar sat up and rubbed his eyes as he shook his head. I motioned Sajen inside.

"I wouldn't use a dangerous enchantment inside a Haven," Kyrundar said through a yawn. "That would be irresponsible."

"Glad you got some sense in your head since your early years at Harcos," Sajen quipped.

Kyrundar laughed and joined us in the middle of the room. "How did you know we were here?"

Sajen nodded to his right. "I'm in the room next door. Was sleeping lightly and heard someone come in and smelled shifter and elf, so I listened in long enough to determine it was you two." He crossed his arms and donned the stern expression of a suspicious instructor. "I have questions about what I overheard."

Kyrundar turned pink to the tips of his pointed ears, and my face felt like I'd sat far too close to a bonfire.

"We haven't broken our vows," I said in a rush at the same time as Kyrundar protested, "There's no rules against flirting!"

Sajen's eyebrows climbed, and his mouth pulled to the

side in a poorly disguised smile. "Mmmhmmm."

"Why are you here?" I asked, desperate to change the subject.

"Why are you both blushing like newlyweds?"

"We only kissed, all right?" Kyrundar exclaimed. "That's not against our vows."

"Once," I added, as if that somehow made it better. There may have been more than one kiss, but it was only one instance.

Kyrundar eyed me like he was worried that was a declaration I wouldn't kiss him again. Perhaps I shouldn't.

Sajen's too-intelligent eyes moved slowly between us. "Interesting," he murmured. Then he lightly shook his head. "I arrived the night before last and have been waiting for you. You said in your letter you were headed north to charter a ship along the Glacorian coast, so I hoped I could catch you in Gamnica."

Jealousy that Sajen had made the journey so quickly stirred up my dragon fire, but I quenched it. My inability to shift wasn't Sajen's fault, and he hadn't meant any unkindness by his comment. Besides, we'd have been faster if we hadn't gone to Ravensburgh first and hadn't been dealing with assassins.

"You found something, then?" I asked.

Sajen's mouth thinned with displeasure. "Yes. Potentially bad news. The description of your original attackers eventually led me to an inn, but I lost their trail for a couple of days—until a servant boy recounted a conversation he'd overheard."

Nervous energy built in my stomach. Could this be the lead I'd been looking for?

"I noticed the lad watching and following me, and I finally caught him. The boy was terrified—and with what he heard, who wouldn't be?" Sajen shook his head, his expression heavy. "His conscience drove him to tell a rengir, but it still took a lot of coaxing to convince him it was safe to tell me. He'd seen a couple of your attackers meeting with a cloaked woman, all armed to the teeth. The woman said their orders were to kill Eilmaris, and Ilifir if he got in the way, but she would go ask their archon what to do about Rouven and the risk to the league if a rengir found him before they did."

I gaped at the gryphoni. No wonder the poor boy had been frightened after encountering such brazen violence and disregard for all things holy. That wasn't what truly mattered, though. "You're saying Gautindar Rouven is also an enemy of the league?"

Kyrundar made a disgruntled sound. "Or a former member. How do we know we can trust him? If he realizes killing you might place him back in the league's good graces—"

"We don't know that." My fingers twitched at my sides. "And we don't have another option for removing the curse."

"For all we know, Rouven designed this ice curse," Kyrundar muttered.

"We also don't have any evidence he did," I said firmly. "Assuming we can find him, we won't mention the league until after the curse is destroyed. He won't know they're after me until I'm back at full strength."

Kyrundar's jaw tightened, but he nodded.

"That's why I had to try to catch you before you boarded a ship and it became harder to find you, despite the precious little information I found," Sajen said. "Whether Rouven has always been the league's enemy or is a deserter, it's best to be on guard. That's the reason I came in person instead of sending a message. I'm going with you. You've been attacked twice—"

"Three times," Kyrundar said. "A night elf tried to smother her the night before last."

Sajen swore under his breath. "Even the Order has only three night elves out of three hundred members. I'm definitely accompanying you."

I pursed my lips. "We've handled it so far, and I don't want to make you a target as well—"

"To the contrary. They could be targeting you because you're the only threat to their existence. If more people know what you know, the number of targets becomes unmanageable and more likely to draw attention they clearly wish to avoid." He glanced between us meaningfully. "Unless there's any reason you wouldn't want me along...?"

My blush returned, but I shook my head. "No, I see your point."

"You're welcome to join us," Kyrundar added.

"Good." Sajen grinned. "What's your plan for finding Rouven?"

"Asking around to find deliveries of Nyksian mead to a Glacorian inlet."

Sajen blinked. "That's it?"

I nodded, unwilling to admit aloud we had no better ideas.

"Then you two should get dressed and we should start searching." He left, closing the door behind him.

The mention of *you two* reminded me that Sajen knew we'd kissed, and I didn't want to deal with my feelings about that right now. I avoided looking at Kyrundar while I grabbed my things and changed behind the screen. When we emerged into the hallway, Sajen was waiting with his war hammer hanging from his hip. We headed outside, but Sajen stopped just past the front door.

"Let's split up. Kyr, why don't you ask around in the city center. Zidra and I will go to Klavon's Port and talk to the sailors and dockworkers. We can meet back at the Haven to discuss our findings."

I wasn't certain if I was more relieved or panicked at the prospect of going with Sajen.

Kyrundar shook his head. "I should—"

But Sajen held up his hand. "Truthfully, I need to talk to Zee about something we discussed before you two left Laedresh."

My mouth went dry. I wasn't sure what Sajen wanted, but it definitely had something to do with Kyrundar, and I didn't want to talk about him. Us.

The troublesome ice elf in question looked between Sajen and me. "I'll see you soon, then." He hesitated before he struck off toward the city center.

Sajen started in the opposite direction. "Shall we?"

Feeling like I was back at Harcos and about to get

scolded, I fell into step beside Sajen. How fitting that now, as at the Academy, I was only in this situation because of Kyrundar.

Gravel crunched beneath our boots, and the cry of a seagull carried over the rhythmic crash of the waves on the nearby rocks. The briny air off the sea had a cold edge that nipped at my ears and nose.

After several heartbeats of nerve-wracking silence, Sajen said, "So. Kissing."

I wanted to bury my face in my hands, but I forced myself to keep walking with my arms loosely at my sides. A dozen responses tangled in my mind, but my mouth felt too dry to speak.

A triumphant grin crinkled his face. "It's about time."

"What?" I squeaked.

"First, of course, I'm delighted that you're accepting more help and that the two of you are working together through everything you're facing. More importantly, I'd hoped this would be the result of you two being forced to spend days together." His knowing smile grew. "If gambling weren't against our vows, the instructors at Harcos would have been placing bets on when you two would get engaged."

My jaw fell. "That's—what? Ridiculous! And we're not! That kiss was probably a mistake, and—"

"A mistake?" Sajen stopped but was forced to catch up to me when I kept walking. "Why?"

I took a fortifying breath and released it slowly. "Kyrundar distracting me is part of why I'm in this situation at all." I motioned to the bandage on my arm. "Sort of. I don't really blame him anymore, and without him I wouldn't have any idea where to look for Rouven. More importantly, I'd be dead several times over. He's as honest and genuinely kind as he appears."

Sajen bumped his arm against mine. "That sounds more like an argument for a relationship than against one."

"There are more reasons." I kicked a stone out of the gravel path. "I don't know if I can release all my past hurt from his behavior, even if I was wrong."

He cocked his head. "What do you mean by wrong?"

"Well... I resented him, but I've learned I misunderstood him. He isn't using me for glory or pitying me for being a wyveri rengir. I was hurt by a situation that existed only in my mind, I suppose." Said aloud, that sounded ridiculous even to me.

"Changing your emotions can be difficult, even once you realize they were based on a false reality."

That made me sound like a petulant child. "I did forgive him. I'm not holding my own stupidity against him."

Sajen nodded. "All right. Good."

I felt like I'd been tricked into discarding an argument against a relationship, but I wasn't upset about it. Still, I rushed to the next problem.

"He's an elf. If I wed an elf, my father will feel hurt, and my mother might decide that's the final straw and disown me."

"Why under Iskyr's great sky would they do that?"

As we left the coast and entered the noisy streets of the

shipping district, I stepped closer to Sajen so I wouldn't have to shout. "Wyveri have suffered so much and tried so hard to distance ourselves from the actions of our ancient king that many wyveri see marrying an outsider as a sign you're ashamed of your own people. They think it makes wyveri look undesirable if we don't want to marry our own kind."

Ironically, I'd discovered that this attitude only made wyveri look more suspicious to the other peoples of the empire.

"Even wyveri who do intermarry usually pick another shifter. An elf?" I stepped around a mud-filled pothole and dodged a boy pushing a wheelbarrow full of fish. "Forget ever introducing Kyr to my family."

"That would be hard," Sajen acknowledged softly. "Is that all?"

"Isn't that enough?"

"Is it?"

A group of sailors loitering on a street corner watched us pass. I was wearing trousers and a knee-length tunic today—in dark red, which Kyrundar had definitely noticed—without my armor, but I still had my insignia pinned on my chest and my sword at my hip. The sailors' gazes roved over our weapons and insignias before they turned away. The shouts of dockhands and the stench of fish pressed against me.

I nibbled on my lower lip, wishing we were somewhere less chaotic where I could think. Yet I didn't really need to think about it. In my heart, my reasoning rang hollow. I had disappointed my family and clan the moment I took my vows. It wasn't as if I visited the Islands anymore now that I was in the Order. I couldn't fall much further in wyveri regard.

But I had a chance to improve my standing if I turned my back on Kyrundar.

Sajen already knew how I felt about the Merit ceremony and why I hated accepting help. What did it matter if I told him the truth?

Glimpsing the docks, I turned down a side street. "If I marry him, I can forget about ever outrunning the Kyrmaris moniker or proving my value. I'll lose any chance of impressing my mother and convincing my people that I am meant to be a rengir. How can I abandon everything I've worked so hard for?"

"Hmmm." Sajen didn't speak until we reached the end of the street and started walking down the dock toward sailors loading crates onto a ship. But instead of approaching the ship officer barking orders to the crew, Sajen marched past them to the end of the dock. He rested his crossed forearms on top of a piling and gazed out across the Aizurgon Sea.

I hesitated, looking between my friend and the ship's mate, wondering if I should start interviewing sailors by myself. Instead, I stepped up to Sajen's side.

He nodded slowly, his gaze unfocused. "I see your predicament. On the one hand, you can part ways with Kyrundar for the uncertain possibility that you might do something grand enough to silence the voices of doubt, perhaps get a second Emperor's Merit all by yourself, and win the admiration of every person in the empire, the acceptance of your clan, and the begrudging love of a mother you shouldn't need to impress. On the other hand, you can enter a relationship with a sometimes irritating and overly casual ice elf you work well with and like and who loves, accepts, and admires you as you already are."

Words failed me. I stared at Sajen, torn between wanting to yell, stomp away, or break down in tears. Yet I could formulate no coherent response to shout at him. Storming off would hardly be the action of a respectable rengir. And I hadn't cried in front of another person since I was a child.

"Unless you don't like him," Sajen said with a noncommittal shrug. "But then we wouldn't be having this conversation, would we?"

No, we would not.

"Give it some thought and ask Iskyr for guidance." He straightened. "Shall we split up to investigate? With Kyr's people skills, he's probably already learned something useful. If we take too long to return to the Haven, he may worry something has happened."

I waved dismissively. "He'll just check the bond and..." Realizing what I'd accidentally revealed, I trailed off.

Sajen's eyebrows arched toward his hairline. "Surely you don't mean a heartbond?"

"Yes," I said, my voice so choked the word was scarcely audible.

"You're not married?" he said, somehow both a statement and a question.

I groaned. "It was a side effect of Kyr using his magic to pull the ice curse back through my body and contain it to the puncture site. Unwanted, unintentional, and…"

"Not as unwelcome as you expected it to be?" Sajen laughed and turned his face toward the pale-blue sky. "Ah, Iskyr. Knew it would take more than a small nudge to get through to these two, eh?" Still laughing, he turned back toward the bustling dock. "Come on, Zidra. Let's go search for the hermit who hopefully holds the answers you need."

TWENTY-TWO

KYRUNDAR

The emotions I sensed through the heartbond weren't truly concerning, but they weren't reassuring, either. Whatever Sajen was talking to Zidra about made her uncomfortable, but not alarmingly so. I released the connection, because her emotions were distracting me from my purpose.

While I hated separating from Zidra, I had to admit Sajen had a point. Zidra was the person to talk to impatient port masters, grumpy clerks, and self-important merchants. I was the person to uncover the gossip in dining establishments.

The scent of delicious roast veal pulled me into a tavern. The barmaid had never heard of Rouven, nor had the tavern's proprietor, and they just chortled when I asked about Nyksian mead. After the maid delivered my veal handpie, I wandered over to the other guests. The wolf shifter couple hadn't heard of Rouven and didn't know where to buy Nyksian mead, and the balding human sipping an ale while he balanced a ledger only grunted in response to my query.

After the tavern, I meandered over to a bakery. The light elf woman tried to talk me into buying all kinds of baked goods, but I stood my ground and bought a single iced cinnamon bun. If they'd had any apple turnovers, I'd have purchased one for Zidra. The baker hadn't heard of Rouven and didn't know where to buy Nyksian mead, either.

"Heard any fascinating gossip, then?" I leaned against the counter with a conspiratorial smile.

She looked up from rearranging pastries in the display case. "All kinds, but not any I reckon would interest a rengir." She considered. "Well, there was that brawl last week."

"Brawl?" That wasn't helpful, but was it something I should look into as a rengir?

"A couple sailors got into a tussle in the street, right in front of my shop. Then their friends took sides, and the city guard had to break it up. I heard they were fighting over who was going to do shopping for some rich old hermit." She shook her head. "Fighting in the streets for a few extra gold coins from some eccentric old fool. Unseemly behavior."

"Old hermit?" I asked eagerly. "An ice elf, by chance?"

She turned up her palms. "Not sure. The sailors would know, though."

I thanked her and wandered back out to find some sailors. At this time of day, most restaurants had very few patrons. At last, I found a tavern where three men who looked promising were eating in the back corner. The blond human had a sun-beaten face, the green-eyed and tanned forest elf wore a loose shirt tucked into fitted trousers that were unusual for an elf, and the brown-skinned human's muscles strained against the shoulders of his shirt.

I approached a young man wearing an apron and ordered an ale, which the lad brought out quickly. I carried my drink over to the three men and motioned to the remaining chair at their table. "Mind if I join you?"

They took in my swords and insignia before nodding slowly.

"Thank you!" I slid into the chair and sipped my drink. "Are you sailors?"

The forest elf nodded. "We work on the *Wraith*. You're an ice elf, right?" His gaze fixed on my earrings, his brow puckering. "I heard Kyrundar Ilifir, one of the Emperor's Merit recipients, is an ice elf with a light elf mother."

I lounged back in my chair with a relaxed smile. "That's true, I am."

All three men sat taller, glancing at each other with wide eyes. The sunburned human rested his forearm on the table near me, as if barely restraining himself from touching me. "Do you need help with anything, Rengir Ilifir?"

I took another sip. "Have any of you heard of an ice elf named Gautindar Rouven?"

They all shook their heads, looking disappointed.

"Then do you know anything about a rich old hermit who pays sailors to do his shopping?"

"Old Frostbite?" the sunburned human said.

"Who is that?"

They said together, "Nobody." The other human snickered.

I chuckled confusedly. "Er…"

"That is," the elf said quickly, "a mean old ice elf has been living in one of the Glacorian inlets for…close to six months?"

His friends murmured their agreement. I almost danced in my chair.

"He says his name is Nobody. I suppose he just hates people that much. All the sailors have taken to calling him Old Frostbite, both because of his temperament and because he's surrounded his inlet with ice magic." The elf shrugged. "At least, that's what I heard. I haven't been that way recently, but some elves say they can sense his magic a mile away."

"I've heard Old Frostbite skates out with a sack full of gold to passing ships when he wants something," the dark-haired human said. "And he asks them to bring him back expensive food and drinks. Sounds half mad to me."

"Does he ask for Nyksian mead, by chance?" I pressed.

"Possibly. We've not been hired by him."

"Know anyone who has?"

The elf frowned. "The crew of the *Ishara*, for sure, but they left port a few days ago."

As they didn't have much more to offer, I thanked

them and left with a spring in my step. I almost headed back to the Haven, but checking in on the heartbond confirmed that Zidra was still by the docks. I could meet them there…but the Cherry Blossom Teahouse was only a street away. Their tea wasn't as good as that at the Blooming Lotus, but I liked the place. More importantly, it was frequented by bards and troubadours who were good sources of gossip. If I could get the name of someone who had actually met Old Frostbite or the location of the magic-protected inlet, Zidra would be impressed. And I'd get tea out of the deal.

Mind made up, I proceeded to the teahouse. Upon entering, I spotted a ginger human with a lute hanging on the back of her seat. I grinned. Our eyes met, and she jumped to her feet.

"Kyrundar!"

"Laine." I helped myself to one of the three empty chairs at her table. After the host took my order, I leaned back and looked to Laine. "How is troubadour life?"

"Same as always." She grinned back. "Dusty roads and demanding audiences. Speaking of which, *please* tell me you have new Kyrmaris stories. I need material to incorporate into the song I'm writing about you two receiving the Merit together."

Something twisted inside me, but I kept my smile in place. "I'm afraid not."

The host brought over my tea, and I thanked him and poured myself a cup before continuing the conversation. "I'm actually looking to get information."

Laine sighed melodramatically. "Are you hunting for a mission or investigating something specific? Because I've been trying to get someone to look into a death, but the two rengir I've talked to said there's nothing they can do since the city inspector ruled it wasn't murder."

I frowned. "A friend of yours?"

"No, but an occasional patron." Laine refilled her teacup, her expression pinched. "A wealthy merchant who loved hosting parties, Teague Carlower. I performed at his townhouse in Cadevelde three weeks ago, and at the end of the night, he was drunkenly ranting about how he'd been threatened to include strangers in his next caravan. He said he wouldn't be threatened, even by a group of powerful heretics who are infiltrating the government to take over the empire."

Alarm coursed through me as I remembered the shifter assassin insulting Iskyr. "Heretics?"

She shook her head and sipped her tea. "I'm not sure what he meant. All I know is the next day, Carlower was dead. Suffocated, the physician said, but without signs of a break-in or struggle, and there was nothing lodged in his airway. Like he just...choked on nothing."

Or like he was strangled by a night elf's shadows. "Are you putting any of that in a song?" I asked, trying not to sound too worried. I didn't want assassins to target another friend.

Laine's eyes widened. "Void-cursed monsters, of course not! If there is a group of people up to conspiracy, sacrilege, and murder, I don't want their attention. Besides, conspiracies and fear-mongering don't elicit the emotions that make audiences loose their purse strings." She smiled sweetly and leaned closer. "What audiences would love to know is where Kyrmaris went together after the Dawning Festival."

Just then, the door to the teahouse opened. A wave of anger flashed through the heartbond without me accessing it. Trailed by Sajen, Zidra marched over, her expression deceptively calm. Her gaze moved purposefully from me to my teatime companion to the lute hanging from the back of Laine's chair and back to me. She sat in the unoccupied chair to my left, across from the troubadour, and skewered me with a look.

I considered moving my chair away from Laine, but that would make me look guilty. I wasn't doing anything wrong, and Laine was just an acquaintance and source of information—but I didn't know how to politely explain that to Zidra in front of Laine.

"Telling more stories?" Zidra asked.

Accusation hid behind the sharp question. I winced. She was probably wondering if I was telling every bard, clerk, troubadour, and busybody in Gamnica about our recent adventures and her current predicament, and I couldn't really blame her.

I smiled reassuringly. "Hearing them, actually. Zidra, this is Laine. Laine, Rengir Zidra Eilmaris."

"The honor is assuredly mine." Laine rested a freckled forearm on the tabletop and leaned forward. Her ginger hair slid over her shoulder and hung dangerously close to her half-full teacup. "Do I understand there are new Kyrmaris stories to be told? Ilifir is being irritatingly tight-lipped." She slid her narrowed eyes over to me and affected a dramatic pout.

On my other side, Zidra stiffened. Sajen watched both women before lowering himself into the seat opposite me. He tilted his head with a far too merry expression. Easy for him to think this was funny when he wasn't the one caught between a suspicious wyveri and a cunning human who was adept at flirting, cajoling, bribing, and otherwise convincing people to give her sensational gossip.

"Traveling makes boring stories," Zidra said dryly.

"Exactly." I nodded as if that settled the matter. Zidra studied me for a moment before returning her attention to Laine.

"Then what were you two discussing?" Zidra's mouth pinched downward.

"Rumors and shadows of rumors and the ever-shifting mists of secrets hinted at but left unspoken," Laine replied, a bit of performer flare mixing with snappishness. She leaned back and pointedly turned toward me. "Did you have any other questions?"

"Do you know anything about Gautindar Rouven?"

Laine shook her head. "Doesn't sound familiar, sorry." She tossed back the rest of her tea and stood. "Always a pleasure, Ilifir. Iskyr guide you all."

"And you," the three of us replied in unison.

The troubadour nodded to each of us in turn, then slung her lute on her back and departed.

"I wasn't flirting," I said. "I'm not interested in Laine."

Zidra stared at me, and then her posture eased and she nodded. "Did you learn anything useful?"

"I've gleaned several bits of interesting information. What did you learn? And talk about?" Hopefully it wasn't obvious I cared less about what they had learned than what they had discussed. I doubted they'd tell me the latter, though.

"We have a lead, but we wanted your opinion, so we went looking for you."

The corner of my mouth pulled up, and I tried for my most flirtatious tone as I asked, "How did you find me?"

Zidra blushed. "You know very well how."

Sajen chortled and leaned back in his chair, observing us as if thoroughly enjoying himself.

"I assume you know how as well, then?" I asked.

"Indeed."

Did his crooked smile mean what I assumed it did? "Any thoughts on the matter?"

"The route is unexpected, but the destination is not."

Sajen's approval bolstered me.

Zidra slid down in her chair. "What matters right now is Rouven."

"Agreed." I drained my tea and stood. "But I am out of tea and out of coin to pay for more, so shall we discuss this back at the Haven?"

"Out of coin?" Zidra stood, and Sajen followed suit. "How? That old woman—"

"Was incredibly generous," I said mildly. "I'm sure the

238

copper coins she gave us were incredibly precious to her. They don't go as far in a port city as I imagine they would in her village—"

"You spent it all on *tea?*" she demanded.

I opened the door for her and Sajen. "Of course not. This wasn't my first stop. I can't loiter in an establishment without buying something. That would be terribly rude."

"And that poor woman thought her donation would enable us to help more people," Zidra muttered.

Sajen pressed his lips together, poorly hiding his amusement.

"It did!" I insisted. "Because my purchases enabled me to talk to several people, and those people gave me information that may help us help others. Maybe indirectly," I admitted in response to Zidra's narrowed side-eye. "But getting you healed means you'll be able to help more people, and I have some interesting tidbits on Rouven and the league."

That got her attention. She went from reluctantly trailing after me to striding ahead of me so quickly I had to rush to keep up, even though her legs were much shorter.

Once we were back in our room at the Haven, we tossed pillows on the floor and sat in a circle.

"What did you learn?" Zidra asked before I'd even fully settled.

"What did you two talk about?" I parried.

Her gaze flicked to Sajen, then fell to the wood-paneled floor. Sajen's relaxed posture and neutral expression revealed nothing. Neither spoke, and finally I had to accept that whatever they had discussed, they weren't going to tell me.

Which made me suspect they had discussed *me*, but it seemed I would never know. Annoying.

"We spoke to an ice elf ship captain who recently sailed down the coast," Zidra said. "He said there's an inlet partway up the Glacori coast that is covered in powerful ice magic wards and traps. The mouth of the inlet is sheer cliff faces, though, so there's nowhere to dock. We'd have to fly in."

"It seems dangerous, but worth checking," Sajen said.

"That fits with what I learned." I related the information about Old Frostbite.

"That settles it," Zidra said. "We need to find a ship that's leaving soon and will sail past this inlet." She started to get up, but I held up my hand to stop her.

"First, though, I need to tell you about something Laine told me." I repeated her story about Merchant Carlower and my suspicions about night elf involvement.

Zidra drummed her fingers on the wood floor, then rose to her feet with grace that could make an elf jealous. "Well then. First, we need to write to Archon Aekyrdra with what we know."

I nodded. As the current leader of the Order of the Rengir, Aekyrdra could send notices to every Haven in the empire, and she met regularly with the Council of Archons and high-ranking imperial officials. If anything happened to us, the Order would still know everything we did about the league of assassins. Which admittedly was very little.

"Then," she continued, "we need to go down to the docks and charter passage."

"That gets us to the inlet," I said, "but not past Rouven's ice traps." Assuming Old Frostbite was the right cranky old ice elf. *Please, Iskyr, let him be the right man. And let him be trustworthy and willing and able to help.* "I can't guarantee I can disarm the traps or protect us from all of them. In fact, sometimes such traps are designed to be triggered if other magic tampers with them."

Sajen stood as well. "I can fly over the inlet to do reconnaissance. If I carry you, perhaps you can sense if there's a way in."

Zidra blinked. "Surely no one could maintain magical traps over an *entire* inlet."

With a sigh, I shuffled to my feet. "I suppose we'll find out soon."

TWENTY-THREE

ZIDRA

We spent the next hour reviewing all the information to put in the letter to Archon Aekyrdra and figuring out how to say everything more concisely. Once I was satisfied, I made two additional copies.

One letter I sent directly to Aekyrdra. The second I sent by a different messenger service to the headmaster at Harcos Academy, with instructions to read it and then deliver it to Aekyrdra. The third I sent by yet another messenger service to the Riverfront Haven in Laedresh, again with the same instructions. There was almost always at least one rengir at the Riverfront Haven, so someone would receive it sooner or later. Kyrundar teased me about being paranoid, but I wouldn't risk the league intercepting a single letter.

Aekyrdra was smart enough to figure out why she'd

gotten multiple copies. The Order hadn't voted to retain her as archon three times in the last forty years for no reason.

By midafternoon, we had booked passage for three to Seath Inlet—according to the ship's captain, the home of Old Frostbite. Unfortunately, the *Tristan* wouldn't set sail until early the next morning.

Although it was early for supper, neither Sajen nor I had eaten anything since we bought muffins for breakfast. Kyrundar said he knew several excellent places to eat depending on what we were in the mood for. Sajen wanted fried fish and offered to buy our food, so Kyrundar merrily led us across the sprawling city to a restaurant at the end of White Gull Wharf. True to its unimaginative name, white seagulls circled and cried overhead.

The Sunbathing Seal, marked by a large sign with a painting of its namesake, stood at the end of a crowded row of shops built on the pier. I paused at the end of the pier, gazing out over the gentle waves of the Aizurgon Sea. A cluster of shapes stood out in stark contrast against the pale blue of the sky on the horizon.

The Wyveri Islands.

Shaking off an odd mixture of heartbreak and homesickness, I followed my companions inside.

Sunlight streamed through large windows, and chandeliers provided additional lighting. Despite how many tables and chairs crowded the space, the vaulted ceiling and warm glow made the place feel open and airy rather than oppressively cramped like many taverns. The tables and floor were clean, and I took a deep breath. No stench of sweaty patrons and spilled ale; just a slight lemony scent underlying the smell of cooking food.

Kyrundar grinned at me. "I thought you'd appreciate the ambiance, Zee. And the lack of patrons at this hour."

I turned toward him, my eyebrows knitting.

Before I could formulate my question, he added, "I know sometimes the crowding, noise, and smell of restaurants overwhelm those overly keen wyveri senses." He waved for me to follow and made his way to a table in the corner, positioned beneath a window looking out over the bay.

Kyrundar took the chair with its back to the window, and Sajen took the chair to his right. I slipped into the chair with its back to the room. I may not have been able to shift, but my senses were sharp enough that I'd know if an assassin tried to attack me from behind.

Still, I didn't feel uneasy. The Sunbathing Seal was well-lit, and the few clients scattered around the room were well-dressed. This pier didn't attract ruffians. Besides, from where he sat, Kyrundar could see the entire room, and I trusted him to notice anything concerning behind me. He wouldn't let anything happen to me.

Thankfully, the window behind Kyrundar didn't face the Islands. I wasn't sure I could have stared at my people's home while sitting across from the ice elf I was falling in love with and still kept my appetite.

A young man wearing a black apron over his dark clothing came and told us their selection for the day and took our order. Like Sajen, I opted for the fried cod with a side of peas. Kyrundar chose baked herring stuffed with herbs and a side of roasted asparagus, and I started to doubt my choice. Just thinking about the food made my stomach rumble.

While we waited, we sipped spiced light ale. None of us spoke, but the silence was comfortable. The silence of friends who don't need to fill every moment with conversation to feel connected. It was a marked difference from the silence I had often experienced at home, where the lack of conversation often was a judgment that I wasn't worthy of being addressed or a false sort of peace that was merely the absence of arguing.

Such thoughts turned my mood sour, so instead I pondered our upcoming journey. I'd never been on a ship before. Every time I'd had to cross the sea, I'd flown. Even the wyveri merchant caravan I'd traveled with had all flown—we'd carried the hyzli dogs in padded kennels and the other goods in crates. It was exhausting and required crossing the sea only in fair weather, but it was faster and cheaper than a ship. Wyveri merchants would rather take multiple trips than bother with ships. How much of that was simply irrational pride that we didn't *need* ships, a practical concern because of how difficult it could be to find safe harbor on the rocky shores of the islands, or a paranoid defense because having no ships meant we built no docks and no one could land on our shores, I wasn't sure. It was probably stubborn pride and how reluctant most matriarchs, like my mother, were to change how things were done.

Realizing I'd failed to keep my thoughts *off* the wyveri and my family, I searched for a conversation starter. Anything would be better than brooding.

"Sajen, have you decided if you're going to take a new partner?"

As soon as I asked the question, I wished I'd thought of a better one. The human firemage who'd traveled with Sajen had retired from the Order a little over a year ago due to a combination of injury and old age. While I knew Sajen wouldn't be offended, the subject of rengir companions came too close to my strange situation with Kyrundar.

Sajen sighed. "I teamed up with other rengiri before I met Lars, and I've partnered with a few since he retired, but none of them have been the same. I know I'm being picky. Lars and I fought side by side for three decades. We knew each other's habits and quirks and could communicate without a word. It takes time to build that kind of rapport."

"Indeed." Kyrundar raised an eyebrow at me. "When you find someone you work well with, it makes sense to keep working with them if nothing is stopping you."

"A shame humans age so much faster than us. Without a heartbond, at least." Sajen chuckled. "But do you know what the rusty old suit of armor did? He got married."

I blinked at Sajen. "He what? At his age?"

"I know! Hasn't got half his hair anymore and what he does have has faded from black to the same white as an ice elf's." He nodded in Kyrundar's direction. "Seventy years old, but he met a human widow a little older than him in the rural town in Neaston that he retired to. They got married a few months ago. I said that seemed fast, and they said life is too short to wait, especially for humans." His wide smile faltered. "I wasn't able to attend the wedding. A downside of traveling so much is it's hard to reach a rengir in a timely manner."

But then Sajen shrugged. "Ah, well. I met the lucky lady when I stopped by on my way to Laedresh. I tell you, the way those two carried on like youngsters on a honeymoon nearly had me blushing." He lifted his tankard in a mock toast. "You two aren't half as bad."

My cheeks heated, but I was saved from answering or listening to some flirtatious comment from Kyrundar by the arrival of our food. Kyrundar's herring was still sizzling, and the herbs smelled amazing. Sure, just about anything was delicious fried, and my own food did look tasty, but his looked better. If only I could have both.

"Eyeing my food when you have your own, Zee?" he teased.

"Wondering if I made the right choice," I admitted.

"Well then." Kyrundar grabbed my plate and pulled it over in front of him.

"Excuse you?"

He laughed. "Let's share. Half of each?" With his knife and fork poised about the plates, he looked to me for confirmation.

"That...sounds good."

"Hmmm." Sajen ducked his head over his plate to hide his smile. I decided to ignore him.

The fried cod was excellent—Sajen praised Kyrundar for his choice of restaurant—but the herb-stuffed herring was delightful. I had just scraped the final bit of lemony sauce onto my last bite of asparagus when Kyrundar sat up straighter. His sharp gaze landed on something over my shoulder.

My hand went to my sword's hilt, and I turned in my chair. A man with tan skin and wavy brown hair that hid his ears approached us. But I didn't need to look for further signs of his race. I knew him.

And there were only three people I wanted to see less. Based on the way his gaze fixed on me and his mouth had pinched into something near a scowl, he wasn't happy to see me, either. I'd rather have been approached by an assassin.

I pried my fingers from my sword's grip and stood. My joints felt wooden as I faced him and inclined my head in a small bow. "Artur."

Kyrundar stepped to my side. Rather than feeling a reassuring presence, I wished he weren't there. "Friend of yours?" he asked amicably.

"This is Artur Eposeth." I motioned toward the intruder, wishing I were anywhere else. "My cousin. Artur, this is Rengir Kyrundar Ilifir and Rengir Sajen Hargren."

Artur bowed his head to each man in turn.

"What are you doing in Gamnica?" My question came out strained, revealing more of my discomfort than I'd hoped.

"Filling in as an extra guard for Thesian. He's taking a

caravan to Fairow. One of his men fell ill at the last moment." Artur's dark eyes flicked toward Kyrundar and back to me. "We heard about the Emperor's Merit."

My heart nearly stopped. What did my family and clan make of it?

"We'd assumed the stories claiming you are close with the ice elf were exaggerated or confused, perhaps lies originating from the elf himself. I see we were wrong, or you wouldn't be having such a friendly meal with him."

I wished my tankard were full of water instead of a couple sips of ale. Not that I could turn around and retrieve it without being rude.

"Do you have a problem with ice elves?" Kyrundar asked in a tone as cold as his magic.

"Not particularly," Artur said with an equally icy stare. "Simply disappointed to see that the firstborn daughter of one of our matriarchs abandoned her birthright only to be unable to make a name for herself without the aid of an elf."

"Lying is against our vows," I said, belatedly grasping at the only accusation for which I had a response. "Kyrundar Ilifir is an honorable man, a devout rengir, and a recipient of the Emperor's Merit. Do not disparage his character, and certainly do not do so within my hearing."

Artur grunted. "Your mother will be disappointed to hear that the rumors are true, regardless of his character. Your clan expected more of you than to let someone else carry you to renown."

"Renown is hardly the chief concern of a rengir." Sajen's

chair scraped across the floor. He stood and moved to stand on my other side. "Zidra earned the Merit, but even without it, she is a fearsome and cunning warrior, a kind soul, and a dedicated and pious servant of Iskyr. She deserves your pride and respect, and if all you have to offer is scorn, you may go and leave us in peace."

Artur took in Sajen's bulk, appearing unimpressed. "A wyveri who requires others to defend her is hardly deserving of my respect."

"She requires no defense," Kyrundar said. "We defend her simply because we care about our friend. Perhaps you have no friends and so cannot understand."

My companions' words both bolstered and crushed me. Nothing they could say would change Artur's mind. Wyveri treasured their superiority too much.

Artur shook his head, his expression sad. "You are weak, Zidra. And your weakness harms the clan. The Merit gave us hope, but you're just as inadequate as we suspected. It's unfortunate your nephew is too blinded by hero worship to see that."

The building panic in my chest came to an abrupt halt. "What about Zarik?"

"You haven't heard?" Artur's eyebrows leaped up. "He broke your brother's and sister-in-law's hearts and left last winter for Harcos Academy. He wants to be a rengir."

"Because of *me*?"

"Because of you," Artur confirmed, but the way he said it made it sound like I'd convinced Zarik to become a criminal.

"At least Zidra isn't the only wyveri with any sense," Kyrundar muttered, plenty loud enough for shifter hearing.

"How could Zarik have decided to become a rengir and I didn't know about it?"

Artur wrinkled his nose. "Zarik doesn't want you to know because he doesn't want any special treatment at Harcos or from the Order. I imagine your parents and sister didn't tell you because aside from the difficulty of getting a message to a rengir, when Zarik made his announcement, your mother declared she'd never speak to you again. If you'd achieved the Emperor's Merit without the accomplishment weakened by your partnership with an elf, perhaps she would have changed her mind, but I don't see that happening now."

Some fragile hope in my chest cracked with a physical pain that threatened to bring me to my knees.

"That is quite enough," Kyrundar snapped.

"May Iskyr treat you with the same regard with which you treat his servants," Sajen declared—a blessing turned curse that sounded particularly ominous in his deep voice.

Somehow, I found my voice. "Excuse me."

I barreled past him and out of the Sunbathing Seal. Kyrundar fell into step beside me before I made it far down the pier, but he didn't say anything as I tore through the city and back to the Haven. More people filled the streets as evening approached, and focusing on not bumping into anyone provided me with a distraction from my bruised emotions.

But once the door shut behind us in our room, there

was nothing to keep my mind off Artur's words.

Kyrundar watched me, his expression strained, like he wanted to speak but had no idea what to say.

My thoughts crashed into each other, tangling together. "I was right," I whispered. "My people are ashamed of me. A shared Merit is a failure, not an achievement."

"You deserved the Merit, Zee," Kyrundar said. "And they may not all think that. He's one person, and your family seems a bit…harsh. They don't speak for every wyveri. They certainly don't speak for every Laedreshian citizen. Those townspeople we saved didn't see you as inferior. I don't see you as inferior."

I only half heard him. My cousin, my parents, my brother and sister-in-law, presumably also my sister, all of them saw me as a failure and blamed me for losing Zarik, too. Could I ever do anything that would change their minds?

Kyrundar eased closer and lightly grabbed my shoulders. "He was cruel. He chose to be cruel, knowing his words would hurt you. And your parents and sister— they're wrong to treat you as they have. They're wrong to disdain you for having a different set of skills than they wanted or a different career than they envisioned. You are not in the wrong here. It's not your fault they can't appreciate you for who you are, for the person you were made to be."

My throat tightened. I blinked rapidly, determined to remain strong and in control.

"Artur is a fool, and worse, a mean-spirited fool. Your parents and sister are shortsighted and selfish. Their behavior and words hurt because they're designed to, and because they're based on lies. Do you understand?"

I stared at the ends of his white hair lying against his blue tunic. Perhaps he was right, perhaps he wasn't. I wasn't certain I understood the point he was making, but I couldn't respond. If I tried to speak, I'd break.

Kyrundar placed the side of his forefinger beneath my chin and tilted my head up until I unwillingly made eye contact with him.

"You're allowed to be in pain, Zee," he said softly. "You're allowed to admit it hurts. That doesn't make you weak or make your family's cruel and stupid opinions right. It means you're a person with a heart that can bleed, like you're supposed to be. And neither Iskyr nor I will judge you or turn away from the tears you have every right to cry."

His eyes glistened as if he, too, were barely holding back tears.

A shudder went through me. "Artur didn't even know..." My words turned into a choked cry. A sob wracked my chest, and the tears I had locked away no longer obeyed my commands but fell hot and fast down my cheeks. But I had to say the rest.

"What if he learns I'm wounded?" I wasn't even certain Kyrundar could understand my keening words through my sobbing. "That I can't shift? What if I have to quit being a rengir? What if he realizes you're half light elf, and that I've always known and don't care? And if Zarik is training at Harcos, why didn't he visit me? He had to have attended the ceremony, but he didn't seek me out. Is he ashamed of me?" The last word was drawn out on a hiccuping wail.

All ability to speak abandoned me, and I could barely see.

Pressure on my shoulders tugged me forward, and then I collided with Kyrundar's chest. His arms encircled me. Usually someone touching me while I was crying would have been overstimulating, but Kyrundar's embrace felt right in a way I couldn't explain.

"Let it out," he whispered.

I broke.

Sagging against him, I grabbed fistfuls of his tunic and buried my face in the soft fabric. My body shook with my weeping. Some distant part of my mind was embarrassed of my gasping wails muffled against his chest, but I couldn't stop. Years of suppressed hurt and the last several days of fears and doubts had built pressure, and like water that had found a crack and burst through a dam, the flood couldn't be stopped.

Kyrundar squeezed me closer. His hand stroked my back.

By the time my crying subsided and I could breathe enough to pull away and wipe my face, my head ached. Exhaustion pulled at my limbs. I backed out of his arms and stumbled to my pack, from which I retrieved a handkerchief. My cot squeaked as I sat heavily on it. I turned away from Kyrundar to blow my nose. Embarrassment at last caught up to me.

"I'm sorry—"

"Don't you dare be ashamed of crying." Kyrundar sat next to me on the edge of my cot. He wiped his eyes, and his voice was hoarse. "The holy texts would not say that Iskyr keeps a record of our tears so that he may comfort those who mourn and execute justice for the afflicted if we were not meant to weep over suffering or injustice. And your family has treated you unjustly. Every wyveri who has judged you for being a rengir and every person who has judged you for being a wyveri has hurt you. You can cry as much as you need to."

I was already tired of crying, yet listening to the raw emotion in his voice, I nearly began again. Instead I took deep breaths and massaged my forehead as if that might help my headache dissipate.

After a few minutes, Kyrundar slid closer, so his leg brushed up against mine. Despite the layers of fabric between us, the gentle pressure of his knee against mine felt oddly intimate.

"Zidra," he murmured. "Are you ashamed of being a rengir? Ashamed of how well you did at Harcos, or of how many people you've protected and monsters you've slain? Do you think you've failed to honor Iskyr as you vowed to do?"

I took a few slow breaths and tried to ignore how much I wanted to lean against him. "No. Perhaps I could do better, but—"

"That's not what I asked." He chuckled softly. "Do you honestly believe you're doing anything wrong?"

"No," I whispered. "But—"

"Do you think Iskyr is ashamed of you or displeased with you? Or do you think he smiles on your efforts to protect his people and follow your vows?"

I swallowed. Everything I had been taught told me that Iskyr cared and would not be ashamed of my honest efforts. *Iskyr? Is that true?*

"I'm certain Iskyr is pleased with you," Kyrundar said. "If you know you've done nothing wrong and Iskyr approves of your actions, then the blatantly wrong and vicious opinions of people like your cousin aren't what matters. Right?"

A reassuring calm tinged with pride brushed across my consciousness, so quiet and still I almost missed it, yet underlain with the power of Iskyr that I sensed whenever I had a premonition.

My heart still ached, and I felt like a wrung-out rag, but Kyrundar was right. I nodded and whispered, "Thank you."

He placed a hand on my shoulder, firm enough to be comforting but light enough I could have easily shrugged him off if I'd wanted to.

I didn't want to, and I refused to examine why too closely.

"Do you need to talk about it more? Or do you want some time to yourself? Or shall we do something to distract you?"

A weak laugh emerged shakily from my lips. "I tend to avoid comforting people. I never know what to say or do." It shouldn't have come as a surprise that Kyrundar knew what to do. He was good with people—even sobbing wyveri, apparently. "How did you get so good at this?"

"I had parents who believed in allowing emotions, even uncomfortable ones. My father often rants about human men who speak as if they have no emotions. They do, of course; they simply don't know how to handle them, and then most often they misdirect them into anger, and then they can't handle someone else expressing an emotion they've always denied. My parents did their best to ensure I didn't grow up to be like that."

"Your parents sound wonderful."

His shoulders caved. "I'm sorry—"

"Don't be. I don't want to let my hurt over my own family cause me to resent others for having a good family."

"Still." He rubbed my shoulder. "What do you need?"

My head ached, my eyes felt puffy and itchy, my nose was still stuffy, and my limbs dragged on me like heavy weights. "Sleep."

"All right. Sleep. I'll go out so I won't disturb you—"

"No!" I grabbed the edge of his tunic in my fist. He stared at me, taken aback by my loud outburst. "I…" My mind caught up to my actions, and horror at my weakness shoved my fear aside. "Never mind." Slowly, I released my grip on his tunic. "I'll see you later."

"Zidra," Kyrundar murmured. "If you want me to stay, you need only ask."

I swallowed. His piercing gaze held mine, as if compelling me not to look away. "Will you stay?"

He didn't ask why. Didn't force me to admit to my fear

of an assassin finding me while he was gone or the aching loneliness that filled my chest at the thought of being alone.

"Always."

TWENTY-FOUR

KYRUNDAR

After I put up an ice barrier, Zidra fell asleep quickly. I wasn't tired, but I didn't leave. I didn't know if I'd reached for the bond to check on her, if she'd shared her emotions willingly, or if her feelings had been so powerful they had traveled through the heartbond without her knowledge, but I'd felt her fear. Her worries of being assassinated, yes, but also her dread of being alone—abandoned and unwanted.

I would not let her wake and think I had left her.

So I sat on my cot and kept watch. Sajen checked on us, and I let him know Zidra was sleeping, then returned to my post. When my eyes grew heavy, I went to sleep myself.

The sound of Zidra moving about the room woke me before dawn. A candle flickered dimly in the corner, casting long shadows as she huddled over her pack.

"You're up already?" I rubbed grit from my eyes and sat up. "What time is it?"

"Sorry, I didn't mean to wake you. Bells tolled five a few minutes ago. I can put the candle out—"

"It's fine." I yawned and tossed aside my blanket. "No sense in going back to sleep now when we'll need to be at the docks in about an hour and a half. I'll just be groggier if I try to sleep for less than an hour."

"Sorry—"

"No need to apologize, Zee." I smiled wryly. "You did get to sleep early last night."

Her shoulders hunched, and she didn't answer as she rearranged things in her pack.

"Are you all right?" I asked softly. "And you can be honest. You don't need to pretend for me. I'm not judging you. I'm not upset with you for being a person with feelings, and I honestly want to know."

Her sigh made the candle flutter, but the tension in her shoulders eased. "Is it terrible that I like that I can tell whether you're lying?"

I frowned. "I do usually make a policy of telling the truth."

Zidra huffed a quiet laugh. "I suppose you do. It was unfair of me to assume you were like my family, hiding derision or ulterior motives behind your words."

My heart ached for her. "Unfair, maybe, but also understandable." Abruptly, I straightened, the last of my sleepiness draining away. A sly smile crept across my face. "Wait. How do you know I wasn't lying? Are you accessing the heartbond, Zee?"

She bowed her head farther down over her pack, so her thick curls hid the side of her face. "Maybe."

"Mmm." I slipped off the cot and padded over to kneel by her side. "Do you *like* being bonded to me, Zidra Eilmaris?" I whispered near her ear.

She shivered. "Don't."

"Don't what?"

"Flirt."

I drew back a little and watched her closely. "Why?"

"I told myself I wouldn't kiss you again until the curse is removed."

My mouth fell open. "*Why?*"

She finally lifted her head to peek at me. "If removing the curse removes the heartbond, then I'll know if it's just the magic affecting me."

"And if it doesn't?"

Her lips pursed. "I don't know."

My mood deflated. "I suppose I should get dressed," I mumbled, more to myself than to Zidra.

We didn't speak much as we finished getting ready and then waited for Sajen. We made our way through Gamnica in silence, past sleepy townspeople going to their shops. Sajen kept glancing at us both through narrowed eyes as if he suspected something was off, but he didn't ask.

As per our agreement with the *Tristan*'s captain, we took up posts to keep watch for sea serpents. We'd offered to help the crew, but the idea of untrained hands getting in the way had made Captain Hulme grimace. Although the *Tristan* had a single mast and square sail, it was long and wide, with two decks and a high sterncastle, and as such, it had a crew of forty people. While not a common problem, sea serpents did occasionally attack ships off the Glacorian coast, so standing on the edges of the upper deck was both useful and kept us out of the crew's way.

Of course, Hulme was happy to host rengiri on his ship, regardless—probably hoping our presence would ensure favorable winds and safe ports. He had offered his cabin in the sterncastle for our comfort, but Zidra had immediately refused. I smiled fondly at her, although her back was to me as she stood at the ship's bow. She was the most hardworking and honorable rengir I knew.

But as it turned out, she was also the least seafaring rengir I knew. Within an hour of our casting off, Zidra stumbled away from the ship's bow toward the hatch to the lower deck, looking rather green. Alarmed, I started toward her, but Sajen reached her first.

"Seasick?" he called.

Zidra nodded and pressed her hand to her stomach. "I'm going to go lie down—"

"That won't help," Sajen and I said in unison.

Zidra grimaced. "Then what will?"

"Switching positions, for one." Sajen motioned her toward the spot midship where he had been standing. "Less movement in the middle than at the ends. Keep your eyes on the horizon and try to breathe slow and steady. I'll ask the captain if he has any ginger…"

Reluctantly, I left Zidra in Sajen's care and returned to my own post. I wasn't sure it would help with a physical ailment, but I tried to send soothing sensations through the heartbond anyway. Maybe that was overstepping given her apparent hope that destroying the ice curse would remove the heartbond, but if she really didn't want me to do it, surely she'd send some kind of angry message back. Since I didn't sense any displeasure from her, only annoyance that seemed more directed at the rocking of the ship than at me, I decided she at least didn't mind.

By nightfall, Zidra had grown accustomed enough to sea travel that she was able to fall asleep below deck, but sleep evaded me. The creaking of the ship and muffled sound of ship hands occasionally calling to each other on deck kept me awake despite the rhythmic swinging of my hammock. Or maybe it was my confused thoughts about the woman lying little more than an arm's length away. She kept pushing me away and pulling me in only to push me away again, as changing as the tides. My heart couldn't take much more of this. If she wouldn't commit one way or the other, I'd take matters into my own hands and leave.

Everything in me rebelled at the thought, but I knew there was no alternative.

Tomorrow we would reach Seath Inlet, where I prayed we would find Rouven. Then he would save Zidra's life—I had to believe he could.

After that?

Either I'd start courting Zidra officially, or we would part ways.

Iskyr...

I fumbled for words to express the yearnings of my heart.

Do what you will.

Iskyr had placed Zidra and me in the same class at Harcos, had put us both in the Order, and had linked us with a heartbond. Perhaps there was a reason.

As much as it hurt to admit, though, that reason could just be saving Zidra from the ice curse and assassins.

I wouldn't be angry about that, though. If Zidra and I weren't meant to be together, at least she was alive.

I didn't remember falling asleep, but a man's voice and someone gently prodding my shoulder woke me. I lurched upright and tumbled out of the hammock, landing with a thud on the unforgiving wood floor.

"Sorry!" Boots scurried backward, likely belonging to the sailor who had awoken me.

"Ow." Rubbing my hip, I sat up with a groan.

"Are you all right?" Zidra dropped to a crouch next to me, her eyes wide with worry.

Grand. Falling out of my hammock like an idiot was such a good way to convince her to stay.

"Kyr?"

I forced a smile. "I think my pride took the worst of it."

She rolled her eyes and stood. "Your pride could take a few hits."

I caught her hand before she fully straightened. "You were worried about me, though." I winked. "Admit it."

"Obviously. Who is going to sense Rouven's traps if you break your skull falling out of bed?" Yet she didn't pull her hand free of mine, and the corner of her mouth twitched with mirth.

My lips curved into a full smirk. "On second thought, I think you'd best check me for injuries. Just in case."

Zidra pressed her lips together and raised an eyebrow as she looked me over. "No blood. You're fine. We're nearly to the inlet." She tugged on my hand. "Get up."

I pushed to my feet and let the added momentum of her pulling propel me forward. We bumped into each other, and I snaked my free arm around her waist.

"I don't know," I whispered as I gazed down into her coppery-brown eyes. "I'm feeling a little lightheaded."

Pink tinged her cheeks. "I'm starting to believe you've never flirted before. This is terrible."

Leaning closer to her ear, I murmured, "Then why are you breathless?"

Someone cleared their throat, and Zidra nearly leaped out of my arms, wrenching her hand free of my grasp. Stifling a sigh, I turned to face the sailor. His skin had taken on a ruddy hue as he stared determinedly at a post off to my right.

"We'll be passing the Seath Inlet within a quarter hour. Rengir Hargren has already headed to the deck." He bobbed an awkward sort of bow and turned sharply on his heel before marching away at an impressive speed.

"I think that's the first time I've seen you make someone uncomfortable," Zidra said dryly. She darted around me and followed the sailor.

Well, she wasn't angry I'd broken her no-flirting request, so I counted that as a win and trailed after her.

On deck, the air was cold and sharp with the taste of

salt. The bright edge of the sun crept over the coastline to the east, casting the mountainous coast in shadow and setting the peaks ablaze in glowing orange. Something stirred in my chest at the sight, familiar yet foreign. While I was growing up, we lived near my mother's family in Bryluthia. But we'd visit my father's family in Glacori on the other side of the Ithemorca Mountains most summers. Many pleasant memories included watching the sun melt behind the mountains as the stars came out.

Zidra stepped up next to me and leaned against the railing, squinting at the horizon line and taking deliberately slow breaths. For a moment, I let my mind run wild, imagining taking her to meet my family, watching white ermine bounce through the snow, and showing her all my favorite places in Glacori and Bryluthia. Well, not all of them. I'd already shown her the pond where I'd learned to ice skate and my favorite ice elf cathedral a few years ago, after we'd finished a mission together in Glacori. My wistful mood evaporated.

Looking back, I don't know how I'd mistaken her disinterest in my tour for mere exhaustion when she was probably resenting me for elbowing in on another of her missions. At the same time, it felt equally foolish that I'd thought I needed to show Zidra places that I remembered fondly from my childhood but also hadn't realized how much I cared for her.

Zidra shivered and wrapped her arms tighter around herself. Only the bustle of sailors going about their tasks around us stopped me from putting my arm around her and pulling her close. Not that I cared what they thought, but if Zidra was unsure about our future together, she might care.

My magic tugged inside me, drawing my attention from Zidra to the coast.

Captain Hulme pointed at an indentation along the coastline. "There it is."

I nodded. "I can sense potent ice magic."

"I suppose it's time, then." Sajen shifted into his huge gryphon form. I could barely see over his lion back without going up on my toes, so I was relieved when he crouched down for me to clamber onto his back.

Zidra turned toward us. "Be careful. Both of you."

"When am I not?"

A sound rather like a laugh rumbled deep in Sajen's chest, but Zidra gave me an unamused look.

"All right, when is Sajen not careful?"

She shook her head. "Iskyr guide you and bring you safely back."

Sajen lightly bumped his eagle head into her chest, then lumbered to his feet and took to the air.

With the increased altitude and speed of Sajen's flight, the air over the Aizurgon Sea went from chilly to frigid. I drew on my powers to keep myself warm, thankful that Sajen's fur and feathers meant he didn't need my help. Using my magic to keep someone else warm was much more complicated and taxing.

Sajen slowed and banked lower when we reached the inlet. A vertical blue line of ice shimmered on the rock faces on either side of the entrance, the magic so potent I could sense the warning and danger laced into the ice without effort. As agreed, Sajen turned aside and flew over the steep cliffs to the south rather than directly over the water or the lines of magic.

I gathered my magic into my hands, ready in case I needed to protect us against a magical attack. Snowflakes swirled around my fingers, and I sent threads of magic to test the borders of the inlet.

At the end of the inlet, a cabin sat tucked under the protruding rock of a cliff. A man stepped out, his white hair tied at the back of his neck. He craned his head back to watch us approach. Sajen slowed even further. The man raised a hand, and a blue-tinted glow swirled around his fist. Snowflakes grew to ice chunks.

"We come in peace!" I withdrew my own magic to almost nothing, just enough that I could still react quickly if the man didn't listen or couldn't hear me. "We'd like to talk!"

"What?"

"Rengiri! Here to talk! Peacefully!"

The man didn't respond or move to attack. Sajen dipped down as if preparing to land on the pebbled beach in front of the cabin.

"Not yet," I cautioned. "The air is half-choked with ice magic, and by the way he's scowling at us, I'm not sure he isn't going to attack."

Sajen turned instead to fly across the width above the beach. The man watched us cross once and back again.

"Permission to land and talk?" I shouted as Sajen passed the cabin a third time.

At last, the man lowered his hand, although blue light still spiraled around his fist. But then some of the stifling ice magic surrounding the inlet relented.

"Land cautiously and be ready to take off again," I advised.

Sajen bobbed his head and dove, forcing me to grab a fistful of feathers with a stammered apology.

We landed several paces from the cabin and the man. White pebbles scattered from the impact of Sajen's landing. I jumped down, and Sajen shifted back to his true form. We both bowed our heads. The wrinkly-faced ice elf just crossed his arms and grunted.

"Thank you for allowing us to land," I said. Given the old man's attitude, I deemed it best to give some information before I asked for any. I pointed to the insignia pinned to the breast of my tunic. "I'm Rengir Kyrundar Ilifir, and this is Rengir Sajen Hargren. A friend of ours, Rengir Zidra Eilmaris, requires specialized magical medical attention. Are you Gautindar Rouven?"

The man stared back at us, his expression like that of a toddler asked to eat vegetables. Was he deaf? I didn't remember enough hand signs to communicate without any words. Or was this not Rouven at all?

"How did you find me?" he snapped, his voice rough as wood bark.

A calm sense of Iskyr's reassurance nearly made me slump with relief. "It wasn't easy, but the powerful ice elf hermit with expensive tastes seemed a good guess."

Rouven grunted again. "I'm retired. And a hermit. Leave me alone." He turned toward the cabin.

"Wait!" I held out my hands, begging him to halt. The moment he slowed, I sprinted across the rounded stones and skidded to a halt within arm's reach of the man we'd traveled so far to find. "Please! We've been to Merael's, and they couldn't help us. Physician Mirlanwen told us to find you. I don't know where else to go if you don't help. My friend, my…the woman I love is going to die." My voice cracked.

"I'm still retired," Rouven grumbled, although with less vehemence. He stepped toward his house, but I grabbed his arm. His other hand snapped up with speed that belied the age spots on his skin, and I barely had time to raise a defense before our magics crashed into each other with the sound of shattering ice.

I moved back and held up my hands in a conciliatory gesture. "I'm sorry. But you might be the only person with both the power and the medical knowledge to save her. The only way I'm leaving here is with your permission to bring Zidra back or because I'm dead."

Rouven's bushy white eyebrows pinched together low over his eyes, but he didn't fully turn back to me. "What under Iskyr's great sky could possibly be wrong with the girl?"

"She has an ice curse in her arm."

His head tilted subtly. "Zidra Eilmaris… Not an ice elf name."

"Wyveri," I supplied.

His eyebrows sprang up. "And she's not dead?"

"I was able to pull the cursed magic back and trap it at the initial puncture site, but I couldn't remove it."

At last, Rouven turned his back to the blue door of his cabin, his countenance thoughtful. "When did this happen?"

"Er…" I thought for a moment. "Nine days ago."

Rouven pursed his lips and stared out across the inlet toward the sea. I hoped the ship hadn't traveled too far in the time since we'd left. The captain had ordered the crew to shorten sail until we returned, but this was taking longer than I'd anticipated.

"Please," I begged. "If there's any way I can repay you, I swear I'll do it or return with whatever price you demand. Her dragon fire is constantly at risk of burning away my barrier, and it's beginning to affect her arm—"

"Fine," Rouven sighed. "Bring her. Even retirement doesn't annul the oaths I took to use my knowledge and skills for life and healing, and as refusing might doom the girl, fine. Bring her, but I make no guarantee that I can save her. Besides, I admit I am curious to see this barrier you have placed. Never have I heard of such a thing being done."

If I'd had the time, I might have fallen to my knees in gratitude. Instead, I shouted my thanks over my shoulder and ran back to Sajen, who was already shifting.

We quickly found the ship, and this time, Zidra rode on Sajen's back while I struggled to keep up with the gryphon's speed on my ice disk. Show-off flying-type shifters.

When we landed, Rouven was nowhere to be seen, but within moments, he poked his head out of his cabin and impatiently waved us inside.

"I'll keep watch out here," Sajen said as he took up position next to the blue-painted door.

Zidra looked at me. "Are we sure this is really Rouven?"

"As sure as we can be." When she hesitated on the threshold, I grabbed her hand and gave it a gentle squeeze. "I'll be with you. I won't let anything happen to you."

She looked like she might argue, but then she nodded and took a deep breath. Her hand slipped out of mine, and I followed her into the house.

TWENTY-FIVE

ZIDRA

The back of my neck itched as I crossed the threshold into the cottage. Inside, a sizable four-poster bed with its curtains tied back took up nearly a third of the space. A washbasin large enough to stretch out one's legs occupied most of one wall, while a tidy desk and stuffed bookshelf occupied all the space under the large window that faced the water. Random household implements filled shelves built into the walls on either side of the spacious fireplace, and a small armchair sat in the center of the room. Combined with the fact that this one-room house was tucked into the concave space at the bottom of the cliff, situated right beneath all that rock, the cramped space made me want to take flight.

"Cozy," I said, half trying to convince myself that that word could describe the room. "But it seems lonely."

"It seems crowded," Rouven groused. "It's supposed to have only me in it!"

"Why would you choose this?" Even though I liked my time alone, I'd lose my mind without contact with another person for days or even months on end.

The elderly ice elf scowled at me, drawing the lines of his face deeper. "I wanted some peace and quiet away from people who always want something from me."

I watched him closely. "Not because you're running from anything?"

His posture stiffened. "You're here for medical attention, not to ask personal questions."

Not a no. "Maybe I'd like to know who is treating me before I trust you."

"And why should I trust you, hm?" He pointed at my insignia. "Maybe you all murdered some rengiri and stole those. Maybe you made counterfeits."

I raised my eyebrows. "To...what? Trick you into helping me?"

"Or into letting you in." His mouth twisted to the side. "Although I suppose if you wanted to kill me, you would have attempted it now that there's three of you inside my defenses and I'm not actively wielding any magic."

"Does someone want you dead?" I asked, trying to keep my tone casual.

But Rouven's eyes narrowed. "For someone with a life-threatening condition, you seem more concerned with prying into my affairs than securing my medical expertise."

Kyrundar stepped up next to me. "Pardon her. She's

just nervous, and wyveri don't like tight spaces."

Rouven considered this, then nodded slowly. "I suppose that makes sense, given your size when shifted. Well then, come sit on the bed then, girl, and let me take a look."

"There's a perfectly good chair—"

"And if I need you to lie down, we'll have to move, so stop wasting time. Besides, I already put my tools on the bed." Rouven stomped to the bed and turned around to glare at me.

A slight pressure on my lower back marked Kyrundar steering me toward the bed, and I let him. Sure enough, a scalpel, pair of shears, towel, bowl of water, needle and thread, and roll of bandages waited on the foot of the bed. Stiffly, I sat on the edge of the mattress, surprised at its plushness. For living alone in the middle of nowhere, Rouven certainly had made his life as comfortable as possible.

At the healer's prompting, I removed my pauldron. With speedy precision, Rouven used the shears to cut off my bandage and cut away some more of my sleeve. His frown deepened as he looked at the wound. Without speaking, he cleaned the area and wiped it dry.

"Do you feel this?"

I looked down to see his fingertips prodding at the blackish edges of the small dark-red wound in my arm. "No," I whispered.

Rouven sighed and dropped his hand to his side. "I wish we had a fleshmage here. That would help. As it is, if we can destroy the curse—and that is *if*—I'm going to need to cut out the parts of your flesh that have necrotized. Even fleshmages can't bring this back, but they can speed up the healing and help you regrow at least some of the flesh. But if you survive, you're going to have at least a large scar. At worst, you may have a permanent indent in this arm. You may have some tightness there that will never fully go away."

I gulped. It mattered little, although I prayed it wouldn't affect my ability to swing a sword. "Understood."

"Now I'm going to examine the magical part of this malady."

"It may hurt," Kyrundar warned.

Rouven released a frustrated grunt and waved a hand. "Of course it will hurt, boy. It's tainted and malicious magic."

As the physician cupped his hands around my arm, I braced myself. Rouven's magic felt different from Kyrundar's—colder and sharper, like needles of ice exploring under my skin. I gritted my teeth and clenched fistfuls of the soft bedspread. Perspiration beaded on Rouven's face.

Finally, the pain stopped. He released my arm and stepped back with a heavy sigh, his shoulders slumping as if under a great weight. He wiped his forehead and turned to Kyrundar.

"You did well." His tone sounded begrudging. "Exceptional work, demonstrating skill and power." He rolled his neck and straightened. "Which is good, because you're going to need all of that expertise and strength if we're going to save her life. The ice curse has latched onto her, like thousands of tiny barbs—but barbs that have a sort of life to them, that want to grow and spread. As I'm sure you discovered, attempting to remove the curse requires far too much effort and will cause her too much pain. We'll have to destroy it inside her."

"How?" Kyrundar asked the question I couldn't voice, sounding as shocked as I was.

"It basically involves compressing it until it implodes, but let me worry about that." Rouven pointed at Kyrundar. "Your task is to keep the curse and my magic contained. You'll have to strengthen and maintain your barrier and ensure that its size remains consistent and that none of my magic or the curse gets past you. If your barrier fails, I may lose control, and she'll freeze before your eyes. Can you do that?"

I worked my throat, trying to find the words to reassure Kyrundar that he could do this, but the only thought in my mind was *she'll freeze before your eyes* on repeat.

Had we survived three assassination attempts only for me to die now?

I didn't want to die. Not now. Not yet. I'd fallen asleep in the belly of the ship reciting prayers, and I had dreamed—not regular dreams, but dreams I knew were from Iskyr. While they were hazy now, Kyrundar and the heartbond had featured heavily in them, and I knew Iskyr was telling me to trust his gifts and plan. I'd awoken determined that if the heartbond survived the removal of the curse, that would be my sign that the love I felt for Kyrundar was true. And while I'd waited on the *Tristan* for Kyrundar to return, fretting about whether the magical traps would hurt him or worse, I'd realized I regretted pushing him away.

I couldn't die. Not before I'd kissed him again.

I almost grabbed him and kissed him right that moment, but he needed focus, not a distraction. Besides, I wasn't entirely sure I could make my limbs move. I felt half frozen already.

Was that the curse, or my fear?

Kyrundar's wide eyes locked with mine. Then a look of steely resolve overcame his countenance. He nodded once. "I won't let you down. Iskyr, give me strength."

Rouven nodded. "Iskyr strengthen and guide our magic and our skill and protect our patient." He motioned toward the bed. "Zidra, please lie down. This is going to be painful. You may get lightheaded, so I'd prefer you didn't fall. Actually…" He stomped back to the door and threw it open. "You—whatever your name was, with the muscles. It's going to be crowded, but I need you in here."

The ice elf returned, and Sajen ducked through the door, the tight space emphasizing his bulk. "What do you need me for, exactly?"

"Get on the bed on Zidra's other side and be ready to hold her down if she starts thrashing."

Blood drained from my face at the same time as Kyrundar went pale as snow.

"Is that likely to happen?" he asked, his voice strained.

"How should I know? I've never operated on her before, and no one has ever tried this."

Sajen raised his brows and glanced between the physician and me as if questioning whether this was a good idea.

That made two of us.

Three of us, judging by the look on Kyrundar's face.

But we didn't have another choice. Either I died here, or I died when the curse overpowered Kyrundar's magic. Or when the ice magic in my flesh killed my arm.

I lay down near the edge of the bed. Sajen climbed up and sat between me and the wall, while Rouven and Kyrundar stood over me. Rouven fussed over Kyrundar's hand placement, physically repositioning Kyrundar's hands on either side of my wound until at last he was satisfied. His own hands hovered over the puncture, glowing slightly blue, but I didn't feel anything yet.

"Strengthen the barrier," Rouven said, calm and low. "Can you draw it in slightly tighter?"

I winced at the chilly prickling and pulling sensation in my arm.

"Good. More power…good. Hold that. Add more power if needed to keep it that size. That exact size, understand? Good. I'm starting now."

Rouven placed his left hand atop his right and pressed his right palm to my arm between and overlapping Kyrundar's hands. Burning cold stabbed at my arm.

I screamed.

TWENTY-SIX

KYRUNDAR

"Hold it steady!" Rouven shouted above Zidra's horrifying scream.

She jerked, and I had to press down harder on her arm to keep my hands in position. Gritting my teeth, I tried to ignore the pain prickling from my hands up my arms into my whole body—the sensation of malicious ice crystals skittering through my veins. That wasn't what was happening, but fighting against the ice curse as it tried to escape Rouven's and my magic felt like that. I couldn't imagine how Zidra felt.

Her arm moved as if she were trying to tug free, and she screamed again, the sound echoing in the small cabin and leaving my ears ringing. Sajen slammed his forearm across Zidra's shoulders and grabbed her left wrist, stopping her from reaching over to grab at her arm. Or perhaps to pry Rouven's and my hands away.

I squeezed my eyes closed, unable to watch her twisted expression. Losing focus wouldn't help her. *Hold it steady. Iskyr!*

Hold. Help! Steady. Iskyr. Iskyr, please—hold!

My thoughts devolved into incoherent pleas as hot tears slipped past my eyelids. The ice curse raged against Rouven's efforts, and I sent more power into restraining it. Was my barrier keeping enough of the cold away from Zidra's flesh? Was I doing enough? Sweat trickled down my temple, and my knees trembled with the intensity of the power flowing through me while my arms burned from the exertion of keeping Zidra's arm still.

A strange sound undercut Zidra's cries, and it took me a moment to realize it was Rouven, whimpering with pain. His hands trembled between mine.

Then Sajen's voice added to the chaos, but his words were low and calm. "May Iskyr the creator hold you, may Iskyr the guardian heal you, may Iskyr the comforter give you strength." He repeated the words, reciting the benediction over and over at a soothing pace.

I let the cadence of Sajen's prayer run through me like cooling water. My breathing stabilized, and my exhaustion eased. Zidra's screams lessened to groans, and Rouven's hands steadied. I redoubled my efforts and confirmed that neither Rouven's magic nor the curse had escaped my containment.

We can do this. Thank Iskyr, we can do this!

A strange tugging sensation came from Zidra's wound.

It felt like a sudden sinkhole, something and then nothing. Or like the tide rushing out, dragging everything on the beach out to sea. I clenched my teeth and strained to keep my magic from collapsing in on itself.

The magic churned, tumultuous, then stilled. I could no longer detect the malevolent, biting cold of the curse. Then Rouven's hands drew back, and the sensation of his magic vanished.

"Kyrundar," Rouven said hoarsely. He cleared his throat. "You may slowly and carefully withdraw your magic from Zidra. Be sure you leave none of it behind, for her safety. You saved her life, but people aren't meant to have ice magic of any kind embedded in their skin."

I opened my eyes to find Zidra gazing up at me. A shaky smile curved her lips. A broken half-laugh, half-sob wrenched from my chest. She was going to be all right.

"Almost done," I promised. "Just have to get this last bit of magic out."

"Well, then I do need to cut away the necrosis and stitch you up," Rouven said.

Zidra winced. "At least that won't hurt as badly."

"Does that mean I can go?" Sajen ran a hand through his hair, not quite hiding his trembling. "I need some fresh air."

"You can go," Zidra confirmed. "Thank you. I'm sorry for punching you."

Sajen rubbed his chest. "Yes, remember that you escaped my grip and bruised my chest bone the next time you doubt whether you're strong in your di'ora."

She chuckled, although I felt her quiver.

After I removed my barrier, I sent my magic carefully over Zidra's body, checking that I'd left nothing behind. Satisfied, I drew my power back into myself and released her arm. The door creaked and clicked closed as Sajen made his escape.

Zidra started to sit up, but Rouven held out his hand.

"No, stay like that. This may make you woozy. Kyrundar, bring that chair from my desk over here. This old man needs to sit."

While I did as asked, I subtly sought out the heartbond. It was still there.

Bent over the chair with my back to Zidra, I allowed myself a grin. But I smoothed my expression before turning around and left the heartbond alone. I'd wait for Zidra to react to its continued existence before I said anything.

Rouven started by using his magic to lightly chill Zidra's skin, just to dull the pain. I tried to watch, but the moment the scalpel cut into the skin outside the ring of blackened flesh, I spun away. Zidra whimpered. My stomach lurched, and the cabin tilted around me worse than the ship had at sea.

Rouven sniggered. "Warriors always think they can handle surgery. But it isn't the same as blood in the heat of battle, especially when the patient is someone you care for."

After what felt like an eternity of listening to Rouven's reassuring murmurs and Zidra's muffled cries, Rouven declared he was done. I turned around to find the physician wrapping a clean bandage around Zidra's arm and giving her instructions for wound care, including reiterating his strong recommendation to find a fleshmage.

The moment she sat up, I rushed to her side. "How do you feel?"

"Like I almost died." Her weak laugh only added to the twisting in my stomach. "But I didn't. Thanks to you." Her soft, breathy tone toyed with my heart, as did the way she watched me, her golden-brown eyes smoldering like coals. But then she abruptly looked to Rouven, who had moved to his desk and was washing his hands. "And thanks to you, of course. Truly, I am inexpressibly grateful."

"Thank Iskyr. I wasn't even certain that would work." Rouven dried his hands and turned toward us. "How did that happen, anyway? Is the responsible ice elf dead?"

"I believe so," I said. "The ice elf who struck her is dead, although I can't be certain he crafted the curse."

"Good. Most likely he did. They're difficult to keep stable and respond best to the same magic that created them." He sank into the armchair in the middle of the room. "But why would anyone create such a curse and then use it on a rengir?"

"Actually..." Zidra took a deep breath. "We were hoping you might have an idea. Have you ever heard of a league that believes the rengiri are corrupt? And that might want you dead?"

Color drained from Rouven's cheeks, and he went still as a frozen lake. Then he shoved to his feet and pointed at the door. "Out. Get out! I let my magical defenses down to let you in, and that healing was exhausting! If they've followed you—"

"Who is *they*?" I crossed my arms. "Why do you think they'd follow us?"

"I didn't move out here for pleasure. I'm hiding! I knew I'd be found eventually, though," he muttered. "But if they're hunting you, you might have brought them to my door when I'm unprepared—"

"Then we'll help you!" Zidra buckled on her pauldron. "But who *are* they? What do they want? If you can tell us anything to identify them—"

"Ha!" Rouven shook his head. "Anyone who can identify them, who knows too much, who gets too close and doesn't join them, ends up dead or missing or both. If they're targeting you, they must think you know too much."

"What if a lot of people know too much?" she pressed. "I know they consider themselves a league and have some kind of religious motivation, as they call their leader an archon, but they don't honor Iskyr. I know they have assassins, including a night elf. I know they're stationed in Laedresh. And I know they have ties to the murder of a magistrate, and that my investigation into his death started all of this. And everything I know, Kyrundar and Sajen know, and as soon as my letters get to her, Archon Aekyrdra will also know, and then the entire Order of the Rengir and the imperial palace will know."

Rouven studied her for a moment. "Clever. If they start taking out that many people, they'll only confirm their existence and draw more attention, which is the last thing they want." He worked his jaw, then sat back down, far stiffer than before. "What do you want to know?'"

"Anything you do," Zidra said.

She sat back down on the edge of the bed. I almost sat next to her, but not wanting to push her, I chose the wood chair next to the bed instead.

"It started a few years ago, with a human stonemage who came into Merael's seeking treatment for a wound. She tried to claim it was a run-in with a wolf, but the claw marks were too big. Had to be a wolvus. Finally she admitted it was a 'training exercise,' but she wouldn't say training for what or where. I looked into her, and she wasn't a student at Harcos or a rengir or a member of the city or imperial guard. But she didn't seem frightened and said she was safe, so I didn't report it to the guard."

Rouven sighed and slumped a little. "I should have. My silence told them I was trustworthy. I started getting more patients with strange wounds and no clear accounting of how they got them, and not just at Merael's, but at my home. Shifters, elves, humans. Then a man came to see me. A human firemage. He said the Ascendant League had deemed me worthy. He wanted to recruit me to their cause."

"Their cause?" I asked.

"He was vague, but I got the impression he believes that the Order of the Rengir are hoarding some secret source of power that is related to Ascadrion the Earth-Shaker. I suspect they want to bring Ascadrion back, but I didn't ask. I said I wasn't interested. He didn't like that," Rouven said darkly.

"He said he was the archon of the Laedresh conclave,

and that the 'sovereign' of the League would be disappointed. He implied that they have bases all over the continent and that one day they will take control of the empire, and he said I should join them while I had the chance to do so willingly. I said I'd think about it, just to get him out of my office. I thought he was insane."

"They started threatening you?" Zidra guessed.

The physician nodded, his expression sagging into deeper wrinkles. "I started finding notes implying I was being watched and claiming that bad things would happen to me and my wife if I said anything about the League."

"You're married?" Zidra gasped.

"Indeed, although it doesn't feel like it when I haven't seen her in over eight months." Rouven's sigh was mournful. "I sent my wife away to be with her family in southern Glacori. The 'archon' of the Laedresh conclave visited me and told me he'd asked the archon of another conclave to keep an eye on her."

My fingers tensed, digging into my thigh as I imagined the fear and fury Rouven must have felt.

"So I asked an acquaintance to secretly send word to my wife, telling her to change her name and move to a secret location. I hoped the league only wanted me for my power as the head of Merael's, so I retired. That didn't stop them, and they were angry they had lost track of Winni. They made it quite clear that I knew too much to walk away." He stared out the window. "So I came here. Far away from my Winni, and far from any major towns where the Ascendant League might have conclaves."

Silence fell over the cabin, heavy and uncomfortable.

"Do you have names?" Zidra asked quietly. "Descriptions?"

Rouven scowled. "And make myself more of a target? They're difficult to hide from. Even if you can take down one of their conclaves, there's all the others to worry about."

"If we can take them alive—"

"They're fanatics," he scoffed. "They aren't rational. I doubt they'd give up any information they might have. Besides, that large of a society doesn't stay a secret unless they keep secrets from their own members."

That made sense, but we couldn't pretend this Ascendant League wasn't a threat, no matter how ridiculously grandiose their name was.

"Telling you would only put me and my family in more danger." Rouven shook his head. "I'm—" He cut off with a gasp, and his head snapped toward the door. "They've found us."

The door slammed inward and crashed against the wall. Breathless, Sajen stuck his head inside. "Three people approaching! Human, shifter, and an elf, and they don't look friendly."

TWENTY-SEVEN

ZIDRA

No. No, they couldn't have found us—not yet. Not before I'd had a chance to tell Kyrundar I'd been wrong. Over the last few days, the heartbond and Kyrundar had become a part of me in a way I never would have imagined. A part of me I didn't want to lose.

I wanted to keep the heartbond, to keep Kyrundar.

But now wasn't the moment to tell him.

Sajen had already left, the door swinging shut behind him. Kyrundar and Rouven jumped to their feet, but Kyrundar turned to me, his eyes worried.

"Are you—"

"I can fight." I stood and squared my shoulders. For the first time in over a week, I stoked my dragon fire. Claws erupted in place of my fingernails, scales formed on my neck and jaw and horns grew from my scalp. My fangs became more pronounced, and my eyes shifted to slitted red dragon eyes, sharpening my vision.

Kyrundar's eyebrows raised. "You are terrifying and beautiful, and is it bizarre that I am so attracted to you right now?"

My last fear, that maybe he wouldn't want me now that I didn't need him, was banished.

"A little," I said, even though I couldn't help a teasing grin.

Rouven made a gagging noise. "Enemies approaching, rengiri. Save it for when you're in your own room."

I shared a smirk with Kyrundar, but then Sajen's shout of "They're landing" wiped the mirth from our faces.

"Maybe you should hide those features, though," Kyrundar said. "Let the fact you can shift again be a surprise."

With a sigh, I nodded and shifted away the wyvern traits. My ice elf strode toward the front door, and I hurried after him.

"We'll handle this," I told Rouven as I passed him. "Just stay—"

"Not on your Order insignia, girl."

"Do you know how to fight?" I asked tentatively.

Rouven harrumphed. "Of course I do. And I'm tired of hiding. They want to end this, let's end it."

"We aren't responsible for—" Kyrundar started, but the older ice elf waved dismissively.

"Kyrmaris!" Sajen roared. "Get out here!"

I lifted an eyebrow, but the moniker didn't bother me

the way it used to. We raced outside, Rouven on our heels.

Sajen, in his gryphon di'yar, paced along the pebbly beach in front of the cabin. Several paces away, another, larger gryphoni landed, and two figures slid off its back.

One was a human man wearing light-gray robes that made his fair skin look colorless beneath his sandy-blond hair. He carried a staff and looked over our group with haughty indifference.

But the other man captured my attention. Dressed in a close-fitting tunic and loose trousers, fingerless gloves, and tall boots, all in dark blue, and with two long daggers strapped to his hips, he appeared the quintessential picture of an assassin. He was tall and slender, with pale-gray skin, silver eyes, and silvery hair braided back from his face to reveal the long points of his ears.

Night elf.

"Come to try again after your last failure?" I gripped the hilt of my sword.

Truthfully, assassins had no honor, and Sajen and the other gryphoni had already shifted. I had no obligation to meet these men in battle in my di'ora. But it still felt wrong to do otherwise. I would do the honorable thing and face them in my true form before I unleashed my di'yar.

"Thank you for leading us to Rouven," the human said with a lifeless smile. "I didn't like having someone who knew my face and name but refused to join our glorious endeavor running loose in the world."

"Go to the void, Dandrio Kane." Rouven sniffed, as if even speaking to the man were below him.

"That's *Archon* Kane to you."

"To me?" Rouven sputtered. "I'm no member of your infernal League, and you're an affront to Iskyr. You're not an archon any more than I'm a monk."

"Enough of this." Kane raised his hands, and globes of fire burst into existence above his palms. "Time for all of you to die."

Metal scraped against hard leather as the night elf drew his long daggers and Kyrundar drew his twin swords. The shadows cast by the cliff above Rouven's cottage grew, expanding and darkening as if reaching out to swallow us. I drew my own sword and slid my feet into a ready position.

With an earsplitting cry, the enemy shifter lunged. Sajen released an eagle screech and bounded forward. Standing on their back legs with their massive wings spread wide, the two gryphoni crashed into each other.

Kane threw a fireball at my head. I dodged, and the ball of flame crashed into the pebbled beach. Kyrundar was already moving forward to attack the night elf, who had wrapped himself in shadows that would make him harder to strike. Leaving my companions to their matches, I yelled a battle cry and rushed Kane.

A barrage of sharp icicles flew around me and hurtled toward Kane. I missed my next step as I glanced over my shoulder. But it wasn't Kyrundar—it was Rouven, who had an expression on his face that made him look like a being of wrath incarnate.

Streams of fire melted the icicles before they reached Kane, but I darted around the flames and swung my sword.

Kane cursed and leaped back. The tip of my sword scored a line in his gray robes but didn't go deep enough to draw blood. I snarled and vowed that my next strike would not miss.

But as Rouven started up a barrage of ice from the right, Kane raised an impenetrable wall of flame around himself. I paced, watching for a weakness. Such use of magic would be exhausting; he wouldn't be able to keep it up for long.

I looked toward the rest of the battle. Both Sajen and the other gryphoni had taken to the air, cartwheeling as they clawed and slashed at each other. I spied blood on both, but it was unclear who was actually wounded in the frantic chaos of feathers and fur. Threads of glowing blue ice magic tangled with vines of darkness in the shadows beneath the cliff next to the cabin, the only indication of where Kyrundar and the night elf fought.

I began to sweat from the heat of Kane's cyclone of fire. Even Rouven's astonishing barrage of ice and snow wasn't making it through.

I had done the honorable thing and engaged a non-shifter foe in my di'ora. I owed them nothing more. I moved to a position where I had sufficient room.

The time for holding back was past.

"Rouven!" I shouted over the screeches of the gryphoni and the low roar of Kane's magecraft fire. "Hold a moment!"

The old ice elf curled his upper lip, but he lowered his hands, and his relentless stream of ice magic ceased.

A moment later, Kane dropped his wall of fire. He sneered. "Ready to give up already, rengir?"

"Ready to end this."

Kane laughed. "And if you wouldn't die the moment you shifted, I might believe you."

I smiled darkly. "Why do you think we needed Rouven?"

The false archon's cocky expression faltered. "No one has ever survived being struck by an ice curse. Even Rouven couldn't remove it."

"Not by himself, no. But once again, you've underestimated Kyrmaris. You won't again."

My neck grew, my horns and tail sprouted, my thumbs elongated into thick, sharp claws, and my body expanded as my arms and fingers transformed to massive claw-tipped wings. Within moments, the transformation was complete. I rested the bend of my wings on the ground and looked down on Kane's slack face from my fifteen-foot height. Then I stretched my head forward until my mouth full of long, razor-sharp teeth was scarcely more than a foot from his face and released a bellowing, screeching roar that reverberated in my throat and made the ground vibrate beneath my feet.

Above us, Sajen and the enemy gryphoni disengaged and turned toward me. The shadows and ice thinned, and I caught a glimpse of Kyrundar and the night elf gaping at me.

Kane scrambled backward. Between his hands, he conjured a fireball the size of his torso. With a yell, he threw the white-hot ball of flame. I closed my maw and turned my head. The fireball exploded against the side of my scaly face, and I didn't feel a thing.

My laugh sounded like a low, hiccuping growl.

After over a week of being caged, my dragon fire burned with vengeful, animalistic intensity. My wyvern nature prodded me to eat Kane, but I would regret such an inhuman action later.

"Phasta!" Kane shrieked.

The gryphoni dove toward Kane. Sajen started to follow, but as I raised my head and opened my mouth, he wheeled aside and out of my way.

I breathed out a jet of fire that made Kane's human magecraft fire look like a child's firecracker. Flames enveloped the gryphon. The rumble of my dragon fire mostly drowned out the gryphoni's screams. I tracked the shifter's fall until my fire breath gave out. The charred remains of the gryphoni crashed to the ground, lifeless.

While Kane stared in horror at the remains of his soldier, an icicle a handsbreadth in diameter speared through his chest. Rouven lowered his outstretched hand and watched as Kane dropped to his knees and then fell flat on his face. The icicle turned to a whirl of tiny snowflakes and vanished, leaving Kane's still form bleeding out on the stones.

"Zidra!" Kyrundar's shout sent my heart racing.

When I looked over, he was standing beside the cabin alone, bleeding from a few shallow cuts, including one on his cheek, but he appeared to be all right. He pointed up toward the oddly dark shadows covering the entirety of the cliff face.

"I can't see the night elf, and he's fleeing!"

Even with my wyvern eyes, I couldn't penetrate the unnaturally dark and solid shadows churning on the rocky cliff. I spread my wings and took to the air, stirring up little clouds of dust along the beach. Rouven raised his arm to shield his eyes and hunched against the wind.

I unleashed a wyvern screech and moved closer to the cliff. As expected, the loud, high-pitched sound made the night elf flinch. His shadows wavered, and I focused on a darker spot near where the walls of the inlet met and where bits of loose pebbles rained down from the elf's ascent. A deep breath through my nostrils confirmed the night elf's location.

I beat my wings to rise higher, then swung my legs forward and reached with claws as long as a human's forearm into the darkness. The wind generated by my wings dispelled some of the shadows like mist. Solid shadows tried to fight my feet, but between the strength of my muscular, scale-covered legs and the elf's split focus as he tried to cling to the rock wall and fend off my attack, I pushed through. The pungent scent of terror filled my nostrils, and then my right foot found his body. My talons wrapped around the night elf, and I pulled him, screaming, from the cliff.

The corner of the inlet was too tight for me to turn around in, so I flew upward and circled around before I dropped the struggling elf onto the beach. Cushioned by his magic, he landed on the white stones without injury and stumbled to his feet—but too late.

Kyrundar threw a barrage of icicles that tore through the night elf. The writhing shadows vanished, and he sprawled across the ground, never to rise or assassinate another person again.

With a triumphant bellow, I flew a little ways down the beach, safely away from Rouven, Kyrundar, and Sajen, who had shifted back to his di'ora. It felt so good to be back in my wyvern di'yar, I was tempted to do a few laps around the inlet to properly stretch my wings, but there would be plenty of time for that later.

I landed in a spray of white gravel. The moment I finished shifting, I ran to meet Kyrundar.

Twenty-Eight

Kyrundar

As Zidra landed, I broke into a run. I raced past Sajen, Rouven, and the corpses without a glance, although I held my breath for a moment as I passed the smoldering remains of the gryphon shifter. Zidra shrank from a towering creature of heart-stopping awe down to her usual beautiful self with tan skin and a gorgeous halo of frizzy brown curls.

Remembering her reticence to kiss me, I started to slow. But the moment Zidra finished shifting, she sprinted toward me. My soaring emotions lent speed to my legs, and I wished the skittering pebbles weren't slowing my progress.

We collided, our arms going around each other, and she squeezed me just as tightly as I embraced her.

"Zee—"

"Wait!" She pulled back a little, although she didn't

release me, and tilted her face to meet my gaze. Her eyes glistened with unshed tears, but a wide smile made her face nearly glow. "I was wrong, and I've been foolish and ridiculous and rude, and I don't know why you've put up with me for so long, but I want you, Kyrundar Ilifir. I want this heartbond and I want the stupid Kyrmaris moniker and I want to know you'll be with me on my next mission and every mission after that. And I want to kiss you. Iskyr above, I want to kiss you, and I'm done pretending I don't."

That was an invitation if ever I'd heard one, but I couldn't act on it just yet. Still, it took me a few moments to stop staring at her with a boyish grin.

"I want all of that, too," I murmured. "But first, I need your answers to two questions."

Her honey-brown eyes danced with a wildness that made me want to release the dam of my resolve and kiss her until I couldn't think straight. She nodded. I licked my lips, nearly crumbling when her eyes tracked the movement.

"Zee, do you love me?"

She jolted in my arms and blinked. "Did I not actually say that in my speech?"

I shook my head.

"I love you," she said, her voice quiet and warm and slightly rough. "I've been blind not to have seen how much I love you."

I drew her closer and dropped my forehead down to hers. "Zidra Eilmaris," I murmured as my eyes drifted shut. "Will you marry me?"

Her arms tightened around me. "Yes."

My heart danced in my chest, and if I hadn't been holding her, I might have jumped up and whooped in a decidedly un-elvish way.

I loved Zidra, and she loved me. Nothing had ever felt more right.

Then her lips were on mine, and all rational thought fled. I moved a hand up to cradle the back of her head. My fingers tangled in her curls. I couldn't draw her close enough. Her fingertips traced up and down my back, sending pleasant shivers down my spine.

Suddenly the realization that we were standing on Rouven's beach in full view of both Rouven and Sajen broke through, and I eased away, reluctantly breaking our kiss. She started to pull me back in, but I moved my hands to rest on her hips so I could hold her at arm's length.

"We have an audience," I whispered, my amusement barely contained.

She leaned to the side to peer around me. Her eyes widened, and a blush spread over her cheeks.

I released her and took her hand instead, and we walked back to the others. Sajen grinned, a sparkle in his eyes that said he was barely restraining himself from teasing us. He held one arm against his torso, and dark blood stained his sleeves.

"Sajen," I exclaimed. "Are you all right?"

He waved his other hand. "A bit scratched and bruised, but fine. Rouven already agreed to stitch up the worst of it."

For his part, Rouven looked thoroughly grumpy, the old goat.

Zidra surveyed the bodies and winced. "We made a mess of your beach. I'm sorry."

Rouven shook his head. "This is probably for the best. With their archon and best warrior dead, the Laedresh conclave will be in disarray and have to retreat into the shadows to lick their wounds."

"Best warrior?" I asked.

"Perhaps best assassin would be more accurate," he said. "Kane had boasted about the night elf, called him their prized weapon and the envy of several other conclaves. The League as a whole will probably feel the sting of this defeat, but the loss will also make them angry. Their Sovereign will be most displeased."

"I'm sorry to make things harder on you—" Zidra started, but Rouven held up his hand.

"Actually, this will likely help. I can't identify their archon anymore, so I'm not as big of a threat." He looked around the inlet. "And this hiding place is discovered, anyway. I think I'll find my wife. We'll do what she always wanted and make our way together."

Zidra lightly squeezed my hand, and I returned the gesture. Now that I had her, I wouldn't ever choose to part with her.

Rouven sighed. "Now I have to wait for the next ship to come by."

"Only if you want to take your things," Zidra said.

"Are you...offering to carry me?" Rouven's jaw went slack.

"Only if you're comfortable with that."

Sajen and I both gaped at her. Shifters rarely allowed someone to ride them, but wyveri never did.

"What happened to 'no one rides on my back'?" I demanded.

"I owe you my life," she said to Rouven, ignoring me. "This is the least I can do."

"There's nothing here I'm overly attached to. Let me stitch up your friend and grab a pack with some clothing and my coin, and then we can depart for Gamnica." Rouven hurried inside.

Sajen started to follow but then paused in the doorway. His mouth twitched as he fought a grin. "You two worked things out, then?"

Zidra leaned against my shoulder. "We're getting married."

An idea occurred to me. As members of a holy order, all rengiri could officiate weddings. "Would you do the honors in Gamnica?"

Sajen snorted. "Absolutely not."

My mouth fell open. "What?" I demanded at the same time as Zidra sputtered, "Why ever not?"

"I'm not letting Kyrmaris have a secret wedding in travel-worn clothing in a random sanctuary in Gamnica. You're getting married in a proper ceremony in Vairdros Cathedral with a crowd, as is right for the only co-recipients of the Emperor's Merit and the darling couple of the empire."

Zidra and I looked at each other, the indecision I felt mirrored on her face.

"I would like to see you in a wedding dress…"

"Don't say you can't afford one," Sajen interrupted. "Announce you're getting married, and the dressmakers in Laedresh will be climbing over each other to have the privilege of making your dress. Let them keep it for display afterward, and I'm sure they won't charge."

"Are you coming, rengir?" Rouven shouted grouchily.

Sajen rolled his eyes and entered the cabin.

"The idea of you not keeping your wedding gown makes me sad," I said.

Zidra shrugged. "It's not as if I can carry it around on missions, so I wouldn't be able to keep it, anyway."

"Then are we doing this? Getting married in a crowd, with everyone staring?" I couldn't imagine that sounded appealing to her, even though it did to me.

She bit her lower lip as she thought it over. "We'll hear so much complaining if we don't."

I laughed. "Agreed." I could already think of several rengiri, friends, and family members who would never let me hear the end of it—Sylathria included.

She kicked the pebbles, her gaze fixed on her boots. When she spoke, her voice was tight and scarcely audible. "My family won't come."

I squeezed her hand. "You want to marry me, right? There's no moral or ethical reason we shouldn't get married?"

"Of course not!" She frowned up at me. "I did very much mean it when I said yes."

That pulled a crooked smile from me despite the serious point I wanted to make. "We'll be wed before Iskyr and the people who believe in us, like Sajen. You have nothing to be ashamed of. If your family won't honor what Iskyr himself has blessed, that is their wrong choice to make. Their opinions or approval don't change the reality that you are a great rengir, an Emperor's Merit recipient, and the woman I love with every beat of my heart."

Zidra nodded, and I felt her painful sense of insecurity and shame ease into calm. The heartbreak didn't fully fade, but a quiet acceptance filtered through the heartbond—along with a deep love and fiery longing that set my heart racing.

She swayed closer. "After our big public wedding, we have to go to a remote location for our honeymoon and tell no one where we're going."

"Deal." I bent down and kissed her but had to end the delightful experience far too early when Sajen emerged from the cabin.

Zidra placed a light peck on my cheek, then withdrew to shift.

Sajen rolled his shoulders. "Well, I suppose I had best carry you, or you'll never keep up with Zidra."

"Are you in good enough shape to shift?"

"Oh, certainly. In fact, the magic involved in shifting will help me heal faster."

I wrinkled my nose. "Seems a little unfair, though. I should go with my betrothed. You can carry Rouven."

"Ha!" Rouven burst out of the cabin with a massive bag he could barely lift and slammed the door behind him.

"This is my one chance to ride a wyvern, and I am *not* passing on that."

Sajen slapped my back. "I think you'll have future opportunities for Zee to carry you. And it's still an honor to be carried by me, you know."

"Yeah, sure."

We parted ways with Rouven in Gamnica, then returned to Lighthouse Haven for much needed rest and baths. The next morning, we finally had time to wash our clothing. While everything was drying in the sunshine, Sajen bought food for our journey. Zidra and I took the opportunity to sit in the garden and care for our weapons.

"How are we traveling back to Laedresh?" I asked while oiling my swords.

Zidra looked up from running a sharpening stone down the edge of her blade. "I suppose I'll carry you. Wyveri have more stamina than gryphoni over long distances."

I narrowed my eyes. "On your back...right? Not in your claws?"

She shrugged and returned to sharpening her sword.

"Zee. On your back, right?"

Even with her head bowed, she couldn't hide her growing smile. I plucked a withered blue flower and tossed it at her, and it bounced off her shoulder.

Zidra laughed. "Of course, Kyr. I'm not going to let my fiancé dangle from my claws all the way to Laedresh."

Once we were outside the city, though, I discovered mounting and riding a wyvern was tricky. Her scales were slicker and the space between the ridges on her back narrower than I'd realized. She bobbed up and down during flight more than Sajen did. Truthfully, riding a wyvern wasn't as glorious as I'd imagined, but it was thrilling and fast.

When we arrived in Laedresh, we visited Archon Aekyrdra first. She had already notified the Council of Archons and the imperial advisers, who had dispatched an imperial investigator to Rupich to investigate Nevros and Malvoy. She promised to pass on our new information and send a notice about the Ascendant League to every Haven in the empire.

Then we told her about our engagement. I'd never seen an archon look giddy before.

"I'll notify the town criers, and obviously we'll send word to the Havens," Aekyrdra said in a rush.

"Oh, that's really not necessary." Zidra curled down in her armchair, looking like she hoped the furniture would eat her alive.

"Of course it is! Kyrmaris is getting married!" Aekyrdra's smile made her light-bronze skin nearly glow. In fact, her green eyes shimmered with forest elf magic. "Three weeks out should give guests time to travel. I'll officiate, naturally—"

"Actually," I interjected with an uncomfortable chuckle, "we asked Sajen to officiate."

Her eyes dimmed. "But you'll be getting married at Vairdros, and that cathedral is under my authority. I do of course understand if you want your friend to do it…"

Zidra adjusted in her seat. "I would also love if you

officiated, but I don't want to insult Sajen. Perhaps you could talk to him?"

With that settled, we retired to Riverfront Haven—at my insistence, as I preferred its relative seclusion, although Zidra caved quickly.

Tailors, seamstresses, restaurant owners, and decorators lined up as soon as the announcement was made. We opted for small donations from many vendors and promised we would post a sign listing their donations. Of course, we also suggested that we hoped our wedding would help the businesses secure more clients in order that their generosity could continue in the future toward others as well.

Two days before the wedding, the capital was crowded with a swell of visiting citizens and rengiri. It was so difficult to avoid well-wishers that we had to sneak out well after nightfall to pick up Zidra's gown and my wedding tunic without getting mobbed.

"The novelty will wear off," I promised Zidra as we walked back to the Haven in the dark, deserted streets. "At the very least, in a decade, some other rengir will be awarded the Merit, and we won't seem as special."

She wrinkled her nose. It was adorable. "Unless the next recipient is another couple, I'm not sure we'll ever be not-special."

"Good." I draped the linen bag containing my wedding attire over my left arm so I could loop my right around Zidra's waist and draw her against my side. "Because you're incredibly special, and I'd hate for you to ever forget it."

She huffed a laugh. "You're ridiculous."

"Ridiculously in love."

She opened her mouth to respond, but as we turned a corner, the streetlamp ahead of us snuffed out. A figure in a hooded cloak stepped out of the shadows, and then several more hooded people emerged from between buildings.

Zidra and I stepped apart. She drew her sword, and I drew one of mine, our bags of wedding clothing still clutched in our other hands. At least the cobblestone street was dry. If we did have to fight, our clothing might survive.

"Our archon and two of our strongest brothers go to kill you," the first figure said in a low voice. He sounded masculine, but the hood hid his face. "You return and announce a wedding, yet our archon and warriors have not returned."

"They're dead," I said flatly. "Want to join them?"

The apparent leader made a low sound of anger. "You—"

"We," Zidra interrupted, "are Kyrmaris. The greatest rengiri to ever live. And we are going to find you. Not just those of you here, but every member of the Ascendant League, from the lowest recruit up to your precious Sovereign. We will hunt you all down and stop you if it takes the rest of our lives. You have tried and failed four times to kill us. We will not let that go. By now, every rengir in the empire knows of the Ascendant League, as does the archon of every true religious order. We are all hunting you. The League will fall, of that you can be certain."

The other figures squirmed, and some drew back a few steps.

"Misguided pride." The leader's sneer sounded in his tone. "You won't find us. We'll retreat into the shadows, fade so far into the background that everyone will think you fabricated the League's existence. We have been patient. We can continue to wait for the right time to strike. If that isn't within my lifetime, so be it. But the League will rise. We will conquer. Of *that* you can be certain, Kyrmaris." He said the nickname with disgust. "Farewell, rengiri." He spat and then retreated into the space between the houses.

The others scattered in every direction.

"Do we go after any of them?" Zidra asked, but she made no movement to pursue or shift—although shifting in the narrow street would have been unwise. "These buildings are full of working-class families. I smelled shifters, elves, and humans among the League members, but I can't say what magics they have. A firemage could be disastrous, but any fight among these old wooden buildings would endanger children."

"Not to mention rengiri attacking people within the capital would prompt complaints and possibly an Order inquest." I reluctantly sheathed my sword. "Besides, I don't want to risk ruining your gown before I see you in it."

Zidra laughed and slid her sword back into its scabbard. "Then let's go. The sooner we can sleep, the sooner it's tomorrow. And then we'll have to sleep only one more time before our wedding."

I sheathed my sword, pulled her in close again, and kissed her forehead. "I can't wait."

TWENTY-NINE

ZIDRA

Wedding guests filled every seat, prayer alcove, and side chapel in Vairdros Cathedral and spilled out into the street, according to the matronly priestess attending me. I stood in the back of the cathedral, hidden behind tall wood-paneled screens. Although the makeshift room had been convenient for getting ready and staying out of sight until the proper time, I had spent the last two hours listening to the gathering crowd. The screens had begun to feel like a trap, and the noise and scents were approaching overwhelming.

I didn't know most of the people in attendance—everyone from commoners to rengiri to archons to nobles and officials. The priestess thought Emperor Valesiart himself was watching from a secure, hidden side chapel, but I refused to think about it. Also in attendance were

Sylathria and Kyrundar's parents and siblings and several of his extended family members, all of whom I had met over the last week in a blur of names I'd already forgotten.

My nephew Zarik was somewhere as well, which was bittersweet. He'd accepted my invitation to talk, and our conversation had been good, if awkward. I hoped I'd convinced him to avoid some of the mistakes I'd made, to reject the lies wyveri culture had instilled in us. Still, I respected that he wanted to keep our family ties a secret. Competitive Harcos students could be judgmental, and Zarik was young and both proud and self-conscious. It was enough to know that he was not ashamed of me and was excited to attend the wedding.

Still, Zarik's presence highlighted the painful absence of my parents and siblings. Releasing my desire for their support and feeling confident in Iskyr's approval was proving to be a slow process, but I was getting there.

I closed my eyes and reached for the heartbond. Bubbling joy and anticipation tumbled from Kyrundar, alongside the steady reassurance he had been sending me unceasingly since we separated this morning. My impatience to wed him grew.

Soon. Any moment now.

I turned to the tall mirror standing in the corner and checked my reflection one last time. My white gown had gauzy sleeves that flowed down past my hands and fluttered lightly as I walked. Silver beads arranged in the shape of flower blossoms trimmed the heart-shaped neckline, and delicate chains and silver rings formed a belt at the bottom of the lace-covered bodice. A large teardrop-shaped pale-blue gemstone that matched Kyrundar's earrings hung from the V-shaped point of the belt. The same gauzy fabric as the sleeves overlay the skirt. My curls were pinned back with silver pins tipped with pearls, and crushed mica dusted my cheeks, giving them a sparkling shimmer. I felt beautiful, and I couldn't wait to see Kyrundar.

Finally, the choir started to sing. Taking one more steadying breath, I nodded to the priestess. She smiled and moved one of the screens aside. I stepped out into the center aisle.

Blue and red ribbons and flowers adorned the ends of the packed pews and wound around the towering columns. Matching petals were scattered over the stone floor between me and the altar. Blue for Kyrundar's ice magic, red for my dragon fire.

As I drew nearer to the front of the cathedral, the choir mostly covered the crowd's murmurs. The joyful atmosphere filled the air with palpable energy. The scents of all of those people and flowers and the incense rising from the altar mixed together. Even with the center aisle cleared and no one touching me, the press of so many people and all of the overwhelming sensations made me want to freeze or flee. As I walked the length of the nave toward where Aekyrdra and Kyrundar waited in front of the altar, my heart pounded, and a headache built behind my forehead.

But then I met Kyrundar's gaze. His ice-blue eyes, glistening with tears of joy, captured mine. Breathtaking desire rushed through the heartbond. My own eyes watered, and a smile stretched my cheeks. I struggled to walk in time with the choir's serene song. As long as I kept my eyes on Kyrundar, though, I could do this.

I barely heard Aekyrdra's short speech as I focused on Kyrundar—his hands clasped in mine, the smile on his face, his joy in the heartbond.

Somehow, I made it through reciting my vows without either breaking down in tears or becoming tongue-tied due to so many eyes watching me.

At last, Aekyrdra said the words I had been waiting for.

"In the sight of Iskyr and all of those gathered here today, by the authority granted to me by Iskyr and the Order of the Rengir, I hereby declare you husband and wife. People of the Laedreshian Empire, I present to you: Kyrmaris!"

A roar went up from the crowd.

I tapped my toes, growing more impatient by the moment.

Aekyrdra raised her hands for quiet. "You may now kiss the bride."

Kyrundar grabbed my waist and braced one hand against my upper back as he dipped me back so fast he stole my breath. I gripped the front of his white and silver tunic to steady myself. Then, his eyes glittering and a lopsided smirk on his lips, he bent down and kissed me.

My eyes drifted closed. It was a good thing he had a firm grip on me, because my legs turned to jelly. I released his tunic to wrap my arms around his neck and bury my fingers in his silky hair. He deepened the kiss, and for a moment, I could no longer hear the cheering crowd. Nothing existed but me, my ice elf, everywhere our bodies touched, and the hungry movement of his mouth against mine.

We separated, and Kyrundar whipped me back upright. I stumbled a little and laughed as I caught myself against his chest.

He held me close and pressed a soft kiss to my forehead.

I groaned. "I want more proper kisses."

"Then we'd better get out of here," he said with a mischievous grin.

My heart fluttered. He started to turn toward the front of the cathedral, but I grabbed the sides of his head and pulled him down into another kiss. His hands tightened on my back, and a soft groan escaped my lips.

He pulled back and sighed contentedly. "I love you, Zee."

I opened my eyes and gazed into the face of the man whose heart I was so blessed to have. "I love you, Kyr."

At last, we turned and waved to the crowd. And as the bells of Vairdros Cathedral rang out and the crowds cheered and tossed handfuls of dry rice, we ran down the center aisle and into the next chapter of our lives—together, as we were always meant to be.

NEXT IN TETHERED HEARTS: TIES OF DUST

A girl hiding in plain sight.
A prince trying to save the peninsula.
A very inconvenient enchantment.

Flora owes her role as a royal bodyguard to her ability to control Dust—the invisible magic created by movement. She doesn't precisely pretend to be a man. She just doesn't correct those who assume the Siqualian princess's bodyguard must be a man…which is everyone. Including the delegation of the foreign prince to whom the princess is betrothed.

Prince Cassius's sole purpose in seeking a marriage alliance is to bring strength to the region before outside forces succeed in splintering the peninsula further. When a misunderstanding magically tethers him to the princess's scrawny bodyguard, he thinks his plan couldn't go more wrong. Until the bodyguard reveals herself to be far from the teenage boy he'd assumed—it turns out his plan can go much more wrong.

Flora and Cassius find themselves in an uncomfortable bind—especially as their own hearts become as great a threat to the proposed marriage alliance as the outside forces determined to prevent it. When Cassius's enemies emerge from the shadows, and their tether puts Flora in even greater danger than Cassius, both will have to decide what they'll fight to protect…even if it means choosing between their hearts and their kingdoms.

Although it's a fully standalone story, Ties of Dust *also serves as a prequel to Deborah Grace White's upcoming fantasy series* Magic of Dust and Movement.

TETHERED HEARTS

Ties of Legacy by Melanie Cellier
Ties of Starlight by Celeste Baxendell
Ties of Deception by Alice Ivinya
Ties of Bargains by Tara Grayce
Ties of Death by Constance Lopez
Ties of Shadow by Alora Carter
Ties of Frost by Selina R. Gonzalez
Ties of Dust by Deborah Grace White

ACKNOWLEDGMENTS

I always tell myself I'm going to make my acknowledgments short this time, but I have so many people to thank. And, as anyone who follows me on social media or my newsletter probably knows, I'm verbose, lol.

First, thank you to Mom and Dad for being the very best patrons-of-the-arts a daughter could hope for. ;) Mom, thanks for always reading my books about as many times as I do.

Thank you to Constance and Alora for inviting me to another multi-authors series—it was an honor to collaborate with you again! And thank you to the other lovely ladies in the group for helping make this series a success.

Thanks to Brooke M. for suggesting the name Laine and to Alexis for suggesting Kane. Thank you to everyone else who has given me name ideas, even if I didn't end up using them.

Thank you to my beta readers, Mom, Alexis, Becky, and Claire, for your encouragement and for suggestions that helped make this book stronger.

Kelly, thank you for the accountability-buddy sprints and impromptu mini retreat/getaway, for talking through a nagging plot issue with me and helping me find a solution, for beta reading, and for re-reading and giving more feedback on rewritten scenes.

Kate, thank you for being an angel of copyediting and not only moving my commas and *that*'s and *only*'s to where they belong and dealing with all of my other repeated grammar sins, but also helping me iron out some uneven sentences. I do not deserve you. (Tell Shara next time I'll name a cat after him instead of a terrible ship. :P)

Appreciation and credit to the Jesse's Teahouse social media account for introducing me to the Chinese Gongfu tea ceremony, especially the video at Wang Fu Teahouse in Beijing, to YT channels Altitude Tea and Path of Cha (and tea master Chen Xiangbai) for Gongfu videos, and to Hankook Tea for their video of a Korean tea ceremony by Yeonok Kim, and to the beautiful Chinese and Korean cultures, for inspiring the tea ceremony in this book.

Dear readers, thank you for taking a chance on this book, whether this is the first book of mine you've read or the twelfth. And if you leave an honest review on the book review site(s) or retailer(s) of your choice, thank you even more! Reviews really do help indie authors.

Finally, all thanks to the LORD my God, my creator, guardian, and comforter, the source of my worth and guide for my life. Soli deo gloria.

www.ingramcontent.com/pod-product-compliance
Lightning Source LLC
Chambersburg PA
CBHW061633190726
48289CB00006B/1590